"...well-written and compelling with a great mix of surprising, very satisfying twists."

  - **D.J. Palmer**, USA Today bestselling author of *The New Husband* and *My Wife is Missing*

"Like Frederick Forsyth, Campbell spins a startling tale grounded by personal experience."

  - **John MacLachlan Gray**, Golden Globe-winning author and playwright

"...thrilling international intrigue worthy of the best James Patterson plot."

  - **John Harlan Hughes**, author of the critically-acclaimed *Dead in Tangier*

NOTHING THEY WON'T DO

BENJAMIN CAMPBELL

TEUTOBURG FOREST PRESS

While all of the places and many of the events in this book are real or based on real events, the characters and their dialogue are all fictitious. Any similarity to any person, living or dead, is purely coincidental.

Teutoburg Forest Press

www.TeutoburgForestPress.com

ISBN: 979-8-9862026-0-0

1

June 2017
London, England

THE PAPERS CALLED it a random terror attack. Only Mason and a handful of people in the British government knew the real story. The posh neighborhood of Kensington had a peaceful serenity about it that evening, as the locals were going about their business at the end of a typical workday. Nestled among its narrow one-way streets and high brick walls, which hid the mansions of some of London's best-known aristocrats, bankers, and celebrities, was the Elephant and Castle Pub.

All over England, the one safe refuge, the place all are accepted no matter where they hail from, is the local pub. The Elephant was far enough off the beaten path that tourists rarely found her. Inside, at a seat by the window, thirty-year-old Mason Wright was having dinner with his fiancée and an old friend. There was a relaxed familiarity about the three of them, with each other and with their surroundings. It was the kind of place where one hour easily turned to three as patrons lounged on leather seat cushions surrounded by oak paneled walls, polished wood and brass décor, and great wall-length windows that looked out on the pub's sidewalk dining and the rest of the neighborhood. The smell of steak frites hung in the air that in a bygone era would have been thick with cigarette smoke.

Not one to go looking for trouble, but never one to shy away from it, Mason had experienced more than his share on both sides of the Atlantic. In fact it was trouble that had brought him to Europe three years before, as more of an exile than an expat. But all that seemed far away on this night. As he savored the delicious aftertaste of his second pint of Guinness, Mason also savored the moment, reflecting on his recent good fortune in both business and love, and how far he had come in such a short time. He pushed any thoughts of past events from his mind and turned his gaze to the outdoor terrace to watch the other patrons enjoying the tranquil evening as the setting sun bathed their tables in its final caress of the day.

"Another pint, Mason?" said a woman with a thick eastern European accent, as her hand gently touched his left shoulder.

He looked up to see Lena, their exceptionally attractive Polish waitress, gazing down at him as if he were the only person at the table.

"Thanks, Lena. Sure. Anyone else want another round?" Mason asked the others, both of whom nodded in agreement.

As the waitress walked away, his friend continued staring at her until she was back behind the bar, finally looking over at Mason with a mischievous grin. Mason simply raised his eyebrows and forced a big, closed-mouth smile, innocently looking over at his fiancée—at which point they all started laughing.

His fiancée shook her head and reached over, running her hand through Mason's thick brown hair.

"That's okay," she said. "I'm used to women flirting with him. I'd do the same thing in their shoes. It's impossible to resist those big, beautiful eyes." She often told Mason that he had the most mesmerizing eyes she had ever seen, exuding kindness and charisma in equal measure. "Besides, I know he got that all out of his system when he lived in Paris, before we started dating," she added.

She placed her slender, beautiful hand back on the table. Mason gently put his on top of it and gave it a long squeeze. As he gazed lovingly at his bride-to-be, something outside the window caught his eye. A tall man with a long, unkempt beard and a brutal scar across his left cheek walked briskly past the pub down Gordon Place. Besides the scar, nothing about the man seemed particularly out of the ordinary. With his stylish jeans and untucked shirt he seemed to fit right in. Yet the more Mason looked at the guy the more concerned he became. The stranger reminded him of a man he had met before and had spent the last eighteen months trying to forget. Mason noticed the oblong case the man was carrying. To the untrained eye, it looked like a case for a musical instrument. But Mason knew otherwise. In fact, he believed he knew the make of the weapon inside. And while owning a long gun is not illegal in the UK, everything in Mason's experience was telling him that something about this guy was off. He tried to get a better look to assess the man further, but a waiter at the table just outside their window blocked his view. By the time the waiter had moved, the man was gone.

Still looking out the window, Mason abruptly said, "Hey, do you guys want to head back to the flat? It's getting a bit noisy in here." A glance towards the bar revealed that the locals were now three deep along the full length of the bar, talking and laughing while waiting for their next pint. The others acquiesced and Mason motioned to Lena to cancel the last round and bring the check. Mason put cash in the little leather folder containing the bill and stood up. "Give me a second to run to the loo before we go," he said, then emphasized, "You guys wait here."

Two minutes later his mobile phone rang. He was both surprised and worried to see Spencer's caller ID. Phoning from his cell was against protocol and something he only did in an emergency. Spencer Hughes-Smyth was a senior officer at MI6, who had once pressured Mason to help the agency on a case that had gone horribly wrong. They had not spoken in nine months. Mason's instincts went from worried to being on high alert. First the guy outside, and now this.

"Spencer. What a surprise to hear from you."

"Hello, Mason, where are you right now, right this second?" Spencer asked in an urgent tone.

"I'm in the bathroom at the Elephant and Castle Pub on Gordon Place, a few hundred meters from our flat. We were just leaving to head back home."

"No! Stay right where you are! I'm in an unmarked police car coming your way on Kensington Gore. I know the place. We'll be there in four minutes. We'll pick you up. Do not walk home!"

"Okay. What's going on?"

"We've just received word that Abdul bin Hakam disembarked from a ferry at Dover two days ago. He's now ISIS's top man in Europe. We've been trying to find him for months ever since the jihadi internet chatter indicated he had left Syria. We suspect he has been hiding amongst radical groups in Brussels. But we now have photographic evidence that he's here in the UK. This means we need to provide you and your fiancée with security until we can catch him."

"Shit. I didn't know he had moved to Europe. Why wasn't I told? And why is he still alive? Didn't you have a contract on him?"

"Yes. We still do. We've been bloody close a number of times but he's managed to slip away every time. Sorry, ole boy. Didn't want to worry you unnecessarily. Anyway, I'm telling you now. We believe his primary reason for coming to London is to launch a terror attack similar to the Bataclan massacre in Paris. But we, uh, we also have reason to believe that he is looking for you personally, to avenge his friend—who you dispatched at that house in Notting Hill eighteen months ago. I'm so sorry. I wish I had never dragged you into all this."

Mason flushed red as an icy chill ran up his spine. *I cannot fucking believe that this nightmare just won't end.*

"Mason? Are you still there?"

"Yeah. I'm here. Okay. Listen, you say you have a picture of him, yes?"

"Sure, we have several."

"Can you text me one, like right now?"

"Roger that. Just give me a second to find it."

After three or four seconds, Mason added, "Spencer. I need it right now."

"Sorry, it's taking me a minute. Listen, I'm going to be there in three minutes.

Besides, you don't need a picture to recognize this guy. He has a massive scar down the left side of his face. You can't miss him."

"Fuck!"

"Mason? Mason? Are you there?" The line went dead.

Mason flew out of the bathroom, knocking a guy waiting into the wall. He plowed through the crowded pub like a bowling ball to get to the other side, trying to make sure his fiancée and buddy were still at their table. But he spotted them through the large window, waiting outside on the sidewalk. Mason sprinted to the side door. Just as he was throwing the door open with both hands, the sound of a deafening gunshot shattered the peaceful evening.

Terrified screams filled the air. Desperate patrons scattered in all directions. Everything blurred as if occurring in slow motion. Some ran for their lives, some flipped tables on their sides in an attempt to shield themselves, others spread out prone on the sidewalk. One woman curled up in a ball in her seat and cried uncontrollably, with no protection whatsoever between her and the gunman.

"Get back inside, there's a guy shooting from those bushes over there!" an old man lying flat on the patio shouted. Mason instinctively dropped to a crouched position in the open door-way, then winced in horror as he recognized the lifeless body lying on the blood-soaked sidewalk in front of him.

2

June 2014
Paris, France

MASON DIDN'T SLEEP a wink on the flight from Dulles to Charles de Gaulle. Being jammed in the cheap seats at the back of the plane would have made sleeping hard enough. But it was almost impossible given that the heavyset guy in the seat behind him had to go to the toilet every half hour throughout the flight and was incapable of getting out of his own seat without violently grabbing the back of Mason's to pull himself up. As he rode the RER into Paris, all he could think of was getting to his hotel and laying his head on a pillow.

The one-star hotel Mason had chosen was more of a dive than he had anticipated: just a sink in the room, separate toilets and showers down the hall, and towels that reminded him of the old dish towels his mom used in the kitchen back home. He had to walk down four flights to the ground floor and pay three euros in order to get the key to the shower. An underpaid Portuguese woman working the front desk, whose French was worse than Mason's, spoke with such a mumbled accent that it was almost impossible to understand her.

The hotel was in the famous cinquième, or fifth arrondissement, near Sorbonne University. Quaint cobblestone streets were lined with welcoming bistros, small sidewalk cafés, and five-hundred-year-old buildings; an impossible amount of charm packed into a single square mile on the left bank of the River Seine. And while Mason was drawn to the beauty and atmosphere of the famous neighborhood, it was all secondary to his mission: to improve his French, ace the interview his business school professor had arranged for him, and land a job.

The intensive French school he was enrolled in, called Eurocentre, ran a no-nonsense program with a teaching staff of seasoned professionals. When he first arrived he was given a five-minute oral exam to assess his current level of fluency. Afterwards, Madame Gouzon explained, in French, "We teach to twelve levels of fluency, level one being a complete beginner and level twelve being someone who speaks like a native Parisian. I believe you are currently somewhere between level five and level six. In order to conduct business properly in French you will need to be at least at level nine. Where did you learn French originally?"

"I minored in French in college but have not spoken it much in three years. How long does it typically take for someone to move up a level here?"

"It varies greatly depending on the student. But for someone studying full-time, five days a week, six hours of class instruction per day, plus homework, you could expect to move up one level every two months or so if you really apply yourself."

Mason thought, *Shit. I've only got enough money to last two months over here, possibly a bit more if I eat like a bird and never take a taxi.*

"It would also help if you did not associate with Americans, or anyone who speaks English with you. If accelerating your fluency is the goal, you must immerse yourself totally in the language and not come out of it, no matter how much you may long to relax and fall back on your mother tongue."

TWO WEEKS later on a weekday afternoon, Mason found himself in the school cafeteria, known as La Cantine. He ate lunch there five days a week, primarily because the prices were subsidized by the school and a full meal only cost about three euro, but also because the food was fantastic. As he approached the hot buffet line the server said in French, "Salut, Mason. How are you today?"

"Salut, Omar. I am fine, my friend. Just fine. Could I have the coq au vin today, please? It looks so good. I could smell it all the way down the hall. Did you make this or did Josette?"

"Josette made this today. It's a favorite dish of hers."

"I believe you all only do this job for fun and that your real job is in the evening at Tour d'Argent. Where I come from you would have to be in a five-star restaurant to eat like this."

"Thank you, my friend. That's very kind of you."

MASON TYPICALLY DINED ALONE, studying while he ate. But on this day he was pleasantly surprised when a slender young Brazilian woman in his class named Thais shyly approached his table.

"Hi, Mason, would I be bothering you if I sat here and ate lunch with you?"

"Hey, Thais, not at all. Of course, pull up a chair. Where are all your Brazilian buddies today? I don't think I've ever seen you without them."

"I believe they are all asleep still. We went to a nightclub last night and did not arrive home until after six a.m. It seems I'm the only one who managed to still attend class today," she said, as her hand gently brushed her long, raven-black hair away from her face. As she set her tray on the table her purse strap slipped from her shoulder. The little purse fell against the table, overturning and spilling its contents on the floor. Terribly embarrassed, she bent down to pick up her things. Mason came around to help her.

"I'm so clumsy today. Perhaps I should have stayed in bed like the others."

"Don't be silly. That could have happened to anyone. If I wasn't so slow I would have caught it for you."

They sat back down on opposite sides of the little table. Mason closed his notebook as Thais quietly collected herself and then began to eat. Finally, she looked up with a curious smile and said, "So, what's your story, Mason? Sometimes my friends and I try to guess about your background. All we know is that you're American and that we always see you studying alone, and that you're really smart in class."

With a pleasant smile of surprise on his face, Mason replied, "I didn't mean to be unsociable. All you had to do was ask."

"Okay. So, I'm asking now," came Thais's reply, with a mischievous look.

Checking his watch, Mason said, "Well, um, we'd need the rest of the day for the full story, so I'll just give you the abbreviated version. I was born and raised in Virginia and went to college there at the University of Richmond. And until a couple of months ago, I was a first-year MBA student at a business school in Boston."

"Which school? Wait. I'll bet I can guess—Harvard."

"Why would you guess that?"

"My dad went to Stanford, and he said you can always tell when someone went to Harvard because they never just say the name of the school. Instead, they like to say 'a school in Boston.'"

Mason laughed. "Your dad's a smart man."

"Why did you say 'until a couple of months ago'?"

Nodding slowly, Mason replied, "Well, I got into some trouble in the city one night a week before final exams and they...uh...they threw me out."

"Oh my God. I'm sorry. It must have been serious. What happened?"

Mason hesitated, taking another bite of his meal while continuing to look at his plate. "I'd rather not go into it. It was an accident, but it made the news and it was just a bad scene. I thought it was an overreaction on their part to throw me out of school over it, but I get that they have a reputation to uphold. Anyway, they told me that if I want to return someday to finish the program they would likely let me come back, as long as I've done something, how did they phrase it, 'exceptional in a professional business setting for two or three years,' and stayed out of trouble. I don't know, maybe it's supposed to be some kind of penance. So, I'm over here trying to achieve that."

"Sorry, I'm a bit confused. What does that mean?"

"You're not alone. I don't know what it means either, or if it's all just bullshit. But either way, I need to get a real job and do well at it. And that's why I'm here in France. Are you sure you want to hear this long story? Let's talk about you."

"No, no. I am very interested in your story. It's not something you hear every day. Please, continue. You're here in France looking for work."

"Actually, I'm here in France just for one interview, which I'm supposed to call and ask for once my French is good enough to speak at a professional business level."

"*Quoi?* I don't follow you."

"It's not your typical story. I'm in a bit of a jam, actually. I applied for and was rejected from five different jobs in the US. It seems no one over there wants to hire the guy who just got kicked out of school. Things were looking really bleak. And then, by the grace of God, one of my B-school professors called me and offered to help me find a job through his network of contacts. He asked what I wanted to do, and I told him that my dream had always been to work in Europe, more so now than ever. He said he was willing to ask around. It turned out he has an old friend who was in his section when he was at Harvard, who apparently is an important French industrialist. He said his friend is willing to give me an interview for a position he has in mind. But the interview will be in French, of course. So, I'm here to improve my French enough to convince this guy that I can work in France."

"Wait. You are saying that you moved to France to study French just for one interview? That cannot be correct. I think there must be more to this story. Do you know what the job is, or if you even want to do this job if you are successful in your interview?"

"Nope. There is nothing more to the story. I don't know what the job is other than it's a sales position for a tech company."

Thais stopped eating and put her silverware back on the table, as she stared at Mason with a look of incredulity, her beautiful mouth hanging slightly open as she searched for her next words. "How is this possible? Who does this? And how will you even get work papers to work in France if you get the job?"

"I understand your reaction. My parents and friends are convinced I've lost my mind. And I don't know about the work papers either. If it's meant to be I'm sure it will get sorted out somehow."

Thais continued staring at him in disbelief.

He continued, "I know it sounds insane, but I was desperate to just get away from the States—from the rejections, from job applications, and from the humiliation of everyone around me knowing I missed the chance of a lifetime. And this one opportunity came up and it gave me something to hope for—a shot at working in Europe. I know that it's a long shot, but who cares. A long shot is a lot better than no shot."

"What will you do if you don't get the job?"

"I try not to think about that. I guess if I have to go back home in a couple of months when my money runs out, at least I'll have learned to speak French fluently. Maybe I'll get to use it someday in the future. Who knows? I can't think that far ahead."

ON THE FINAL day of Mason's second one-month term his professor Patrice called him up to his desk at the end of class.

"I just wanted to let you know that I am recommending you for level eight for next term. Your dedication to your studies and the speed with which you are learning is really quite impressive."

"Thank you for the kind words. It means a lot to me."

What Mason did not tell his professor as he left that day was that he would not be returning for a third term, because he was broke. Even with a cheap hotel and eating on a budget, living in Paris for eight weeks had been so expensive it had drained what little money Mason had in the bank along with a thousand-dollar gift from his concerned-but-supportive parents. He was now surviving only via racking up debt on his credit card. By his calculation he could last roughly ten more days before his card would be maxed out. If the job did not pan out, he would need to call home to ask for help in buying the plane ticket back to the US. He emailed his professor to ask if he could do a WhatsApp call the following day.

"Bonjour, Mason! How is the French coming along?"

"Hi, Professor Bellini. It's coming along quite well, thanks. It's been tough on my poor brain, but I'm loving it. I think I'm ready to have my meeting with your friend Monsieur Le Lidec."

"Okay. If you think your French skills are up to par now."

"I'd love to stay and practice longer, but there are other circumstances that require that I pull the trigger now. I have come a long way. I think I'm ready."

"Very well. I will reach back out to Jean-Pierre and arrange the meeting. By the way, I spoke with him recently and he gave me some more insight on the opportunity. He owns a majority stake in a promising young software company called Soft Control International, or SCI."

"That works. Anything with sales is a fit. And software sales is a great fit. What kind of software do they make?"

"They make motion and robotics control software for large manufacturing companies. Le Lidec tells me that the one thing he is most worried about is their ability to grow fast enough to beat out potential competitors and lock up market share. He needs hungry salespeople."

"Well, that is definitely a fit. They don't come much hungrier," Mason said with a laugh. "I do have one question though. Won't there be some challenge with the fact that I'm not an EU citizen and don't have a work permit?"

"We discussed this. Le Lidec is incredibly plugged in with the French government. And in the world he lives in, a lot of things that are officially not possible, are possible. He said if he likes you then there are ways he can take care of that."

"Okay. Well, I guess I'll cross that bridge if I make it that far. I'll stand by to hear back. Thank you again."

The next day, Mason received a phone call from the billionaire Le Lidec's personal secretary, inviting him to dinner at his Paris home—two weeks later. *Two weeks from now!? My credit card won't last that long. I guess I'm going to have to play hide and seek with the owner of my hotel.*

L e Lidec lived in the seventh arrondissement in what was closer to a palace than a home. In France these are known as hôtel particulier. As a tourist, one would likely walk past them and never know what's behind the tall, nondescript walls, often ten or twelve feet high. Once inside the walls, these mansions, most of which are three or four hundred years old, typically have exquisite grounds complete with formal gardens and swimming pools.

On the appointed evening, Mason arrived precisely on time and rang the buzzer. While waiting he thought, *The French may be socialists on the surface, but the ultra-rich continue to live as well as the kings of old.* A white-gloved butler answered the outer gate and showed him into the palace.

Jean-Pierre and Mason hit it off right away. "We Europeans are passionate about our history. It's rare to meet an American who knows so much about it, let alone one who speaks French so well. What a pleasant surprise on both counts," Jean-Pierre said with an air of approval.

"With a father who's a history professor, it's hard to grow up and not share a passion for the stories about where we all come from," Mason explained.

Their discussion spanned the ages from Charlemagne to World War II. They differed slightly on Louis XIV, the Roi-Soleil. Jean-Pierre was proud of his greatness and the things he built, such as Versailles.

"I have a slightly darker view of him," Mason countered. "I believe there is a strong case to be made that his oppression of the French populace did more to lay the groundwork for the French Revolution a century later than the actions of any other king—French or otherwise. And what's more, his treatment of his finance minister, Nicolas Fouquet, was unforgivable."

Le Lidec nodded and said, "I cannot disagree with your position. However, is it not possible that both positions can be true at the same time?" They both laughed, and Mason raised his glass as a sign of respect to his host's diplomacy. It was an enchanting evening in the truest sense of the word, made complete by the fact that they drank the best bottle of wine Mason had ever tasted, a 1982 Chateau Margaux.

They also spoke at length about Mason's time running the construction company he worked at in Virginia after college, and especially his motivation and approach to expanding the modest business into other markets. Le Lidec prided himself on being able to assess people quickly based on their character and their abilities. He liked Mason on both counts.

"The thing SCI needs most right now is aggressive salespeople who know how to prospect for new clients. I believe Americans tend to be more willing to do this type of work. And besides, being American not only helps when selling into other countries in Europe because of your English, it also helps because if you make cultural errors by being overly aggressive, customers will forgive you."

Pausing for a moment, a look of concern came over Le Lidec's face. He slowly reached for the wine decanter and poured Mason another glass and then topped up his own. He looked Mason in the eye and said, "Mason, I'm going to need to know what happened that night in Boston, before I will be able to render a judgment on whether or not I want to hire you. Professor Bellini gave me a rough outline but suggested I get the details from you."

"I understand. And I expected that you would ask this question. Indeed you have every right to know. A fellow classmate, a Brazilian named Vicente Machado, and I were out in town one Friday night, shortly before exams. We had been drinking but neither of us was drunk. We were waiting in line outside of the Black Rose pub near Quincy Market. There were two African American gentlemen in line in front of us. When the bouncer removed the rope across the door to let them in, a large drunk man directly behind us in line complained loudly, using offensive language, that these men were being allowed in before him and his friend. This made Vicente angry and he grabbed the man by the collar of his shirt and forced him to apologize to the gentlemen ahead of us. After this the drunk man and his friend left, yelling something that we couldn't discern just as they turned the corner out of sight. Several minutes later we heard a woman behind us scream. We turned around just in time to see that the drunk had returned—with a knife—and was in the process of lunging at Vicente with it, as he yelled something to the effect of, 'See how tough you are now, motherfucker!' Vicente tried to jump clear but the man managed to stab him in the lower right gut, puncturing his small intestine and cutting a four-inch gash along his side."

Mason was coming to the most difficult part of the story for him, and so paused for a moment, took a sip from his wine glass, and continued, "My reaction was purely reflexive, so much so I don't even remember deciding to do it. But as I saw the man stabbing Vicente, I stepped in his direction and punched him in the side of the head with all my weight and all my might. As he was focused on Vicente, he never saw my punch coming. I'm told that the blow connected with the side of his temple, just next to his left eye."

Le Lidec nodded a knowing look, as if he understood at that moment what had happened, and why.

"The man fell like a tree, immediately knocked unconscious. His head hit the metal pole that held the rope across the door on his way down. He never moved again. No one paid him much notice as we were all focused on helping Vicente and treating his stab wound. It was only when the second ambulance arrived that it became clear the man was in serious distress. He died later that night at the hospital, never having regained consciousness."

Le Lidec interjected, "I'm sure you've been informed by now that this spot next to the eye on the temple is one of several well-known pressure points that martial arts experts use to incapacitate an opponent. Only they take great care to hit gently because a full-force blow at that spot is often fatal."

"Yes. The doctors and the district attorney told me later. I had no idea. I would never have hit him there had I known. As I said, it was just an instinctive reaction to try to protect my friend. Of course I was not trying to kill the man. I've never felt so guilty in my life. It's at least part of the reason I'd love to work in Europe—to just put the entire episode out of my life and out of my mind."

"I understand. Who was the man?"

"His name was Seamus Cole. Apparently he was not a very nice man. He had been released from prison on parole less than two weeks before the incident. Nevertheless, he didn't deserve to die just because he wasn't a nice guy."

"And your friend, Vicente? What happened to him?"

"He was in the hospital for about a week but was released in time to take his final exams."

"As I said, Professor Bellini did not share any details with me, just the basic facts. It's clear to me that this was a tragic accident. I'm sorry to make you recount it but I needed to know."

"Of course."

At the end of the evening, as he was walking Mason to the door, Le Lidec stopped to scribble a name and number on a piece of paper. Handing the paper to Mason, he said, "Here is the number of Monsieur Philippe Bourget. He is the CEO of SCI. Call him tomorrow. I think they could use someone like you, and I will tell him this."

"That is such wonderful news. I cannot thank you enough. Really. Thank you so much."

Le Lidec walked Mason out to the entrance gate and opened it. Just as he stepped out to the sidewalk, Mason turned around and said, "If I may, could I impose on you to answer one final question?"

"Of course."

"In researching your background before our meeting, I noticed that your bio on the website of your holding company does not mention Harvard in your education. Forgive my asking, but I'm just curious as to why you would be so modest about your HBS degree?"

Le Lidec hesitated for a brief moment as he stared at Mason. Then, with a confident smile he replied, "That is because I did not finish my degree. I too was asked to leave after my first year. In my case it was for academic reasons. I believe they still call it 'looping out.' I just never got around to going back."

Mason's eyes bulged wide open as if he'd seen a ghost, just as Le Lidec said, "À bientôt," and gently closed the gate.

Still shaking his head with incredulity and newfound confidence, Mason stepped out into the empty streets of Paris. *Who needs the stupid degree. Le Lidec made billions without it!* He checked his watch and saw it was 1:30 a.m. He looked down at the wet cobblestones and then up at the stars in the clear night sky. In the distance he could see the Propreté de Paris street cleaners in their green uniforms hosing down and sweeping the streets, washing the dust, pollen, and dog dejection into the labyrinth of underground sewers beneath the city's ancient streets. The dead silence of the streets at night was an extreme contrast to the emotions screaming through Mason's brain at that moment. An empty taxi pulled alongside him as the driver looked across inquisitively. Mason shook his head and waved him on. He didn't have a single euro in his pockets. With a spring in his step, he headed off into the dark to make the long walk back to his hotel.

ugust 2014
London, England

ON THE OTHER side of the English Channel, a gray-haired gentleman was staring intently at the file in front of him on his massive, weathered mahogany desk. Director Mark Seifert rarely took the time to appreciate the breathtaking views of London and the River Thames out the window of his office. Seifert's office was on the top floor of the MI6 building, the headquarters for the UK's international counter-espionage operations. With the persistent growth of ISIS over the past two years, and their increased attacks in Europe, there was little time for such frivolities as appreciating landscapes. He glanced at the map of the Middle East on the wall and wondered what that map would look like in five years' time. Just then his old-fashioned intercom buzzer rang and his PA's voice came through.

"Director Seifert? Spencer Hughes-Smyth is here for his appointment."

"Send him in," Seifert replied.

Seifert glanced briefly back to the map as the man walked into his office.

"Ah, Spencer. Do come in. Please, have a seat."

"Thank you, sir. I was pleased to receive your request to see me. I hope I can be of service."

"Right. I'll get right to it. I've been studying your file. Cambridge educated; twenty-two years active duty; special forces stationed in Lebanon for two years; fluent in French and Arabic; two tours in Iraq embedded with the US forces; wounded in action with multiple medals for bravery; honorably discharged in 2009—recruited by our anti-terror unit here shortly thereafter. And twice promoted in the four years you've been with us. Very impressive. In fact, one might say exceptional."

"Thank you, sir."

"You know better than anyone the trouble these ISIS fanatics have been giving us. We've been sharing the reports coming out of your group with the PM. And he's concerned that we seem to always be playing catchup. We are consistently one step behind the buggers, instead of one step ahead. Earlier this week the PM authorized a substantial increase in our budget specifically to fight these bloody animals. Effective immediately, I am creating a new unit within the anti-terror group, one dedicated to focusing on ISIS in Syria. And I'd like you to head it up. Of course, it will entail a promotion in title and an increase in pay but more importantly it will give you increased freedom to explore the avenues you believe have merit and to do what has to be done to help combat this scourge more efficiently. You can handpick your team and pursue the assets you need in the field with less red tape and all that. What do you say, ole boy?" Seifert continued.

"In all honesty, sir, this is quite unexpected, and I'm

genuinely flattered," Spencer replied. "Yes, of course, it would be an honor. I will do my level best. Thank you ever so kindly."

"Smashing. Higgins will no longer be your immediate superior. You will now report directly to me. And I will want regular briefings from you in person," Seifert replied. "And as long as you're here, you can give me your first briefing today."

"I thought you might ask, so I brought a file with me that has our latest intel." Spencer placed a file on Seifert's desk. "One important new development we are tracking is an increase in mobile phone chatter about a new way some ISIS cells are planning to move their people into Europe for an eventual attack. They are also seeking new transport channels for the unsuspecting refugee women and teenagers they are trafficking into brothels across Europe. It seems they have a new way to move by ship. We don't know exactly how yet. But we continue to monitor both internet and mobile phone activity. We know that several of the mobile calls that we think are from jihadi burner phones have terminated in western Germany in the Mosel River Valley. We don't know much more than that right now. But I'll have more info for you by the time of our next briefing."

ugust 2014
Paris, England

THE CALL with Bourget was short and to the point. They agreed that Mason would come to interview in person the following day. Philippe Bourget was in his early fifties but looked ten years younger. He was about Mason's height, handsome, with close-cropped hair only starting to gray, immaculately dressed, and clearly in excellent shape. He had been educated at the top French schools as a young man before joining the French military, eventually becoming a full colonel in the special forces. After leaving the military he had been a high-ranking minister in President Chirac's government, before eventually moving into the private sector. He was well-mannered, but like most French people in a professional setting, he was serious, and all business, no happy backslapping or chitchat.

Bourget interviewed Mason for ninety minutes.

"I agree with Le Lidec's assessment. I think you're a natural salesperson," Bourget said. "Your French is good. Definitely not perfect but good enough. In a few months I'm sure it will be excellent. I'm confident you'll spin up quickly on our software suite as well. The key selling points are simple: it's much faster and cheaper to make changes to assembly lines using our software than traditional methods, saving companies more by avoiding lost productivity than they spend on the cost of the software. If you bring that American optimism and energy to prospecting for new clients, you'll do just fine. However, we're a young company. I can't afford to pay you a big salary. The base pay for our sales reps is 5,000 euros per month. The bulk of your compensation will come through commissions. So, get out there and close deals. If you're good, you can easily make three or four times your base pay in commissions. And if you're very good, there may be international opportunity for you in the future in either Germany or the UK, most likely the latter unless you plan to learn German too."

"I'm pretty sure that there is no one on your staff who is as motivated to succeed as I am," Mason replied.

"I don't doubt it. If you want the job, you can start tomorrow."

"I'm in. With both feet. Thank you."

"Great. I'm glad. It seems you're already a bit of a Francophile, but I know you will love living here. There really is no place quite like Paris for expats. Oh, and by the way, one other thing I thought I'd mention: Don't shy away from the Harvard thing. I appreciate that you're embarrassed by having to leave after one year, but in Europe it's not at all uncommon for people to take off a year or two between levels when they study for graduate degrees. The details of whatever troubles you had there are irrelevant and personal. If I were you, I would tell people that you're a Harvard student, working to save money to pay for your second year at HBS. Europeans will hold you in very high esteem upon learning this."

THE NEXT DAY Mason started his new job. Bourget brought him into an office to share with two other young colleagues, Hans von Eiger, a German about two years younger than Mason, and Annabelle Chaude, a twenty-three-year-old French woman who had recently graduated from university. As Mason was settling in at his desk Annabelle looked back and forth between Mason and Hans.

"Are you sure you two are not related? You look like brothers. Same height, short brown hair, big hazel eyes with thick eyebrows, even the same nose. *C'est bizarre*. It's like you're twin models," said Annabelle.

Mason replied with a shy laugh, "I don't know about the model thing, at least not for me, but I agree there is a resemblance. I'm pretty sure no one on my dad's side comes from Germany, but maybe my mom has some German ancestry I don't know about."

Mason thought this small, shared office setup was perfect. Each of them had their own desk and phone, all crammed in the same small room. A short time later, Hans was called into a meeting in the conference room, leaving Mason and Annabelle in the office. Little by little they began to chat and learn about each other's backgrounds.

"Monsieur Bourget says you studied at Harvard."

"Yes. Just one year."

"Your French is quite good, for an American." Mason shot her a look of disbelief. "No, really. Your accent is excellent."

"Thanks. But I have an enormous amount still to learn. I feel like every sentence requires me to think incredibly hard in order to get it right." After a short pause, Mason continued, "Hans speaks excellent French. I'm not used to hearing a German speaking French so well."

"Yes. He was raised in western Germany in a town on the Mosel River, not far from the French border. He told me his parents would speak to him and his brother in French as well as German so that they would be bilingual. But this is common for many families from their background."

"Sorry, what does that mean?"

"His family is aristocratic. He was raised in a chateau. In English I believe you call them castles. It's quite a sad story, really. When he was fifteen years old his parents and his brother were killed in an avalanche while skiing off-piste at Chamonix, in the French Alps. So for the rest of his teenage years, it was only him and his uncle, Baron von Eiger, living in the big castle."

"Oh my God. That is a sad story," Mason said.

LATER ON THAT first day Mason was given a one-hour training on the software by a woman named Kelly O'Callaghan. The moment he walked into her office, he knew he was in trouble. Kelly was twenty-five years old, about five-foot-nine with long dark hair and piercing blue eyes that he was certain knew everything he was thinking. *Come on! She's impossibly beautiful,* he thought. *How am I supposed to get any work done?*

Kelly had joined the company about six months before. She was quickly promoted and was now leading the account management group, as well as training new employees. Unlike everyone else in the office, she spoke to him in perfect English instead of French, albeit with a slight Irish accent.

"Ah. An English speaker. Where are you from?" he asked.

"I'm a bit from all over, really. I was born in Galway, Ireland, to an Irish dad and an American mum. My family moved here to Paris for my dad's work when I was ten years old and I went to

French schools ever since, except college. I went to Purdue University in the US and graduated three years ago."

"Nice. Purdue's a great school. What did you study?"

"Double E."

"Wow. So, you're crazy smart, too," Mason said, impressed by her background in electrical engineering. "Promise me you'll go slowly as you explain how all this works."

"Oh, you don't need to worry about that. It's all quite simple." Kelly laughed as she was calling up the demo files on her computer.

Mason tried to listen to her tutorial but heard next to nothing. He caught himself looking at her lips as she was speaking and had to force himself to look only at the bridge of her nose. A few minutes later as she leaned across her desk to grab a file, he instinctively checked out her body. He thought he was being inconspicuous, until he realized she saw him via the reflection of her computer monitor. He blushed red and immediately over-compensated by turning his head away, looking off to the far right—even though there was nothing in that direction but a blank wall. Kelly continued her tutorial with a slight mischievous smile, but never skipped a beat. Mason was so uncomfortable he just wanted the meeting to end.

When it was finally over, he went back to his shared office and waited for Annabelle to leave the room. He then asked Hans a dozen questions since he'd only heard a fraction of what Kelly had tried to teach him. After the third question, Hans asked him with a knowing look and a raised eyebrow, "Did you not get the tutorial from Kelly?"

"Yeah, I did. But I have a confession—I didn't hear a word she said. I couldn't concentrate." Mason didn't go further, as he didn't yet know how much he could confide in his new officemate.

"Is it because she is so beautiful you were distracted?" Hans asked.

"Yes! Oh my God. What is up with that? How could anyone focus on anything with her in the room?" They both erupted with laughter. *This Hans guy is alright.*

"She is a very disciplined woman, with work and with her fitness. I see her leaving the office with her gym bag every evening at seven p.m. She told me that she works out for at least an hour every day."

"I don't doubt it. I just saw the results with my own eyes."

After his first week at work, Mason decided the next order of business was to find a place to live. He scoured the online listings for a place that was cool, in a hip area, and that he could afford on his salary. Hans and Anabelle both told him that Le Marais, the fourth arrondissement, is where he wanted to be. It was the area behind the Hotel de Ville, stretching back to the Place de la Bastille. Right in its center was the exquisite palace known as Place des Vosges, built by Henri IV in the late sixteenth century. Mason went after work the next day to check out a few of the available apartments. He ended up renting a quaint, four-hundred-year-old rez-de-chausée, or ground-floor apartment, on rue des Tournelles. The one-bedroom apartment was right on the interior courtyard of the building, which had originally been one of the stables for the king's palace. It had stone walls, a tile floor, and a massive, original wood beam that spanned the width of the main living area. The hatchet marks were still visible on the beam from when it was milled in the late 1500s.

On his first night in his new apartment, he sat outside in the courtyard drinking a glass of red wine from an everyday bottle of Bordeaux at his own little table, along with a baguette, some double-cream brie, and a full spread of charcuterie. He savored the moment of where he was and what had happened in such a short time.

6

S *eptember 2014*
London, England

SPENCER HUGHES-SMYTH WALKED into Director Seifert's office at MI6 headquarters in London and proceeded to brief him on the developments of the past few weeks. Opening the thick file he had just dropped on the desk, Spencer pulled out several diagrams and documents.

"We've learned a good deal more regarding the ISIS mobile phone transmissions to and from Germany since our last briefing," he said. "As we noted, the transmissions have been text messages, and some phone calls, in and around the small town of Cochem."

The director interrupted, "Cochem? What kind of bloody name is that for a town? It sounds like someone coughing into their hand, don't you think?"

"Right you are, sir," Spencer responded and returned to his

briefing. "Whoever is receiving these transmissions is shrewd and clearly trying to avoid detection. Since the messages are being sent and received through an encrypted app, we can't read them. We can only discern the phone number and the general location of the phone at the time of transmission, usually to within ten or fifteen meters. But he or she is using disposable burner phones—and never more than once or twice each time—only turning the phone on just as it's being used and then turning it right back off again."

"Cheeky bastards," Seifert said. "You're spot on, Smyth. They definitely think they're outsmarting us. But they'll slip up. These buggers always do."

"I agree, sir. Furthermore, he or she always sends and receives from different locations, at odd hours, making it almost impossible to figure out who it is or where they live. We've put agents on the ground in the area, but it is a matter of pure chance to have someone in the exact area when one of these transmissions occurs. So far no one has seen anything. However, two weeks ago we caught a break. A text message was sent from a known jihadi phone in Syria to a burner mobile phone in Cochem. The phone was only turned on for a few seconds, and then powered off. But it was long enough for the text message to be delivered and, of course, for the burner phone's number and location to register on the network. That one time, the phone's location was right here—" Spencer pointed to the specific spot on the map open on the table, and continued, "within the walls of Reichsburg, a massive castle that sits on the hill overlooking the town. Now given that GPS tracking is only accurate to within ten or fifteen meters, had this been a house in the town we could not have been certain which house it was. But given that it was within the walls of Schloss Reichsburg, it narrows down the possible culprits to just the owner and his staff, or possibly a visitor."

"What do we know about the people who own this castle?" Seifert asked.

"It's owned by Baron Klaus von Eiger. He is the head of an old, wealthy, aristocratic German family. He had a brother who was killed, along with his wife and son, in an avalanche in the Alps some years back. He continued to raise his other nephew, the only surviving heir, Hans, until adulthood. We believe that Hans lives in Paris now and only comes home about once a month, so that rules him out, given the frequency of transmissions. We are checking into the servants as well, but we are told that the baron never has visitors to the castle. We think the baron himself is shaping up to be our most likely candidate," Spencer said.

Seifert asked skeptically, "Why is that?"

"From what we can glean so far, he lost most of the family's fortune in the crash of 2008. Also, and here's where it gets interesting, he owns a shipping company called Von Eiger. Our research indicates that Von Eiger Shipping has been operating in the red for the past few years. Any way you look at it, the baron is short on cash, maybe even desperately short. The question remains: Is he using his ships to transport weapons, jihadis, and/or the women and teenagers they are trafficking, in exchange for cash?"

"This is good work. But of course, it's only a start," Seifert said. "We need ears on the ground over there. Without them we can't know for sure what he's up to and, most importantly, we can't find jihadis and catch them before they attack us in Europe, which is job one. Have you bugged the schloss yet?"

"We're trying. It's turning out to be a bit of a stiff hill to climb, that one," Spencer replied. "He has a modern security system as well as full-time security staff. We've tried several times to break the cable or internet connection and send a repairman, but they never let anyone past the gate. We'll keep working on it. One way or the other we'll figure how to get audio from inside the schloss. We *have* managed to get his internet company to let us look at his traffic. We can see he's using video conferencing apps on his computer. Our IT boys tell us that he's using a VPN to talk directly with people in Syria. But the VPN encrypts the transmission, so again, we've got to get audio from inside the schloss to know what's happening."

Spencer continued, "Also, just this morning we managed to install a tracking device on his car. Since he frequently drives out of the schloss we had a team follow him. He parked in town outside a shop for less than five minutes. But it was enough time for our boys to get a tracker attached under the engine. We did not have enough time to get a bug inside the vehicle, but we'll keep working on it. With the tracker on his car now, the next time there is an ISIS text transmission to a mobile a few miles away from the town, we'll be able to verify if his car is at that location as well. If it is, we'll know for certain he's our man."

"Cracking great work, Smyth. Well done. Stay on this guy and keep me informed. And whatever you do, don't do anything that risks blowing the cover of the operation. Job one is finding out when and where the jihadis will be traveling so we can intercept them. And get me audio from inside that castle!"

"Will do, sir," Spencer replied as he collected his papers to leave. Just before reaching the door he spoke again, "Oh. Uh... there is one other important bit of news, a rather unfortunate bit. We recently began working with a contractor named Crocetti, in Genoa, to give us intel on the comings and goings of different ships from the Middle East. Straightforward stuff, when they came, when they left, how many people came off them, photos and video, etc. Well, it seems he's gone missing. His last transmission was from the commercial port in Genoa three days ago, just as a Von Eiger ship was docking. But we've lost all communication. The local police found his Vespa abandoned behind a warehouse on the dock. Given how much time has passed, we now suspect foul play."

7

F ebruary 2015
    Paris, France

MASON, Hans, and Annabelle had just come back from lunch at their favorite local Normand restaurant, just around the corner from their office in the eighth arrondissement. In classic French tradition they often enjoyed a glass of wine or two with lunch. As they walked up the steps to their office building, Annabelle smacked Mason on his butt. Mason feigned injury and began limping. Hans, who was coming up last, then smacked Annabelle on her behind. She pretended to be outraged, and all three laughed uncontrollably.

Once inside, Mason did a valiant job of regaining his composure, and had almost made it back to their little office when he happened to see Kelly coming down the hall from the other direction. He was just about to say hello when Annabelle walked quickly past him and smacked him hard on the butt again, at which point Mason, Hans, and Annabelle all began laughing again. Mason couldn't help but notice that the pleasant look on Kelly's face immediately turned to a frown.

The office trio would eat lunch together almost every day and go for drinks after work several nights a week. An added bonus for Mason was that Annabelle became his de facto French tutor during the workday. Even though he was fluent in being able to express himself and understand others in French, he still made minor mistakes every day. As he spoke to his office-mates or into the phone on prospecting calls, Annabelle would quietly correct him from across the room no matter what she was working on at the time. She always spoke softly enough so that the person on the other end of the line could not hear. Mason welcomed her corrections which, little by little, were pushing his fluency to a native level.

With each passing day it was not just his French skills that improved. Mason also perfected his pitch convincing large French manufacturing companies to buy SCI software. By his sixth month on the job, he was outselling all five other salespeople. He had not yet completed his first full year on the job and he was already selling more each month than all other sales reps combined. His extreme motivation to be successful at this job was evident in his results.

Mason's social life was also flourishing and had become more interesting than he ever imagined thanks to his friendship with Hans. Annabelle had a serious boyfriend, so she was usually off with him at night. Like Mason, Hans was single, and he and Mason had become close friends. Whenever they were out without Annabelle, their favorite subject was talking about women and what they were looking for in a girlfriend. When Mason would describe his ideal woman, Hans would reply with a knowing smile, "Sounds like you're describing Kelly again."

One evening, as they had drinks at Hans's favorite café in

Paris, Café de Flore, they were engaged in this familiar interchange yet again. Mason tried to clarify his view to Hans.

"It's like I told you on my first day, this job saved my life. I'm not going to do anything to risk it—like having an office romance. Do I think about her? Of course. I mean, she has her shit together more than any woman I've ever met. There's like a perfect harmony of peace and confidence about her. But besides the fact that we work together, I get the sense that she's a 'serious relationship' kind of girl. I don't think I'm in a place in my life where that's the right path for me just now. So, I don't think it'd be a smart move on either front."

"It's too bad. Because if you ask me, I think she likes you. I can tell by the way she looks at you," Hans replied. "And to be honest, I think perhaps you like her more than you are willing to admit, ja?"

Mason tried not to grin as he shook his head and added, "Why haven't you asked her out?"

"We actually did go out two or three times when she first joined the company. But it's like you say, she is a serious relationship kind of person and I have never been inclined to mislead a woman into thinking I have greater affections than I really have just to get what I want, and so we decided to just be friends."

Mason was impressed by Hans as he grew to know him better. He also had another question he had been meaning to ask him. Feigning a quizzical look, he asked, "Did I hear Annabelle correctly last week when she made reference to you having a date with some mystery woman? Are you holding out on us? Talk to me, baby."

Hans looked away bashfully and shook his head, saying, "There is nothing to tell, really. I've been seeing a young lady, very occasionally, for about a year. She's an English girl who is studying at Beaux-Arts. But we only go out a few times each month. She has a very active social life with her own friends and fellow students."

"Why don't you bring her out with us sometime? We could do drinks after work, together with Annabelle. What's her name?"

"Her name is Kristen. I don't know. I don't think either of us wants to get too attached as it's doubtful it will go anywhere."

"Does she have a last name? And why would you say that?"

"Her last name doesn't matter. And, well, for one thing, she does not feel she can tell her family we are dating because she is Jewish and I'm German. Her great-grandparents were killed at Auschwitz and my grandfather Wilhelm was a colonel in the Luftwaffe. So she believes there would be difficulty with her family."

"That amazes me. Are there still families who judge people just by their nationality?"

"*Ja*. For sure there are. And not just in England, or France, or Germany; prejudice of many different kinds still exists all over the world."

Mason thought in silence for a brief instant, reflecting on his own life experiences, and said, "Yeah. I guess you're right. It's just different groups for different reasons in each country."

MASON DIDN'T KNOW a lot about Hans's background, other than what Annabelle told him—that he was raised in a castle in a village in the Mosel River Valley in Germany, and that his family was killed in a skiing accident when he was a teenager. Hans had shared this latter point with him as well. Beyond this, all that Mason knew was that Hans seemed to be a genuinely kind, modest person who had zero airs of pretention about him.

Nevertheless, as the two of them became good friends, Hans began inviting Mason to more and more chic parties in Paris and other cities around Europe. Even if he was modest by nature, given the homes, mansions, and villas where these parties were held and the last names of many of the families Mason met, it was clear that Hans hung out in a pretty aristocratic crowd. They went to the party of a young countess in Geneva, then the next weekend, the wedding of a princess in Paris. They went to several parties in Florence at the villa of one of Hans's best friends, a young Italian named Flavio Costadura, who ended up becoming close friends with Mason too. And they went on a number of double dates, sometimes when one of them had a romantic interest in one of the young ladies, many times just for fun.

Mason was fascinated to learn that this world still existed, where people from a seemingly limitless number of titled families still invited each other to extravagant events at palaces and chateaux. And, just as with everyday people from all walks of life, there was plenty of gossip about whose family still had money and who was broke.

ONE DAY IN EARLY MAY, Hans invited Mason to come with him on the four-hour drive to his home in Germany to spend the weekend and meet his uncle, the baron.

8

M ay 2015
Cochem, Germany

"IT'S INCREDIBLE. There is an ancient castle at every turn of the river," Mason said as he and Hans wound their way along the breathtaking Mosel River. Even though he prided himself on not caring about wealth and privilege, Mason was anxious to see where Hans and his uncle lived.

Hans told him along the way that they lived in a schloss called Reichsburg, and that it was on the hill overlooking the town of Cochem.

"No one knows exactly when it was built—but they know that the oldest walls go back to the tenth century, with additions happening at some point in almost every century since."

Hans also shared some of the more interesting stories and myths about their family history.

"My grandfather Wilhelm was part of the bomb-in-the-bunker plot against Hitler, led by Colonel von Stauffenburg in

July of 1944. Hitler allowed our family to keep our titles and assets if my grandad agreed to take his own life, which he did. My dad and my uncle Klaus, who became the baron upon my grandfather's death, were just children at the time but this put a great deal of pressure on them as the only surviving male heirs of the von Eiger family. And, since the skiing accident I told you about, my uncle has no family other than me now. Therefore, he pressures me to get married and carry on the name."

"Why did he never marry?"

"Actually, he did. When I was a baby he was married to the daughter of a rich family from Hannover. But they were not well-suited for one another. He took the burdens of overseeing our family wealth and our shipping business very seriously and so he worked a great deal. And he does not enjoy socializing. His new wife wanted to party and travel and be with other people all the time. So their marriage only lasted a few years. They divorced, having never had children, and somehow he never found anyone else."

"Speaking of family lineage, how far back does yours go? Like, are we talking medieval times, or what?"

"No. Our family's title and wealth are all relatively recent compared to most aristocratic houses. We trace it back to the late 1700s, 1792 to be exact. The story has become somewhat of a legend within our family. It is difficult to know how much is true and how much is myth. We are descended from Gerhard von Eiger. He was originally only a well-to-do local tradesman and the mayor of our town, Cochem. After their Revolution in 1789, the French launched a campaign against German towns west of the Rhine. By night, Gerhard was the leader of a local raiding party that used guerilla tactics to harass the French supply lines, which were forced to spread themselves thinly along the narrow Mosel riverbank to support their army east of here.

"As the story goes, late one night in 1791 Gerhard's group of fifteen men attacked a French carriage traveling with an armed escort of about twenty soldiers. The fighting was fierce and the French fought to the last man, which was rare. All of the French were killed in the fight or the aftermath. Only four of the German locals survived; their leader, Gerhard von Eiger, was one of them. No one knows what was in the carriage, but the myth is that it carried several chests of gold coins, intended to be used to purchase weapons and supplies for the French army. All we know is that the following year Gerhard had the money to buy Schloss Reichsburg and shortly afterwards, in the fall of 1792, was elevated to the status of baron."

Hans continued, "But he did not live long after this. He was killed fighting the French just two years later as they took over and held the entire Mosel River Valley for the next twenty years. But there is a bizarre end to the story. They say, as Gerhard was dying in the tent of a medic after having been struck in the throat by a musket ball in battle, he desperately signaled for someone to bring him a plume and paper to write a note. When no one was able to produce these items quickly, he tried to write something on his trousers in his own blood. But he died before he could write anything legible. For more than two centuries my family has whispered and daydreamed about what it could have been that he wanted to write down. And that's it. For all we know the story was an invention and passed down through the generations as parlor fun. But in all the centuries no one has found Gerhard's gold. As far as I know, we have grown and maintained our wealth throughout the years starting only from the legitimate assets that he had acquired by the time he was killed, and for the last two generations, mostly through our shipping company. I interned there during my summers while at university."

.   .   .

IT WAS APPROACHING sunset as they finally made their way into Hans's hometown. As they rounded the final bend in the river the breathtaking view of the village suddenly appeared in front of them—the picturesque town of Cochem, nestled in the beautiful green mountains of the Mosel River Valley, with the magnificent schloss towering over the town from the hilltop above. Mason couldn't help but stare out the windshield like an excited child, his mouth hanging slightly open as he was mesmerized by the fairytale-like vista in front of him.

9

H ans's little VW wound up the narrow road from the village to the massive thirty-foot-tall entrance gates of the schloss. A small guard house was built into the wall of the surrounding fortification, with a bay window from which the guard could see arriving visitors. The old gentleman behind the window clearly recognized the car. He gave a hearty wave and a giant grin as he threw the switch to open the enormous gates. Hans and Mason both waved back. They drove into the courtyard. It looked like something out of an old movie. It was not rundown, but nothing was polished or fixed up for show either. It was a very old, historic, extremely large walled castle, that was lived in by a single family—now just the baron. Hans pointed out the western wing where they resided. Much of the rest of the castle was uninhabited or used for storage.

Just as they were about to park, Hans said to Mason, "I guess I should give you warning about my uncle. As I mentioned, his personality can be on the dark side. He never fully recovered from my family's death. He is likely to complain about everything from the economy to the weather, and he will certainly complain about the socialist French. But do not let his negativity scare you. He is a good person."

"Not a problem," Mason replied.

The baron came down the steps into the main courtyard to greet them, clearly happy and relieved to see his nephew return home. He was a tall, slender man, at least six-foot-three, with very short hair on the sides and back and almost completely bald on top. He wore an oxford shirt with a simple wool sweater, slacks, and dress shoes. Like the castle itself, his clothes were of a high quality but old and well-worn. He was still good looking for a man in his seventies, but financial troubles and tragedy had taken their toll and the lines on his face formed creases in a contour of a frown. Mason thought it was touching to see how much he cared for Hans. The baron embraced his nephew when he got out of the car before turning to greet Mason with a more formal demeanor. Mason could have sworn that the baron stiffened his body almost as if coming to attention as he turned to extend his hand to him. But Mason knew that this more formal greeting was typical in German culture. The baron was polite, neither warm and friendly nor cold and distant. His piercing gaze made Mason feel that he was being judged. But he told himself that this could easily just be the way he greeted everyone. The baron insisted that Mason call him Herr Eiger rather than by his title.

After dropping their bags in their rooms, they met the baron in the great hall. The great hall was one of the oldest rooms in the schloss, dating back to medieval times. It had a forty-foot vaulted ceiling with exposed beams and wood-paneled walls, an old oak table in the middle that could easily seat thirty, and a fireplace at one end that was six feet tall and ten feet wide with the largest mantle Mason had ever seen. By the time he and Hans arrived, the baron had already drawn each of them a stein of Bitburger Pils from the keg he kept chilled in the basement, accessible by the tap at his bar off the kitchen. It was his favorite beer, and one that happened to be a favorite of Mason's as well. The baron employed a full-time staff of four: a maid, a gardener, a security guard, and a live-in cook named Sabine.

While Sabine made a delicious, authentic German dinner of bratwurst, wiener schnitzel, and kartoffelsalat, Mason, the baron, and Hans sat by the fire in the great hall recounting some of their more memorable escapades in Paris as well as some of the families they had encountered at the party in Geneva, the wedding in Paris, and the party in the sixteenth arrondissement.

Hans went to shower before dinner while the baron offered to give Mason a tour of their family wing of the schloss. About halfway through the tour, the baron's cell phone rang. It was Henryk, the security guard calling from the front gate.

"I'm sorry to disturb you, mein herr, but there is a Kabel Deutschland van here. The driver says they are coming to upgrade the cable TV service."

"Henryk, I told them before, our service is fine. We do not need an upgrade. Send them away!" The baron turned to Mason. "I'm very sorry for this interruption. The wing we spend the most time in, which we are in right now, is one of the newer parts of the castle. It was designed and built in the early 1790s while Gerhard was still alive. In fact, the library, which I use as my private office, is said to have been Gerhard's favorite room in the castle—for the little time he had to enjoy it. He was a staunch Protestant and an avid reader, personally overseeing the library's construction and choosing the initial volumes with which it was stocked. I'm more of an Old Testament man myself. I'm a firm believer in 'an eye for an eye' when someone has done a wrong to another person, which is why I wish Germany had not done away with capital punishment. Do you believe in the death penalty, Mason?"

Mason was caught off guard by the question, and by the feeling he was being interrogated.

"Um, I don't know. It's a pretty complex topic. Not sure I can sum up my view quickly."

"Very well." The baron changed the subject. "How do you like working at SCI? Do you intend to work there as a long-term career?"

"I don't know. It's hard to say at this point. I can't see that far into the future right now."

"I've been pushing Hans to come back to Deutschland and get into a more serious line of work, such as private banking," the baron replied. "This job at SCI is all he has done since he graduated from Heidelberg. But he needs to get more serious about his future."

Mason did not reply. He understood both the differences in the generations and the baron's personal motivations to see his nephew take a more conservative approach to his career.

As their tour of the castle came to an end, the baron interjected, "Mason, one other thing: since we've only just met, I feel obliged to tell you that we consider ourselves a very private family. As such, I would appreciate it if you respected that privacy by not sharing anything you might learn about us with anyone else."

"Absolutely. I would not dream of doing so," Mason replied. And at that moment, he sincerely meant it.

DINNER THAT NIGHT was pleasant as they discussed the political environments, one by one, in almost every major western country, including the things President Obama was doing in the US, as well as the challenges the English were facing. The baron had studied at Oxford and was still a frequent visitor to the UK on business. He also had strong views on what President Francois

Hollande was doing in France. As Hans had said, the baron indeed harbored a negative view of the French—especially their socialist government. At one point the baron said, "This little midget of a president they have, Hollande—have you ever seen a more ineffective bureaucrat in your life? All these people know how to do is tax and tax and tax more. They will be the death of Europe in the end. And did you see how incompetent he was when the terrorists attacked that newspaper a few months ago, what was it called?"

"*Charlie Hebdo*," Mason responded.

"Yes. That's it."

"This *Charlie Hebdo* attack. Did you see how he looked on the television," the baron continued. "I thought this man was going to cry. How do they consider him a leader?"

"Yes, that was a very trying time for us all. Mason and Annabelle, our officemate, and I all watched it on the internet as it unfolded," Hans said. "The whole thing happened less than a mile from our office in Paris. The man who runs our company, Monsieur Bourget, lost a good friend who worked at *Charlie Hebdo* that day."

"You see why I worry about you being away there in Paris? I wish you would consider my suggestion of going into banking in Koblenz," the baron said to Hans. Mason could see by the look on Hans's face that he did not want to have this conversation, so he tried asking about the baron's shipping enterprise, but the baron made it clear that he did not want to discuss the matter, and instead reverted back to politics.

THE NEXT DAY, Hans gave Mason a tour of the rest of the massive castle and showed him all the places he and his brother used to play when they were young. Like many old mansions in Europe, there were back staircases, secret passageways, and hidden doors in walls. Mason wondered what secrets these held throughout the centuries. One of the passages led from a second-floor closet down a wooden spiral staircase and into a hidden door in the library concealed as a bookcase. The whole place was like something from an old Hitchcock movie.

In the afternoon they explored the grounds outside the main walls of the castle. On the far eastern corner of the property stood the ruins of an old church and a small, ancient graveyard.

"The church fell into disrepair in the nineteenth century. But some of the gravestones are four hundred years old," Hans said as they walked around the back of it to get to the path that led down to the town. After a brief tour of the town, they hung out for the rest of the afternoon in Hans's favorite tavern, Zum Kellerchen.

THE NEXT MORNING, Hans woke up early and headed down to the kitchen while Mason was still asleep. It was Sabine's day off and the baron was busy making breakfast.

"Hans, there's something I've been meaning to discuss with you," the baron said.

"Please, Uncle, not another lecture on marrying the right woman and having a family," Hans replied.

"Well, yes and no. What I want to say will end up there, but it may surprise you. I feel like I should share with you a life lesson that I learned the hard way—a mistake I made as a young man that I've had to live with my entire life."

Hans respectfully said, "Very well."

"As you know, I studied abroad at Oxford for a year while at university. While I was there I began dating a pretty young lady who worked at a local tavern. Our relationship became quite serious and I cared deeply for her. Eventually we became lovers. And, as so often is the case with young people who don't believe that anything unexpected will ever happen to them, she fell pregnant with my child. We were both shocked and frightened. We were not thinking about marriage at that time in our lives and so, I foolishly convinced her to terminate the pregnancy. The procedure was not legal at that time, but as with many things, for the right amount of money almost anything can be obtained. She would not even let me pay for it. That's just how she was. Always independent. I only saw her once afterwards. She met me one last time to say goodbye. I thought she would cool off after a while, but she did not return my calls after that. I wrote her a letter but got no reply. I learned later that she had moved away to another town and I never saw her again. I truly loved her. I would have, no, I *should* have married her. And now look at the irony of my life. The one thing I have always wanted was to have a family, to have children. And here I am an old man and have none. I tell you this only in the hope that you will learn from my mistakes and not repeat them. Also, I did not want you to think me a hypocrite for asking you to take advice that I did not take myself when I was your age. I'm not a hypocrite. I was just young and did not know any better."

"That's such a sad story. I'm sorry for your pain, and for you, if your life has not turned out as you wished. I do not know what I can say to set your mind at ease. I do take my life seriously and I do intend to settle down and have a family when I meet the right woman. I cannot promise you that she will come from an aristocratic family. But if it helps you to know, I am thinking about things more seriously these days."

"That's all I ask," the baron responded. "I know we've talked about this before, but when one is young, one does not realize how quickly life passes, often until it is too late. People from our backgrounds have an extra burden that everyday people do not carry. We have to continue the legacy of the generations that have gone before and secure the legacy of generations yet to come. This is the burden that comes with our privilege. You need to weigh this in your decision-making. You have an obligation to make the responsible decisions early enough in your life to ensure that our family name, our heritage, endures. I need to know that you understand this."

"I promise you, Uncle. I understand."

THE NEXT DAY as they drove back to Paris, Mason and Hans were both uncharacteristically quiet. To make conversation, Hans said, pointing at Mason's New England Patriots cap, "What is the story behind this cap? I have never known you to be a sports fan, but you wear this often."

"It's my hangover hat, when I don't have the energy to shower the morning after drinking too much. Seriously though, this team's quarterback, Tom Brady, is an impressive guy. He has won more Superbowls than any quarterback in football history and is known as a very classy person. I think he's a great role model to young kids. He's super hardworking. He perseveres through any difficulty. And he's kind to everyone—never talking trash like so many athletes do in sports today. He just has a perpetually positive attitude," Mason explained.

"Interesting. I just thought I would enquire since I have not known you to ever follow sports or discuss them."

"Yeah, I don't really follow American sports closely. And it's hard to find the games on TV over here anyway. I guess I'd say I'm more of a Brady fan than a Patriots fan, but the Pats are great, too."

As they crossed back into France, Mason asked, "I heard you and your uncle talking last night. Everything okay with you guys?"

"I believe so. He's been pressuring me for quite some time to join a private banking firm in Koblenz that is owned by an old family friend. He would like me to 'stop playing around and get serious about my life and career,' and find a suitable bride. I feel like I am running out of excuses."

"Yeah, it sucks when adults put pressure on kids to live their lives the way the adults want them to."

"In the meantime," Hans said with a huge smile, "Flavio is having another party at his villa in Florence next weekend. And Pietrojan just bought a large sailboat and wants to take us all out on it the following day. What do you think?"

"Hell yeah," Mason said as they high-fived each other.

10

F ebruary 2005
Damascus, Syria

ABDUL BIN HAKAM was born and raised in one of the poorest suburbs of Damascus. He never knew his father, and his mother never spoke of the man. His mother worked as a cleaning lady for a wealthy family in a neighborhood on the opposite side of town. Her commute to work each day took almost two hours in each direction by local bus, which rarely ran on time. Two doors down in their rundown apartment building lived Abdul's best friend, Nassim Zarwahali.

Nassim's mother died of cancer when he was ten years old. His father, Yusuf, was a handyman at local buildings nearby. Yusuf earned a meager salary but his services were in regular demand, given that all the buildings in the area dated back to the 1960s and '70s and had never been remodeled. Plumbing and electricity were unreliable, and everyone was accustomed to improvising work-arounds in order to survive. The stifling

Middle East heat made life even more challenging in the apartments since there was no air conditioning. Rigging makeshift awnings and window coverings was a common task for Yusuf to help occupants avoid the intense afternoon sun. Although he was poor by most standards, Yusuf was a good man, a devout Muslim, and he tried to raise Nassim as best he could. He was determined to help Nassim achieve a better life than he had.

Since Abdul's mother worked such long hours, Abdul spent more time in Nassim's apartment than he did in his own. Yusuf was the only father figure Abdul had ever known and took him under his wing, teaching him the ways of the world and schooling him in the ways of strict Islamic law and the Koran. In early 2005, when the boys were fourteen years old, Yusuf decided to take his son to visit his dying uncle, Yusuf's brother, who lived in neighboring Beirut, Lebanon. Abdul begged Nassim's father to take him with them. His mother reluctantly agreed and the three of them set off by train for a three-day trip to Beirut—a trip that, before it was over, would instill in the young boys concepts that would stay with them the rest of their lives.

On their last day in Beirut, Yusuf took the boys into the heart of the city to see the beautiful French architecture and experience some of the samke harra—spicy fish in tomato sauce—that the street vendors of Beirut are famous for.

Yusuf had just purchased their lunch from a local stand near the al-Amin mosque while the boys were horsing around on the sidewalk. As he walked up to them with their lunch he was as anxious as the boys were to take a bite. His face had a look of almost childlike excitement as he spoke, "Get ready to taste the best fish you've ever—"

His words were cut short by a massive explosion. The ear-shattering blast shell-shocked all within a two-thousand-yard radius, knocking Yusuf and both boys to the sidewalk. The explosion had come from a suicide bomber in a large truck, who had detonated the massive cache of explosives just as the motorcade of the prime minister of Lebanon, Rafic Hariri, was passing by. Hariri and twenty-one others were killed, including other officials traveling with him, his extensive security detail, and innocent bystanders.

Yusuf and the boys were only two blocks away. Nassim happened to be standing immediately behind his father when the blast occurred. His father's body shielded his as they fell to the ground. Abdul was standing to Yusuf's right, facing the direction of the blast. A piece of metal from the truck struck Abdul in the left side of his face tearing a massive hole across his cheek and back to his ear. Abdul fell to the ground, screaming in pain and bleeding profusely. Yusuf was also hit by shrapnel from the explosion; a bolt from the engine of the truck entered his chest just to the left of his heart, piercing a lung and other vital organs. He held on for several hours, long enough to talk to the boys as they waited for emergency services. He slipped into unconsciousness on the way to the hospital and died the following day, despite doctors' desperate efforts to save him. Although his wounds should have received much greater attention than they did, Abdul was treated and released from the hospital later the same day. The medical staff were simply overwhelmed with life-or-death cases from the hundreds of wounded. His face was hastily and haphazardly stitched up and the boys were released into the care of Nassim's uncle's family.

In accordance with Islamic law, Yusuf was buried immediately. The boys and a few of the uncle's family members were the only ones present at his service. After spending a few more days with the uncle's family, the boys were sent back to Abdul's mother in Syria by train, where they would both live with her. But given that she worked long hours, Abdul and Nassim were now left without almost no parental guidance during their formative teenage years. Apart from Abdul's mother, they felt like they were each other's only family. Their bond became stronger than most blood brothers.

In the days following Hariri's assassination, everyone in Lebanon, including the global press, blamed the young Syrian president, Bashar al-Assad. Not long before, he had famously threatened Hariri and the two were known to be at odds—Hariri, a Sunni Muslim, having consistently pushed Syria to get out of Lebanon, and Assad, a Shia Muslim, determined to maintain Syria's control in the country. To the boys, the details of the evidence didn't matter. Their lives were irrevocably shattered by the loss of Nassim's dad. They both missed him terribly, with a pain in their souls that, prior to this tragedy, they had not even known existed. At a young, impressionable age, they channeled that pain into hatred toward Assad and his regime; they were taught by this very personal life experience that the currency of their culture, from their point of view, was pain, violence—and revenge.

By the following year, the ramifications of this change in their world views were evident to all who knew them. At fifteen, the boys were not fully developed physically, but they had grown significantly. Abdul was already a skinny six feet tall, and Nassim was an even skinnier five foot ten. Both had begun to wear their hair longer and had sworn off shaving, so they had teenage stubble, each well on the way towards growing a man's beard.

One Sunday afternoon, as the boys were returning home to Abdul's mom's apartment, they bumped into Dameer, a sergeant in the Syrian army who lived on the top floor of their building. He was on the way out of the apartment, in the process of tucking his shirttail back into his uniform. They looked at him with confusion, wondering what he was doing in their apartment. He walked past them as if they didn't exist. He slammed the door behind him as he left. Dameer was in his mid-fifties and known throughout the building as an unpleasant person, prone to angry outbursts and physical violence. The boys had been taught that he was someone to avoid at all costs.

The boys found Abdul's mother in her bedroom, crying. A lamp from the bedside table was shattered on the floor, the bed was a mess, and the room looked as if it had been ransacked. Worse, Abdul's mom's clothes were torn, she had a swelling bruise on her left cheek, and bruises on her throat. The boys attempted to console her, but she pleaded, "Please, I beg of you. Do not tell anyone this happened as it will bring shame on me and our family. And whatever you do, do not attempt any kind of retribution. He is a very bad man and terrible things could happen to you and to me. You must promise me that you will not seek vengeance."

Nassim was yelling with rage. Abdul, on the other hand, was stoic and calm.

"Shhhh. It's okay, Mama. It's okay. We won't do anything. You're safe now," he gently touched her hand to comfort her.

Just over a year before, Abdul and Nassim had been like any other young boys. Even though they were poor, they were raised by peace-loving adults who tried to teach them to follow a path of kindness and hard work in life. With the death of Nassim's dad, the subsequent lack of adult supervision, and now this attack on Abdul's mom, any chance of them following a normal path in life had evaporated.

EARLY THE NEXT MORNING, as Dameer exited his apartment on the tenth floor of their building, Nassim was waiting outside his door.

"What the fuck do you want, you skinny little shit?" Dameer asked.

"You," Nassim replied, as Abdul jumped out from the corner behind Dameer and bashed him across the back of his head with a lead pipe. Dameer went down but was not unconscious. He tried to raise his hands in defense, but his efforts were futile. He was too incapacitated from the initial blow, and the fury of the assault from the young boys was simply overwhelming. It was reminiscent of wild animals tearing apart their prey on the Serengeti. The attack continued for several minutes, long past the point where Dameer's wounds would have been survivable. When they were finished, they picked up his shattered body, Nassim grabbing his feet and Abdul lifting under his arms, as inhuman noises emanated from the dying man. With a trail of blood dripping behind them, they carried him to the end of the hallway, where the large window overlooking the parking lot ten stories below was permanently open. They hoisted his heavy body and threw him out the window. Approximately three seconds later Dameer's unpleasant life came to an unceremonious, and permanent, end.

As the boys walked down the stairs back to their apartment, neither of them spoke. Their adrenaline was still running high from the attack and the vengeance they had just unleashed. "Thank you for helping me deliver Allah's righteous justice for my mother," Abdul said to Nassim.

Nassim looked him in the eye and said, "You are my brother. I will always be there for you. I would die for you."

"As would I for you." The two young men hugged and then went back into the apartment.

11

M *ay 2015*
Paris, France

MASON WAS close to finishing his first year at SCI and everything in his life was going well: he had moved to France, perfected his French, found a job, and was crushing his sales numbers. In fact, he had broken every sales record the company had. He was making excellent money and had an amazing social life hanging with Hans, his aristocratic friends, and the beautiful women that attended their parties. It all seemed perfect—except for one thing. He missed having a serious girlfriend, someone with whom he could share his life. And even though he had suggested to Hans after first meeting Kelly that he was not at a point where a serious relationship was on his mind, he was starting to rethink that position. He found himself thinking about Kelly more often, although he was still conflicted regarding whether to ask her out. Somewhere deep in his soul he knew that she was not the kind of girl he could ever just date.

Something about her felt long-term. And that scared the hell out of him.

One day Mason walked into the office and Hans had a big grin on his face.

"Why so happy today?"

"I have received news this morning that will please you," Hans replied. "Have you heard me speak of a woman named Véronique de Montrachet?"

"I think so."

"She is really nice, very beautiful, and a good friend. Her father is a famous French count. They come from an aristocratic family that have been bankers to the European nobility for centuries. Their main home is a chateau called Chaumont in the Loire Valley, just outside of Tours. Her parents keep her a bit sheltered, partly because they are quite conservative, but also because they worry people will be attracted only to their wealth and family name. Anyway, she is having a big party at the chateau in a couple weeks and everyone from our group has been invited—including you, my friend. This will be a very special party."

Mason fist-bumped Hans. "Thank you for always getting me invitations to these things. You're the best."

"Don't be ridiculous. You're part of our group now and always welcome. People would ask where you were if you did not come."

Two weeks later, as Hans and Mason drove to the end of the long, tree-lined drive of the six-hundred-year-old Chateau de Chaumont, Mason was taken aback, not just by how massive the chateau was, but by how exquisitely beautiful it was. Everything about the building and the grounds, every detail, was in order. The massive turrets on all sides, the old bridge one crossed to enter, which used to be a drawbridge, the view from the hill overlooking the Loire River. It was impossibly tasteful in its elegance, like something from a Ralph Lauren ad —the shrubs, the symmetry, the gardens, he could not recall ever seeing a place that was so perfect in its grandeur and harmonious with its surroundings, not even in the movies. *It's hard to believe that there are people who really live in places like this.*

Like most of the fancy parties Mason and Hans went to, the atmosphere was surprisingly casual; no one was dressed in evening clothes, or even blazers or fancy dresses. Véronique greeted guests as they arrived in the spectacular entrance foyer, which was so large it would easily have fit Mason's entire family home back in Richmond inside that one room. She had her dirty blond hair pulled back with a classic French headband and was wearing a knee-length skirt, a simple white blouse, and an Hermès scarf tied around her neck. Her outfit was the picture of French simplicity and elegance.

Mason took one look at her, then leaned over to Hans and whispered, "Good Lord. You weren't kidding. She is stunning. What the hell?! Like, was her mother a model or what?"

"In fact she was, until she met the count and became a countess," Hans whispered back.

Even though these parties were typically informal affairs, given the spectacular surroundings, Mason couldn't help but assume that Véronique would greet them with an air of formality. He was off by a mile.

"My dear Hans, I'm so glad that you could come," Véronique said, while giving him a hug. She then turned to Mason, kissing him on both cheeks. "And this must be Mason, whom I have heard so much about."

"I hope what you heard was all good," Mason replied.

"Oooh, I can't say that for sure."

"Damn. Then it sounds like someone has told you the truth." Mason looked directly in her eyes. "I've already been exposed."

Véronique tossed her head and laughed, then returned Mason's look.

After the small talk, Mason and Hans were led off by a butler to the garden courtyard in the rear of the chateau where the sit-down dinner for one hundred guests was being held. As they walked away, leaving Véronique to greet other guests, Mason leaned over to Hans and whispered, "Oh, brother. I think I'm in trouble. Could she be any finer?"

"My friend, I would counsel you to forget about this girl. Every rich aristocrat in France is forming a queue to try to win her favor. I mean no disrespect to you, but—how do you say in America—'It ain't gonna happen.'" Mason nodded, feigning agreement.

MASON MADE no effort to talk with Véronique during dinner. Instead, he and Hans hung out with the friends they knew best from other parties they had recently attended. After dinner, everyone moved over to the more causal sofas and outdoor furniture set up at the edge of the courtyard overlooking the river below to lounge and continue drinking the endless supply of vintage burgundy being served by the army of waiters taking care of them. After dinner both vintage port and XO cognac were offered as well. And of course, there was an open bar off to the side for those who wanted a more traditional mixed drink.

At one point later in the evening, Mason saw Véronique and a couple of her closest girlfriends slowly moving from group to group, dutifully chatting for just the right amount of time with each, before moving to the next. He knew he only needed one minute alone with her.

He tried to convince himself that he didn't care if she said no to his request for a date. But he was getting more and more nervous as he was about to execute his plan. In fact, he was nervous enough that he knew he didn't want to make his play in front of Hans and the close friends they were hanging with. So, he got up to use the men's room and to time the optimal moment to approach her. As he was returning, he killed some time by getting a cognac from a passing waiter. He then noticed her starting to move between two groups, alone this time. Mason thought it was a good omen. He knew he would not get a better shot than this. He hustled over to where she was so he could "accidentally" walk past her at just the right instant.

"Oh, excuse me," Mason said in playful banter. "You know, you should watch where you're going. I mean, you're walking around here like you own the place."

"Hello, Mason, I do hope you are enjoying our little soirée."

"It is honestly the most tastefully perfect party I've ever been to. Thank you for including me. I sincerely appreciate it."

"Don't mention it. It's very kind of you to say that."

"Listen, I know there is zero chance of us having any time to get to know each other at this big party. I was just wondering if it would be too bold to ask for your phone number? I'd love to call you sometime and maybe take you out, just for a lunch, or maybe drinks or dinner, whatever you'd like." As he'd been taught to do in sales, he just let the request sit there and said nothing more. Their eyes connected during the awkward silence.

Then, to his surprise Véronique replied, "Sure. I would like that. Do you have something to write it down with?"

"It's okay. I'll remember it."

"Okay, I'll only say it once. If you don't remember, then there will be no date." She rattled off the nine-digit mobile number, a single time, with a modest grin.

"Great. I'll call you soon." Mason sauntered back to Hans

and the gang, doing his best to contain the overwhelming excitement he was feeling. He repeated her number in his head twenty times in rapid succession as he walked. When he got back to the sofa, he discreetly typed the number into his phone as a new contact.

Later that evening Mason had gone to the bar to get a round of drinks for himself, Hans, and a few of their friends. When he returned, Hans was standing about twenty feet away from the rest of the group talking intensely into his mobile phone. Mason tried to walk over to hand him his drink, without interrupting. In doing so, he couldn't help but overhear Hans saying, "But that's not a reason to be angry, and certainly not a reason for us to stop seeing each other. Not everyone gets together all the time. We've both been busy. But it doesn't mean I don't care about you. I want to keep seeing you."

Mason discreetly set the drink on the massive stone railing next to where Hans was standing and motioned to him that he'd left it there, and then rejoined the others. A few minutes later Hans came back and sat down.

"Everything okay?" Mason asked.

Hans shook his head, without making eye contact, indicating that he didn't want to talk about it.

Around three a.m., as he and Hans were heading out the tree-lined drive leaving the estate, Mason could not resist sharing the news with his friend.

"It would not be out of line if I went on a date with Véronique, would it?" Mason asked.

"My friend, I explained to you earlier that you should put this girl far from your mind. It simply will not happen. She is on an entirely different level than most of our friends."

"Uh, yeah, well I thought I would just double-check to be

sure I wasn't making a faux pas if I happened to ask her for her number...and if she happened to say yes and give it to me!"

"You are joking with me!"

Mason had already called up the file on his iPhone and turned it to show Hans the contact entry.

"Oh my God. You are an insane man!" Hans shouted, and laughed hysterically. He then demanded that Mason recount every word regarding how he had gone about it, as the little VW came out of the massive main gates and turned onto the empty back roads of the Loire Valley to head back to their hotel in Tours.

12

Véronique de Montrachet had been raised in a gilded cage. So much so that by the age of twenty-three she felt suffocated by her parents' overprotective ways.

For the next few weeks, she spent as much time as she could at her family's hôtel particulier in Paris and she and Mason saw a great deal of each other. After their initial date, which was just drinks and dinner at a brasserie, they saw each other at least once or twice a week—sometimes with Hans, sometimes in groups with other friends, sometimes just one on one for a visit to a museum or lunch.

One day after work, Hans asked him, "Where do you see the relationship heading between you and Véronique?"

"I don't know. I haven't thought a lot about it. I think we're just friends. She's so impossibly beautiful it's hard not to think about becoming more than that. But for now, we're only friends. Why do you ask?"

"I know it's not my business but I'm a bit worried. Everyone hanging out together is great. But you two go out by yourselves enough that she may think it's heading towards something more. Do you think you've said or done anything that might make her think that you're dating?"

"I don't know. The more time we spend alone the more it feels like she might like me as more than a friend."

"I only bring it up to suggest that you might want to be careful there. If I'm right and you two have different views of what you're doing together, then someone is likely to get hurt. I think she may like you more than you know. And if I'm right, you won't be able to maintain your strategy of being neutral forever. This is my humble advice. Do with it what you will."

THE NEXT SATURDAY EVENING, Mason and Véronique went to dinner at Brasserie Bofinger, the nineteenth-century belle epoque jewel of Parisian brasseries in the fourth arrondissement. Mason ordered a particularly expensive wine, a 1990 Chateau Leoville Les Cases, and they took almost two hours to finish the bottle and their five-course meal. After dinner, they strolled through Place des Vosges, her arm through his in classic French style.

"I told my parents that I am staying at my friend Sandrine's apartment tonight," Véronique said. "So, if you want, I can stay at your apartment instead, if you would like me to."

Mason immediately thought of his recent conversation with Hans, but even with the heads-up, he still had not planned on how to handle this situation. "Okay. Yeah. That would be great, if that's what you want."

Turning to face him, she put her arms around his neck and gently kissed him long and sensuously on the lips, replying in a quiet voice, "It's definitely what I want."

Mason made love to Véronique that night, and again the next morning. For the next several weeks they saw each other three or four times a week—lunches, drinks after work, dinners at cafés, and long walks in the beautiful gardens of Paris. Whenever possible, they would sneak back to his apartment to make love, each time as passionately as the first. Everything seemed to be in perfect balance in their relationship, at least so he thought.

One evening after dinner, as they walked along the Seine on the Quai de Bourbon, Véronique said, "What are you doing Saturday night?"

"Something with you, I hope."

"Great. It's settled then. Both my parents will be here in Paris that night and I'd like you to come have dinner with us at our home."

Mason hesitated to answer. Véronique looked over at him with a puzzled look on her face.

"Is something the matter?"

"No. No. I just...I just hadn't thought about us being at that stage yet."

"What stage is that? We're just dating, aren't we? So what could be strange about a young lady bringing a young man she's dating home to meet her parents?"

"I don't know. Nothing, I guess."

"I mean, what are we doing here if we're not dating?"

Like a deer in the headlights, Mason simply froze. There were several things he thought of saying but none of them were primed to come out right. He feared he would make matters worse by speaking at all.

Véronique continued walking slowly in silence, with him following to catch up. After a few deliberate steps, she said softly, "I think you should take me home."

Mason flagged a cab and they rode the ten-minute ride in awkward silence back to her parents' mansion in the seventh arrondissement. As the taxi pulled up in front of the imposing gates, she turned to him and said, "Call me when you figure out what it is you're looking for. But I think it's best if you don't call me until you know what that is." She kissed him on the cheek and got out of the cab.

THE NEXT DAY he and Hans went to lunch and Mason told him everything. When Mason finished recounting how the night ended, Hans said, "I was worried that was happening. What is it that you thought you were doing if you were not dating her?"

"I don't know. I can't explain it. I was just enjoying hanging out with her and making love to her, but I never thought of myself as her boyfriend."

"Why would that be a problem?"

"Because I would never mislead her or her family to think we were going to become serious or that I might eventually marry her."

"Hmm. Help me understand this strange logic of yours. She is one of the most beautiful, fashionable, wealthy women in Europe. And you like each other. Why would you *not* want to become more serious with her or possibly even marry her someday?"

"Because it would never work out."

"Why not?"

"Many reasons. First, our worlds are too different. It's hard enough for two people to make a marriage work when they come from the same background. But it's even harder if they come from such different worlds. Second, I seriously doubt if her family would be excited if she ended up choosing *me,* the American, the Harvard dropout, for a husband. So, I didn't think it was wise to go down that road at all. I'm still surprised that she was even considering it."

"You puzzle me. I would not have thought of something such as this coming from someone as confident as you. I don't know why you would presume that you are not good enough for

Véronique or her family. I believe you have misread this. But if you thought from the start that you were not good enough, then there is a more important question. Why did you ask her out in the first place?"

Mason gazed down at what remained of the steak au poivre on his plate, but was unable to muster a response. Hans eventually filled the void by replying to his own question.

"If I may, I will offer a possible answer. It seems to me that something inside of you likes the challenge of striving to achieve the best, the impossible—the thing that people say cannot be done—such as getting accepted to Harvard when everyone said it could not be done; or selling more than anyone in SCI's history; or even dating the beautiful famous heiress who lives in a chateau, when your friend told you this would never happen. Perhaps you are drawn to the challenge of achieving the best or the impossible things, just to prove that you can, without thinking through whether that goal is right for you, or what you will do with it if you achieve it."

"I don't know. I never really thought about any of those things," Mason said, as he flicked the sole remaining French fry on his plate.

"You have been talking as if you are somehow confused by this situation with Véronique. I am only suggesting that your own decisions may be playing a role in the outcomes you have experienced in life."

After a few moments Mason defensively replied, "Look. I'd like to be rich as much as the next guy. But I don't want to live my life spending someone else's money and being a kept man. I'm not that desperate—well, at least when it comes to money. I'm willing to earn my own."

Nodding slightly, staring past Mason out at the pedestrians walking by on the busy street, Hans said, "I know you are not desperate, about money—or probably anything for that matter."

13

J*uly 2013*
Damascus, Syria

THE ARAB SPRING was in full swing, having already swept across Egypt and Libya, and it was now making itself felt in Syria. Centuries-old hatreds simmering among the different religious groups within the country were beginning to boil over. At the same time, in neighboring Iraq, the sudden withdrawal of the bulk of the US presence there had left a void in the western part of the country bordering Syria. One of the various factions vying to fill this void was a group that called itself the Islamic State in Iraq and Syria, better known as ISIS in the west.

The founder of the movement was a Sunni Muslim named Zarqawi. He was originally part of Osama bin Laden's Al Qaeda movement. Once the US invaded Iraq he split off and became the leader of this equally, if not more radical, group. Zarqawi was killed by US forces in 2006, after which Abu Bakr al-Baghdadi, an equally radical Sunni Muslim, took over with a vision to not just be a stateless terrorist organization, but to establish a physical caliphate in the war-torn lands of western Iraq and eastern Syria.

ISIS gained notoriety early on due to its severe brutality towards anyone who did not follow the strictest interpretation of Sunni Islam. Women were considered to have almost no rights. People from other religions were considered infidels and were forced to either convert or be killed. Homosexuality was punishable by death. And Shia Muslims, including Assad and his regime, were considered blasphemers for believing in a slightly different brand of Islam than the Sunnis, and so were enemies as well.

The ghettos of Damascus were a breeding ground for poor, uneducated, angry young men looking to be part of something bigger than themselves, something that would empower them in their unhappy lives. It was against this backdrop that Abdul bin Hakam and Nassim Zarwahali were living. The twenty-two-year-olds had both been drafted four years prior and were now reluctant Syrian soldiers. Abdul had become an accomplished sharpshooter and Nassim was a corporal in the infantry.

One weekend when Nassim and Abdul were both on leave back home in Damascus, they had a life-altering conversation.

"There is much we need to discuss that I have been afraid to say on the phone or send in a text. I am encouraged by the news. I read that al-Baghdadi continues to win battles and win converts to his new caliphate. I am also told that those who join early will be given positions of power and influence. I think the time is now for us to act on what we have been discussing for years," said Nassim.

"I have read these same things. And I believe that his movement will continue to grow in size and strength. Assad is weak and corrupt. The US hates him and will not support him. His days are numbered. I believe this new caliphate will soon control all of Syria. More importantly, I believe the infidels in the West are weak. They love the Jews, and the women, and the faggots. They are scared to take a single human life. They cannot possibly win against the righteous power of Allah's soldiers. I also think the time is now for us to act. I know a man here in the neighborhood who is rumored to have connections to people who know al-Baghdadi."

"When can we talk to him?"

"What better time than now?"

As THEY WALKED through the crowded markets and backstreets of Damascus, the young men recalled memories from their youth, when they played on these same streets, carefree and unchaperoned. The smell of the grilled lamb and falafel sold by the street vendors, the sounds of people haggling and arguing over the price of goods and trinkets, the pungent aroma of freshly butchered meat hanging in shop windows and from awnings. Together, Abdul and Nassim reflected on that earlier time with fondness, before Nassim's father had been killed and life's painful realities shattered their innocence.

The man they were meeting was a local rug dealer named Kamil. After speaking with Abdul and Nassim for a little over an hour, Kamil was sufficiently convinced of their sincerity and he agreed to tell his friends that they were interested in joining the cause. Later that evening a young street boy hand-delivered a message for them to meet again at Kamil's shop the next day at two p.m.

THE FOLLOWING DAY, as Abdul and Nassim were approaching the shop for their meeting, a van pulled up alongside them just as they arrived out front. Four men stepped out of the van with guns drawn, dragged the two young men back into the van, and blindfolded them as they sped away.

They were taken to a deserted warehouse in a northern suburb of Damascus where a small band of ISIS members were gathered, anxious to find out if these new recruits were legitimate or if they were spies sent by the Assad regime to try and infiltrate the movement. After several days of interrogations and verification of the information they had given, they were cleared to proceed to the final test. Abdul and Nassim were led into a back room of the warehouse that had a dozen supporters standing in it. In the middle of the room sat a young Syrian soldier, still in uniform and tied to a chair. He had been badly beaten. The leader pointed to Nassim.

"You! You say you are good with a knife. Here is your chance to prove it, and to prove your devotion to our cause." He thrust a large hunting knife into Nassim's hand. "The man before you is a Syrian infidel, loyal to the dog Assad. Cut off his head. Say nothing and do nothing but what I command you to do."

Nassim looked at Abdul and back at the men, and then at the young soldier, who had already begun pleading for his life. The leader's voice boomed, "Do it now!"

Nassim gathered his composure, walked over behind the man in the chair, and complied with the command of the ISIS leader. The young man's blood sprayed in all directions, splattering over everyone in the room. The exercise was neither clean nor efficient, but after a minute or two of struggling with the task, Nassim succeeded, holding the soldier's head up as the men cheered.

The next task was assigned to Abdul. The leader walked calmly to the back of the warehouse and opened the door which led outside. There was a man waiting there holding a middle-aged Yazidi woman at gunpoint. The woman was completely naked, covered in cuts and bruises, and had clearly been assaulted and horribly abused. The leader directed the man with the rifle to hand it to Abdul.

"You say you're a sniper. Here is your chance to prove it." He turned to the woman and said, "Go. Run! You are free to leave. Run away." Horrified, the woman begged for mercy rather than run. "If you run, you have a chance. If you do not start running by the time I count to three I will shoot you in the head myself," the leader said without an iota of pity.

As the woman bolted across the field the leader turned to Abdul and said, "Do not fire until I tell you to do so. And when you shoot her, I want you to shoot her in the head. If you miss, then you will endure her same fate."

Abdul took careful aim and followed the woman's movements as she zigzagged across the field. Once she was at a distance of about two hundred yards the leader said, "Now."

Abdul calmly squeezed the trigger. In a split second the woman's head jerked violently and she dropped to the ground, a misty cloud of blood hovering in the air where she had just been.

All the men present waited in silence for the leader's final pronouncement. Abdul and Nassim looked at him solemnly awaiting his decision. After a few seconds, the leader pronounced: "My brothers, welcome these new recruits into our family! Praise be to Allah!"

Cheers erupted from all who were present. Abdul and Nassim, who had felt lost for so long since the death of Nassim's father, were home at last.

14

M *ay 2015*
Raqqa, Syria

AS THEY HAD HOPED, Abdul and Nassim rose quickly up the ranks in ISIS. Two short years later, both men were seasoned soldiers of dozens of combat campaigns. Abdul was a field commander leading a company of one hundred men in battle against the forces of Assad on an almost daily basis. One day, he and a small band of his ISIS fighters had just overrun the last platoon of Syrian army troops still in Raqqa, or what remained of it. They captured the nine remaining men alive, along with the young captain who was leading them.

None of their prisoners was over twenty-five years old, including the captain. Their clothes were disheveled and they were clearly exhausted from days of fighting with limited supplies or support.

Abdul's men made every Syrian soldier kneel on the ground in a row. He walked behind them, firing a single shot from his revolver into the back of each man's head. When he came to the captain, he reached down and grabbed him by the throat, pulled him to his feet, and said, "Why do you continue to fight for that son of a whore, Assad? Why did you not join us? Had you done so, you would have a girl in your bed tonight and live to see the sunrise tomorrow, rather than die like a dog in this alley."

"I have no special love for Assad. But I would rather die like a dog than join your band of devils. You do not live by the principles of God's prophet. You twist his words to your evil desires. You are a scourge on all that is holy and sacr—"

Before the captain could finish his sentence, Abdul shot him in the temple. His lifeless body collapsed next to the bodies of his soldiers. Abdul and his men walked away, leaving the dead men's bodies where they had fallen, to be eaten by the local feral dogs desperate for food.

Later that evening, Abdul returned to his temporary housing in the suburb of Raqqa, bringing with him a new recruit. Al-Baghdadi had sent his nephew, Ziad, to be personally trained by Abdul. The building in which they were staying had been a large, single-family home, once owned by a wealthy merchant. They had commandeered it both because it had been one of the nicer buildings in the area and because it was one of the few still standing. The rest of the neighborhood was completely destroyed. Homes with no rooftops, homes blown in half, some with fires still burning inside them; as far as the eye could see there was nothing but destruction and desolation.

As they walked through the door, the first thing he said to the two other men in the living room was, "What news from Nassim today?"

"Nassim is fine. He is here."

"Praise be to Allah," Abdul replied. A few minutes later, Nassim appeared and the two hugged.

"So glad to see you also lived another day. It was Allah's wish," Nassim said.

"And you too, my brother."

Bin Hakam then said, "Meet the newest member of our team, Ziad, who I told you about last week. It is an honor to have our leader's nephew amongst us." The men embraced Ziad, each in turn.

Nassim interjected, "I told the old bitch in the kitchen to hurry and prepare our food. She is busy with it now. Are you hungry?"

"I could eat an entire goat by myself," Abdul replied.

Nassim asked him, "How went the battle today for you and your men?"

"I brought down many infidels with my rifle. They never knew my position nor saw death coming. And we ended the day by exterminating the last of Assad's dogs in the city. A young captain was leading them. I killed him last, but quickly. He angered me with his judgmental words against us and our brothers and I lost my temper. He was luckier than he knew. I had intended to kill him slowly." Abdul continued, "As for Ziad, he showed himself to be a true warrior on the field of battle today. Killed several of Assad's pigs, as well as a woman who was with them. The woman seemed to take quite a long time to die."

Ziad replied, "When it comes to the women, I like to kill them slowly."

The men all looked at each other in slight surprise and then shrugged their shoulders and laughed.

When he was finished eating, Abdul glanced around the table at his comrades. "I spoke with al-Baghdadi today by mobile phone. He has given me news and updates on many fronts. Brother Abdelhamid has made great progress assembling and training his group. Soon they will be ready to make their journey and strike at the heart of the infidels in Europe. He tells me that he is considering sending you, Nassim, with them. What would you say to that?"

"It would be the greatest honor of my life. When will we know for sure?" Nassim replied.

Abdul said, "Soon, my brother. Very soon."

"And what of you, Abdul? Did our leader have news of when or where you may be called to a higher purpose?"

"I do not know when, but I know that I have been selected to use my skills with a rifle for a very special mission. The honor of ten lifetimes," Abdul replied. The others were quick to inquire, insisting that he tell them more.

"I do not have a time or any other details yet, and I will be limited in what I can say when these things are decided. But, yes, I too will be sent abroad when the time is right to wage jihad against the infidels in the West. But first there is work for me to do here, to find ways to move more refugee women into Europe. The money we bring in from this is critical to funding our caliphate here at home," Abdul continued.

"And now, before I bathe, there is one more important thing I must attend to," Abdul said as he rose from the table. At that, the other men at the table began smiling and nodding in agreement. Abdul walked casually down the hall, opened a door, and walked down the stairs to the small, dark, one-room cellar where there was a filthy old mattress on the floor with two young half-naked Yazidi girls no older than fourteen lying on it, each with a handcuff on one wrist connected to a chain attached to the wall. As their cries for mercy and screams of pain echoed up the stairwell from the cellar, the men at the table continued to eat and laugh.

15

June 2015
Paris, France

FOR THE NEXT few days after his talk with Hans about Véronique, Mason tried to understand what had happened. He concluded that the whole aristo party scene was similar to the way he felt about Harvard. He was accepted into it, and was happy to be on the inside. But he never truly felt like he was a full member of the club. He was more like a welcome visitor. He didn't have any delusions that he was an aristocrat, nor any desire to pretend to be something he was not. To him, a serious relationship with Véronique would have been crossing an inexplicable, imaginary line. Or was all of this just in his mind? Was Hans right? Was this some pent-up issue left over from high school? Mason could not easily arrive at an answer, but he was exhausted by the self-reflection.

For the next few weeks he redoubled his efforts at work. The path to his goal remained unchanged: show amazing sales numbers in France and then get his own office in the UK. This he knew was real. This he knew how to do. This had to remain his primary goal.

In the third week of June, Bourget called Mason into his office one day and said, "I have a question for you. Are you ready to make a change?"

"What kind of change do you have in mind?" he replied.

"We're ready to start developing the UK in a bigger way and we want you to start spending more time over there. It will involve you traveling there quite often. If you are as productive as you have been in France, we will need you to set up a sales and service operation based in London, maybe a team of eight to ten people to start. How quickly that will be needed is dependent on how quickly you can ramp up sales," Bourget said.

Mason was ecstatic. This was exactly what he had hoped for; he did not hide his excitement.

"Not only am I ready to go do it, I'm ready to crush any sales goal you put in front of me, if it will lead to my being able to build and run that operation when you're ready to open an office there."

"I understand. Let's start with bringing in some big deals and we'll see what comes next," Bourget replied.

MASON BEGAN NETWORKING through existing clients and prospecting some new ones to get his first direct sales in the UK. He knew that the best way to crack the market would be to land a few large "anchor" tenants that would generate an interesting buzz amongst other possible clients. Through an existing French client, he managed to get introduced to Finlay Wilton, the chief technology officer for automaker Vauxhall. They used a lot of robotics in their early-stage assemblies and the brand was well known. Mason initially worked the Finlay connection by phone, convincing him of the value of SCI's software. Finlay finally agreed to a face-to-face lunch meeting in London. Mason knew if he could close this deal, it would help kick-start his dream of personally running the UK operation.

Mason and Finlay met for lunch the following week at a chic restaurant on Piccadilly called the Wolseley. The atmosphere was that of a grand European brasserie, with high ceilings and marble floors, columns, and tabletops; yet with a color scheme of black walls accented by white tablecloths and fine china to give the place a cooler, modern feel. As was normal throughout Europe, they took time to get to know each other before discussing anything to do with business. At one point in the discussion, Finlay said with a playful grin, "You know you're a bit of a rare bird. An American who actually seems to have a spot of culture. You know your European history and apparently you speak French well enough to work in France. We don't encounter Yanks like you very often."

Mason was in his element. He loved meeting people and learning about new places and cultures, and it showed. By the time the lunch was over he was confident that he was going to land the Vauxhall account.

16

August 2015
London, England

To Mason, London was not quite as exotic as other European cities because they spoke English. But he loved that it was a melting pot of young people from all over Europe and he was fascinated by London's history. He was particularly passionate about specific aspects of it: World War II history and great leaders, like Winston Churchill, the cabinet war rooms, the old palaces, the ancient pubs, and the historic churches and monuments. Talking with some of the guys he had met at parties in France, who were currently living in London, he learned that the coolest expat area in which to live was South Kensington, or South Ken.

Two weeks after meeting Finlay for lunch Mason closed the Vauxhall deal. And just two days after that Bourget called him to give his blessing for Mason to officially move from Paris to London and lease a tiny one-bedroom flat that would double as his office to "smile and dial" for business. This was cheaper than putting him up in hotels every night and paying for his trips to the UK.

"The Vauxhall deal is exactly the kind of anchor account we were hoping for," Bourget said. "You should consider this the beginning of the countdown until we open a UK office. Please officially start the search for office space, as well as the talent we're going to need: salespeople, account managers, a couple of tech guys, and a finance director. By the way, as you know, Kelly is currently on a six-month assignment in Berlin, helping our new office there get trained up on our software and systems. They'll probably need her for about two more months. After that, I intend to send her your way to do the same thing in London. So that's the timetable. I know it's aggressive. Be working towards it and keep me posted if you think you're going to miss being ready on any component."

"I'll be ready. We will not miss on any of it," Mason said.

MASON STARTED WITH FINDING A FLAT. He found a great little third-floor place on Onslow Gardens, just a few hundred meters from the South Ken Tube station. From this modest home base, he began the process of calling and networking his way into the UK business market for more customers and for the core UK team he would need to hire.

On the personal front Mason was feeling a little burnt out from working so much. In addition to networking business connections in London, he set about meeting new friends as well. His London-based European friends, mostly French and Italians he had met through Hans, kept him pretty occupied with fun social gatherings and meeting new people. And he felt sure that he was increasing the odds of finding a girlfriend by maximizing the number of events he went to—playing the numbers game as he saw it—assuming that this would lead to success just like it does in business.

One Friday night, shortly after arriving in London, he was having dinner at his Italian friend Ludovico's house with a larger than normal group, some Euro expats and some locals, at least four or five of whom he had not met before. A young lady named Pamela sat right across from him. She was English, with a posh accent, a kind face, and seemed both pleasant and talkative. She asked Mason what he did for work and he told her, explaining that he traveled a fair bit back to France, mentioning that he had just come back from a week in Paris. She said that she saw in *Hello* magazine that there had been some royal wedding the past weekend. He smiled and nodded but did not say anything.

"Why the funny look?" Pamela asked. But Mason just shook his head. "No. Tell me," Pamela continued. "Your smile was too spontaneous, so now I want to know. What, were you there?"

His expression changed a bit and he said, "It was really nowhere near as glamorous as the papers made it out to be. I met the groom's sister last year through a mutual friend and we've since become friends. Somehow, I ended up with an invite to her brother's wedding. It was a pretty classy affair, to be sure, but the media loves to over-glamorize that stuff."

"Well, it sounds cool nevertheless. I've been to a few weddings like that here in England. It's fun when everyone gets all dressed up and does the fairy-tale thing, as long as people don't let it go to their heads."

"Exactly. And I swear I was honestly not trying to name-drop that I had been there. I'd rather cut off my arm than be known as someone like that," Mason said. "I know there are people out there like that, but we're like oil and water."

"I believe you, I'm exactly the same way." Pamela laughed and told him not to sweat it.

As Mason and Pam were chatting, a gorgeous young woman waltzed into the room. The only seat left was at the very end of the dinner table, immediately to Mason's right and Pam's left. Mason didn't catch her name. She was extremely pretty, but not the kind, gentle type of beauty that Mason preferred. This woman was more of the Guess jeans model beauty: blond, buxom, with a spoiled, pouty look on her face at all times, like the world owed her something. She knew Pam but seemed a bit put out to be stuck next to the stranger, Mason.

The first thing she mentioned was that she was late because she had been at another gathering with some people she had recently met at Royal Ascot, a multi-day horse race and party that many believe is the social event of the year in England. It has been a tradition since the early eighteenth century and is usually attended by members of the royal family.

"I hear Ascot is a very fancy event," Mason said as he tried to make small talk.

"You didn't go?" she asked, dismayed.

Mason replied, "Uh, no. I've never been," making it clear that he was not from highbrow society. For the beautiful, status-conscious blonde, it was more than she could stand. Not only was she sitting next to this nobody, but he had never been to Ascot. She looked at him like he was a gnat that had landed in her tea. She yelled up the table for some friends to make room for her to come sit between them, and promptly switched seats. Mason looked down at his plate, barely able to maintain his composure. Pam, laughing, looked right at him, shook her head, and said, "That timing was impeccable. What were you saying about oil and water?"

17

Mason's flat in South Kensington was just a few blocks from the magnificent Brompton Oratory, an enormous nineteenth-century Roman Catholic cathedral on Brompton Road, with two-hundred-foot vaulted ceilings, exquisite baroque architecture, and an interior bathed in Italian marble. One Saturday afternoon he was walking by and stopped in, hoping to find it empty. A mass had just started, but he decided to stay anyway. In his homily, the priest referenced the local chapter of St. Vincent de Paul. Mason had never heard of this order within the Catholic Church that specializes in providing companionship for old people who don't have many friends or relatives to come visit them. Something about this immediately struck him as a worthy cause.

The priest mentioned that there would be a meeting of the local chapter of St. Vincent de Paul in the rectory immediately after the service. Mason went and listened with an open mind; he liked what he heard. This was a small commitment in time, and it was an easy call for him.

Mason was assigned a ninety-two-year-old woman named Sally Seton-Wolfe, who lived in a tiny one-room flat in Notting

Hill. The neighborhood looked like any middle-class neighborhood in the area, only in her case the flat she lived in was a single room with a kitchenette along one wall and a tiny bathroom behind a door in the corner. Furniture and belongings that long should have been removed were stacked up in the room. There was only one other chair in the whole room, besides the one Sally sat in. Her seat was a giant La-Z-Boy recliner that doubled as her bed. When standing upright, which was rare, she was about five-foot-five and weighed close to two hundred pounds, with short, thinning white hair that was usually matted to her head from lack of washing. Her myriad of health issues made it painful for her to move around, so she spent almost all day, every day, in her chair.

For a visitor, being in the flat was a challenge to the senses. It smelled of a putrid combination of stuffy attic, hospital, and urine. The government sent a caregiver in for a few hours every day to ensure she got food and was helped to and from the bathroom. But other than that, she sat in that chair every hour of every day, watching TV and, more often than she should, sipping on a bottle of cheap cognac that she had poorly hidden behind the left leg of her recliner.

Sally had been married but her husband was killed in the war before they had children. She never remarried. She had originally been in the theatre and went back into acting and dancing for a time in the 1950s, but her career details after that were thin. She had lived a hard life without many lucky breaks. And now she found herself alone—truly alone. She had one longtime friend who visited once a month, but she lived over an hour's drive from London. Beyond her, and the daily social worker who stopped by, she had no one else. In spite of all this, she tried to be upbeat. She would not wallow in self-pity, at least not in front of others.

On his first visit, Mason found that they shared a common

interest in World War II history. She regaled him with stories of horror and survival and miracles that happened during the war. It was a bit of a chore to carve out the extra ninety minutes from his day, counting travel to and from Notting Hill, but he genuinely enjoyed her company, and the satisfaction it brought him to see how much it meant to her.

ugust 2015
London, England

TWO WEEKS after Ludovico's dinner party, Hans visited Mason in London for a three-day weekend. On Saturday, Mason suggested they go to his favorite outdoor beer garden—a pub called the Windsor Castle—on the north side of Kensington near Notting Hill. As they flagged a cab on Old Brompton Road, neither of them noticed the small navy-blue Peugeot sedan following them.

A few seconds later, Spencer Hughes-Smyth's cell phone rang as he was driving with his wife just two miles away.

"Yes," he answered.

"They've just climbed into a taxi in South Ken. Based on the audio from his flat they're heading to the Windsor Castle pub in Kensington."

"Roger that, I know the place. Good work. Stay with them and let me know immediately if their destination changes."

.   .   .

IT WAS a typical cloudy autumn afternoon, but warm enough to sit outside. The Windsor Castle was packed. Mason and Hans sat at a table in the far corner of the garden, Mason with his back to the pub and Hans facing it. They were starting to work on their third pint each when a middle-aged man and his wife, along with a younger woman, approached the table.

"Sorry, would you mind if we shared the far end of your table?"

"Please. Help yourself," Hans said as the younger woman interjected, "Mason?! Is that you?"

"Good Lord—Pam. What a small world! Well, now you all *have* to join our table."

"This is my second surprise today, Pam replied. "First, my aunt and uncle surprise me by showing up at my flat to take me out for a pint. And now we happen to bump into you. This is so lovely. Uncle Spencer, this is the American expat I was telling you about last week, who was at that royal wedding in Paris."

Standing up to shake his hand, Mason interjected, "Actually it was only thanks to my friend Hans here that I was lucky enough to have an invite."

Pam was with her aunt and uncle, Spencer and Fiona Hughes-Smyth. Spencer was in his early fifties and clearly very fit, medium height and build, neatly dressed in a sweater and slacks, with a full head of close-cropped hair. His wife, Fiona, was only a few inches shorter than Spencer, wearing a simple dress with a cardigan sweater, slightly overweight, with a pleasant face and a perpetually happy look about her.

Like Pam, her aunt and uncle both spoke with posh Oxbridge accents and were clearly well-bred, asking polite questions and showing a genuine interest in both Hans and Mason as people, not just in a superficial way.

Trying to return the polite manners in kind, Mason asked, "What do you do, Spencer?"

Spencer laughed and defaulted to what was clearly a well-rehearsed answer.

"Oh, you know. Not much of anything, really. Technically, I'm supposed to be a government bureaucrat. So, I end up doing a little bit of this and a little bit of that. At the end of the day, I'm not sure what I do, honestly."

"We've often asked that same question but none of us can quite figure out what it is that he does. He's either the worst layabout in the Queen's realm or he does some super-secret job that he can't talk about. We like to think it's the latter," Pam said.

They ended up talking for longer than either group had planned and having one or two pints too many. Eventually Fiona said, "Honey, we should probably get going, as we need to get Pam home and let the boys finish their afternoon."

"Nonsense," came the reply from Spencer. "Our new friends and I are enjoying getting to know each other." He then flagged down the waitress and ordered another round.

19

September 2015
London, England

SINCE GETTING the green light from Bourget the month prior, Mason had been hard at work looking for the right people to hire for his UK team. He had already hired the director of finance, a former finance executive for *The Economist* named Steve Jeffries. A London native, Steve was instrumental in helping Mason understand UK labor laws, how to incorporate locally, as well as networking to find other employees. Together, they had been able to rent a modest office suite in a building on Regent Street, just north of Piccadilly Circus, and make offers to several other members of the core staff needed.

Steve was also a big help when Kelly O'Callaghan finally finished her stint at the new Berlin office and moved to the UK in early October to start training the new team in London. She leased a flat in the Earls Court area, just next to South Kensington, and Mason got Steve and one of the other new hires to come with him to help her move in. Mason remained incredibly attracted to her but, now that his dream of heading up the UK office was coming true, more than ever he was determined not to take any unnecessary risks with his job. And he viewed trying to date someone in his office as just such a risk. Besides, his life was pretty good on the personal front. Although the intensity of his work kept him busy during the day, he was finding time in the evenings to hang out with his London-based Italian and French friends, as well as new friends he was making—going to small gathering at their flats, and enjoying London's historic pubs.

One of his favorite pubs was the Grenadier. The Grenadier was originally an eighteenth-century mess hall for officers of the royal foot guards. In the early nineteenth century it was converted into a tiny, quaint pub situated on a cobblestone mews street in Belgravia. It's said that George IV, among other famous visitors, loved to frequent the place in his day. Small in size, with room for only about thirty people—the wood paneling, the ancient bar, the entire authentic décor make visitors feel they've gone back in time.

One Thursday evening Mason had arranged to meet Steve at the Grenadier to talk about their progress on making offers to the final members of the team. He enjoyed hanging out with Steve, not just because he was great at finance and business, but because Steve was a classic lad's lad—a six-foot-four 250-pound former rugby player who loved sports and loved to drink. Moreover, they could talk about anything: history, women, politics, without the risk of anyone being offended. Around seven p.m. Mason wandered in, ordered a pint of Guinness at the bar, and was happy to see the corner table open up. He sat down to wait for Steve to arrive. A couple minutes later he got a text from him saying that he was stuck on a last-minute call at work and would be half an hour late. Mason texted back, "Take your time. I have a Guinness in hand and I'm holding down the corner table."

Three minutes later, two well-dressed men entered the pub, walked quietly and confidently up to Mason's table, and sat down across from him. One of them looked familiar, the other one he'd never seen before.

"Hello, Mason, long time no see," said the familiar one. Mason couldn't quite make out where he knew the guy from. They both had serious looks on their faces.

"Sorry, guys. Have we met?"

"Pam's uncle. The beer garden—the Windsor Castle?" the man spoke in a hushed tone.

"Oh, yeah. Spencer. Sorry." Mason's demeanor changed from defensive to friendly. "I thought I knew you from somewhere, but you look so proper and serious now that I hardly recognized you."

"Yeah, well. Sorry about that. But it just so happens, we were hoping to talk to you about some rather serious stuff. We could use your help. And most importantly we need your discretion," Spencer replied.

"Uh, well, sure. I'm happy to help if I can, but I'm not sure how a simple Yank like me can be of service," Mason said.

"Well, let's have a talk and see, shall we? Do you mind taking a walk with us?"

"No problem," Mason said as they were leaving. "Are we going far? Because I'm supposed to meet a friend here."

"We know," Spencer said. "He's running a half hour late, so you'll definitely be back in time."

"What the hell?" Mason replied under his breath.

As soon as they stepped out onto the ancient cobblestone mews a sedan about twenty meters away pulled up to where they were standing. The driver got out, leaving the car empty. Spencer opened the back door and motioned for Mason to get in. His colleague got in the driver's seat.

"I thought we were going for a walk?" Mason said.

"Relax, we're just going a few meters down the street to get some privacy," Spencer replied.

Man, this just went from a little strange to fucking weird. Do I just get in the car with this dude? I guess I gotta assume he's legit if he's Pam's uncle, but this is bizarre.

The driver walked alongside the car until it parked back in the corner of the mews and then stood outside while the two men talked to Mason inside.

"Right, I'll get to it because we don't have a lot of time. Thank you for agreeing to talk to us. Can we count on you to keep this entire conversation, and the fact that it even happened, in strictest confidence?" Spencer asked and Mason nodded in agreement.

"Okay, remember the *Charlie Hebdo* terrorist attack in Paris back in January?"

"Of course. I was in Paris when it happened."

Spencer, reaching for a photo, continued, "Well *this* is the terrorist who was behind it. Thanks to the French police, he's now dead." Spencer passed Mason the grainy photo of a Middle Eastern man boarding a cargo ship. "A key issue we try to understand for all terrorists is how they get into Europe. This picture, which we only understood the significance of afterwards, was taken three weeks before the attack, as he was leaving Alexandria, Egypt, heading for Genoa, Italy."

Mason nodded.

Passing him another picture, Spencer said, "And *this* picture shows the name on the stern of the boat as it left the wharf."

"Okay, I give up. What does it mean?" Mason replied.

"Your German friend, Hans—his uncle owns the ship. It's a von Eiger ship."

Mason replied, "Ah. That explains why you guys want to talk to me, because I know Hans. I was trying to make sense of this bizarre meeting." *I'm also now wondering if the meeting at the beer garden was really so accidental.*

"Okay. So, it's a von Eiger ship. So what? That doesn't mean the baron had anything to do with it. He doesn't know every side deal that might get struck with every ship captain," Mason continued.

"Right you are, mate," Spencer said. "If that was it, it wouldn't mean much. But we have a great deal of other intel that implies that he's not only aware of it but that he personally negotiated the deal. Several text messages have been sent recently from jihadis in the Middle East to cell phones located near towers in the Mosel River Valley. Each time to a different number—burner phones. Each time within fifteen miles of Cochem. We know that his car has been at the precise GPS location as the phone that received the last three messages. He also calls someone else via WhatsApp every time he finishes a jihadi call so we suspect he has a partner of some kind, but we can't know for sure. We have enough right now to implicate him in transporting jihadis and women and teenagers that we believe are being trafficked by ISIS operatives, but we don't have enough to prove anything or prosecute him.

"But it's not about getting him. We need him to lead us to the bad guys. We know that ISIS and Al-Qaeda are using his ships to move guns from Libya to Syria. And we know that one of his ships, from the photo, moved the *Charlie Hebdo* ringleader from Egypt to Italy in the weeks before the attack. We believe they paid him a large amount of cash to do it, because he somehow came up with enough cash to prevent foreclosure on his castle just three days after the ship landed in Genoa. What is bringing things to a head right now is that all the chatter we are intercepting indicates that ISIS is going to do something big and very bad in Paris again—in the next few months—and that the jihadis who are going to do it are being moved from Syria by ship, because walking in with the regular refugees through Turkey is too risky for them right now since we have every policeman, border agent, and dog catcher between here and Syria on high alert looking for them."

"Wait. Hold on. You said everyone is looking for them. So, you know who they are?" Mason asked.

"This is one of the key players." Spencer reached into a file folder and pulled out another grainy picture. "His name is Abdelhamid Abbajad. He's a very bad guy. A hardcore jihadi. Thinks all Westerners are infidels. He has Belgian citizenship, but he's been radicalized by Islamic State fanatics in Syria. His writings indicate that he thinks the way to hurt the West is to go after our economies, and the way to do that is to create terror and mayhem in the streets so that people stay home out of fear. Spending drops, then markets drop, sending our economies into recession."

"Okay. I need you to slow down. Can I talk for a minute?" Mason was more than a little concerned now.

"Sure," Spencer replied.

"Who the hell are you guys and why are you telling me all this? I mean, one minute I'm in a pub waiting for my buddy and the next minute you're feeding me a fire hose of secret agent shit. What the hell? And isn't this all classified stuff?"

"Yes, thank you. Those are great questions. And I apologize for not starting with introductions; I thought it was important to first impress upon you how serious this is, that time is of the essence, and that a lot of innocent lives are at risk," Spencer replied. "To answer your first question, sorry, you don't get to know who we are. You know who I am but where I work is not important. Let's just say we are the guys that don't carry business cards. My colleague in the front seat is American. Say hello to Jeff. Jeff, say hello to Mason, my niece's friend who knows the von Eigers."

"Hello, Mason," Jeff said, in a deep voice with an American midwestern accent.

"Jeff flew over here from Langley, Virginia, just for this meeting and to assess you for himself," Spencer said. "Regarding why we are telling you all this? The answer is: because we need your assistance, plain and simple. And believe it or not, you are currently the only person in the world that we know of who can help us out."

20

M ason looked at his watch, wondering how long he had been in Spencer's car, and whether he was going to miss his meeting with Steve back at the Grenadier.

"We've been trying for almost a year to get someone inside Baron von Eiger's office library there at the castle, but nothing has worked," Jeff said. "We've messed up their cable service, their phone service, you name it. Every time we send a 'repair-man' to fix it we can't get near the library or the baron won't let us in at all. The security is too tight, and they almost never have visitors. You are literally the only person we know of who has visited as a guest in the eighteen months we've been watching him."

"We're way out on a limb here, way further out than we like to be," Spencer said. "I had to make a judgment call after meeting you just once at the beer garden. I thought you were worth the risk. Jeff will have to make his own assessment tonight. You seem like a straight shooter. We know your grand-father fought at Normandy and at the Bulge, may he rest in peace, and that he raised your father to believe in his country and that your father raised you that same way, by all we can tell. We are straight shooters as well. So, here's the deal: we are asking you to help us. We want you to visit your buddy Hans, at their schloss, as often as possible in the coming weeks. We need you to listen out for, and look for, any information that might connect his uncle to these terrorists or indicate anything about the timing of their movements—in the unlikely event that you can spot anything like that laying around. But primarily, we want you to put a special book into his library, near his desk, that has a listening device in it. That's it."

"You want me to snoop around and spy on my close friend's uncle, in his own house?"

"That's exactly what we want you to do. And to do it soon, and to not get caught, and to tell no one," Spencer said. No one said anything for the next few seconds while they let the concept sink in with Mason.

Finally, Spencer spoke. "Believe me, we get it that this must seem very disloyal and distasteful to you. We wouldn't be asking if we had any other way. Eavesdropping on the baron is the only way we know of to catch the bad guys before they kill innocent civilians—full stop. And from the chatter we are hearing from our sources, we are almost out of time."

Mason was still silent. He loathed everything about this proposition. His brain was working overtime to find a way out. He decided to be as up front as he possibly could.

"Gents, I'm flattered that you reached out to me to ask for my help. And I get that being part of your plan is probably the patriotic thing to do. But I'm going to need some time to think about this. If I'm being really honest with you, I don't see how I'm going to ever agree to spy on my best friend and his family, especially after how loyal they have been to me. I'm not saying no, categorically. And I'm happy to keep all this just between us. But you should know that it's really unlikely that I'm going to partici-pate in this."

"We thought you might say that. So, we'd like to offer you an additional—what shall we call it—incentive. I believe you're starting a new company here in the UK, yes?"

"Yes, that's correct."

"And I take it you've applied for a corporation license with Companies House, as well as a work visa to be able to work in the UK as a US citizen?"

"Obviously, yes to both."

"Yeah—the odds are pretty much zero that either of those applications will get approved. In fact, we are planning on having a conference call with our French counterparts tomorrow to see that your work visa for France is revoked."

Before Spencer had finished the final sentence, Mason flushed red and began to sweat profusely. He couldn't believe what he was hearing. His emotions ran from rage to primal fear. Within seconds he had caved emotionally on the issue at hand. He couldn't bear the thought of being unemployed again, and sent home from Europe for lack of work papers. Everything he had worked to achieve would have been for naught.

"I can't believe I'm hearing this. You're supposed to be the good guys, and here you are blackmailing an innocent man to do something underhanded for you. It's utterly disgusting."

"Spare us the self-righteous attitude. We're trying to save the lives of hundreds, possibly thousands of European citizens. Do you think we care if one bloody Yank loses his job and gets sent home?"

After a brief pause, Mason said, "Alright. I'd like to revise my earlier statement. I'm inclined to help you. But I'd still like to have a day or two to think about this. It's a lot to process, having all this thrown at me at once."

"You don't have to decide anything tonight. You have the

freedom to make the decision to either help us, or not help us and suffer the consequences. But Mason, listen to me carefully. The one decision you do *not* have the freedom to make is whether or not you keep this meeting and this information confidential. You cannot tell anyone, via any medium of communication, that this meeting ever happened—not Pam, not Hans, not anyone—ever. Is that clear? Should you decide not to honor this demand for discretion, I promise you the ramifications will be orders of magnitude beyond just losing your job."

"Okay. I assure you, I won't tell anyone, ever," Mason replied.

"Alright, one last thing and we're done here for tonight. Take out your phone and take down this number I'm about to give you." Spencer gave Mason a number which Mason keyed into his contacts.

"You can always text me at that cell number, but I ask that you never use my name or give any other important information in the text. It's not a phone, so it won't do any good to call it. And it's untraceable. It comes into a special device that's on my person at all times. I will rarely text you an actual message back. I typically only reply with a number one for yes, a two for no, or a three for okay, as in understood. Rarely anything more. Don't ask me to explain, I'm sure you understand it has to do with traceability. Okay. We're done here."

Spencer opened the door and slid out. The driver waiting outside opened Mason's door and let him out. Spencer put his arm around Mason and walked a few steps towards the Grenadier with him. He turned to face him as he shook his hand and said quietly, "I hope you decide to help us. I'm sorry we have to play hardball on this with you. But we really need you on this one. We literally have no one who can get inside that castle. There are lives at stake, and we don't have much time. Please let me hear one way or the other in the next forty-eight hours. Give me a yes or a no."

Mason nodded and, just as Spencer turned to walk away, said, "I still think that somehow you're wrong about Baron von Eiger."

"Maybe," came the reply with a condescending smile.

"I know him. And he's a good man. What makes you so sure you're right?"

"Because desperate people do desperate things. I've found that it's not the person who tries to get something they really want who becomes desperate. No. It's those who have grown accustomed to already having something which is important to them, and who risk losing it—like an especially important job," he said as he nodded towards Mason, "or wealth and status, or an ancient heritage like a castle. People, even good people, who risk losing things of this magnitude can become truly desperate —and they are the most dangerous people of all, because there is nothing they won't do."

Just then, a device in Spencer's jacket beeped. He looked at it and said, "You need to hustle back in there. Your buddy will be here in three minutes. Thanks for chatting with us."

21

M ason got very little sleep that night. He tossed and turned, considering his options.

If I help these guys Hans's uncle could go to jail or get hurt. They could even lose their ancestral home, all because of me. What a grotesque betrayal of his friendship.

On the other hand, if the authorities miss their chance to arrest the terrorists before they kill innocent people, how am I going to live with that—knowing there was a chance I could have helped stop them.

I wish Hans and I had never gone to the Windsor Castle beer garden that day. But somehow I suspect that Spencer would have found some other way to "accidentally" meet me.

Mason knew he was going to agree to help Spencer. But, before he made his final decision, there was one important thing he needed to do.

The next morning Mason carefully typed a text to Spencer, "Same place, tomorrow, 6:00 p.m.?" He read it three times, and even checked the number again, and finally hit send. A few minutes later he received a text from an unknown number that simply had the number two in it. *What does he mean, no!? What the fuck?* It took him a few minutes to calm down enough to figure out that it was probably something as simple as a scheduling conflict. He texted again. This time he wrote, "Same place tomorrow, 7:30 p.m.?" Within a minute the reply came back, again from the unknown number: *1*. It was on. He felt simultaneously relieved and incredibly nervous.

THE NEXT EVENING Mason left his flat at 7:15 sharp to hail a cab for the short ride to the Grenadier. He took the lift to the ground floor and opened the main door to his building, to find Spencer sitting on his porch railing and a short man casually dressed in a Manchester United football shirt standing next to him, holding a small satchel.

"Hey, guys. I thought we were meeting at the Grenadier?" Mason said, with obvious surprise.

"I know. Sorry about that. We're not big fans of predictable behavior," Spencer replied. "Mason, meet Rupert. Rupert, this is Mason." They nodded at each other.

Spencer stood up and approached Mason, shaking his hand.

"Good to see you, my friend. Let me apologize in advance. It's not that we don't trust you. We do, or we wouldn't be talking. But my friend Rupert here needs to scan you quickly. Can we step back into your foyer for just a minute, off the street?"

Mason obliged. Rupert took a small electronic wand out of his satchel and scanned Mason from head to toe, looked at the device, then looked back at Spencer and nodded, indicating all clear. Spencer then opened the door and motioned for both men to head back outside.

"Cheers, Rupert," Spencer said. Rupert simply waved without looking back and got into a waiting car on the other side of the street, which then slowly pulled away.

"That wasn't a metal detector, was it?" Mason asked.

Spencer laughed. "Good Lord, no. It was a scan to determine if you had any listening or broadcasting devices on you. They make them so small now that they're almost impossible to detect without special technology. Which reminds me, considering the sensitivity of the stuff we're discussing, you wouldn't mind powering down your phone, would you?"

"Not at all." Mason turned off his iPhone.

"Fancy a pint at the Anglesea Arms?" Spencer asked. "It's a nice night to sit out on the front terrace, and the tables are far enough apart that we can speak privately."

Mason nodded and said, "Why not? It's my local. Love that place."

"WHAT ARE YOU HAVING? I'm buying," Spencer said once they were at the pub.

"Thanks, I'll have Fuller's ESB, please," Mason said.

"Excellent choice. We'll make an Englishman out of you yet. Two ESBs, please," Spencer said to the bartender.

Once they were seated on the terrace at the table furthest from any others, Spencer continued, "I was pleased to get your text. I hope you're going to tell me that you're with us."

"I'm an intensely loyal person," Mason replied. Hans is one of my closest friends in the world. And he's already been through a lot more shit than most people deal with in a lifetime. He doesn't deserve to be betrayed by a friend. So, on the one hand, every fiber of my being tells me to run away from you guys. On the other hand, I understand your job. If these jihadi assholes are for real, and if they're coming into Europe to kill innocent people, and there is even a chance that I might be able to help save those lives—then I don't see how I can walk away from it, especially now that you've made me an offer that I can't really refuse without fucking up my life and that of another friend. So, I guess I'm ultimately going to say yes. But there is one thing preventing me from committing, and only you can solve it."

"I'm pleased to hear where you're heading. But hold your next thought for just a minute. There is something I want to emphasize to you before we go any further. If we all play this right, there is no need for Hans, or the baron, or anyone to ever know that you helped us. We are only asking you to get us info that can help us catch Abbajad and his jihadis. If we do that, the mission will be accomplished, and I'm confident that it will give us enough info to bring the baron down. But that won't be your problem. That will be ours. Again, there is no need for anyone to ever know you helped. You can go back to living your normal, anonymous life."

"I hadn't thought of that. But I'm not sure it matters anyway. If I end up ultimately being responsible for bringing down his uncle, I don't know that I could face him after that and pretend to be his friend."

"You need to separate the two things. The way I see it, you could absolutely still be lifelong friends on the other side of this. Either way, it may all be for naught. We don't know what's going to happen so let's not waste time discussing theory. Tell me what the one thing is I can solve for you that will get you on board, and if it's in my power, I will solve it," Spencer said.

"Okay. The cold reality is I have no more idea than a man on the moon if you guys are for real, or if maybe you are the bad guys, and you made all this shit up about von Eiger to trick me into some dirty scheme to eavesdrop on the baron for some crooked business deal. Now I know you can't tell me who you work with or any details at all. Fine, I don't need to know the details. I just need to know for certain that this whole thing is sanctioned by the British government—that you are representing the government. If you can satisfy me of that, I'm in."

"I guess that's a fair question. But I'm not sure what we could do that would still maintain secrecy and yet be sufficient proof for you. Are you thinking some throwback to the cloak and dagger days of the resistance during the war where we get the BBC announcer to say some phrase?"

"Not likely. You could pay any wanker announcer a couple hundred quid and he'd say just about anything on the radio these days. I'm afraid I'm going to need something a bit more substantial."

"What do you have in mind?"

"I'm open to other ideas if you don't like this one. But I'm thinking more like Big Ben," Mason replied.

"What about Big Ben?"

"Tomorrow, at noon, have Big Ben strike the count of twelve, exactly ninety seconds late—not a minute late, not two minutes late—exactly ninety seconds late. I figure, as heavily guarded as the Houses of Parliament are these days, if you guys can achieve that, then you represent the British government," explained Mason.

"It's a tall order, and we might be able to make it happen. I'll have to check. But even if it can be done, it will surely take some time. There's no way we can move as fast as tomorrow," Spencer said.

"Sorry. I have to cry bullshit on that. If you guys are the real deal then the people you're going to have to tap to make this happen can do it in hours, not days, not weeks. Here's my logic: if you're the bad guys, given enough time to come up with a scheme to bribe the right people, you may be able to make it happen. But only the good guys could do it the next day. It's tomorrow. It's noon. Big Ben chimes ninety seconds late—or I'm out."

Spencer forced his face into a position that could almost pass for a smile.

"You're a right bloody pain in my ass, Wright. But you're smart and I like the way you think. It gives me hope that you might end up being a valuable resource. Alright, let's be clear: if I can pull this off, and don't get sacked in the process, then you're in—all the way. There is nothing else, right?"

"Yes. That's it."

"Okay, then what say we meet at 12:05 p.m. tomorrow at the main entrance to the National Gallery. You'll be able to hear Big Ben from there, and we have things to discuss. There's not a minute to lose. We won't need long, maybe fifteen minutes."

"Done," Mason replied.

"Right. Then I need to piss off. I was going to stay and have a few more with you, but I have a lot to get done before noon tomorrow."

Spencer finished what was left of his pint, shook Mason's hand, and briskly walked off into the night.

22

I t was a short walk from Mason's office to the National Gallery on Trafalgar Square. Mason got there fifteen minutes early. He had set his old-fashioned wristwatch to the exact time displayed by his iPhone the previous night—before meeting with Spencer—just in case anyone had the cheeky idea to move the time being broadcast on the cell phone network forward ninety seconds, to make Mason think Big Ben was late ninety seconds. He had even slept with the wristwatch on his arm. As of 11:45 a.m., the time on his wristwatch still matched the time on his iPhone exactly. And then it happened. Noon came and went without a gong from Big Ben.

Mason stopped an elegant lady passing by with an expensive watch on her wrist and asked the time.

"I'm showing 12:01 p.m.," she replied kindly. He thanked her and walked to the edge of the railing, looking out over the square at Nelson's massive column, and Parliament in the distance beyond. It was an extraordinary event. He watched as the second timer he had set on his phone continued to tick, and sure enough, at precisely 12:01:30, Big Ben chimed twelve times. It sent a chill up his spine.

Wow. This is some crazy shit. This is really happening. I can't believe I'm doing this.

By 12:05 p.m. Mason had made his way over to the main entrance to the museum. But there was no sign of Spencer. By 12:10, just as he was beginning to worry, a young teenaged girl broke off from her friends heading into the museum and approached Mason.

"Excuse me, sir. But are you waiting for a gentleman friend named Spencer?" Mason replied that he was. She then said, pointing to the square, "He told me to tell you to meet him at the base of Nelson's column." Mason thanked the young girl and headed over to meet Spencer.

"I know. I get it—you guys don't like to be predictable."

"Walk with me," Spencer said, and after a few steps he said, "Let's get to it. Forget about the baron and what may or may not happen to him. The only thing we care about right now is getting Abbajad before he gets to Paris. We need you to find a way to go through any of the baron's papers that you can find or to listen out for anything that might give information about the movement of his ships or have any reference to the number thirty-six. I know it sounds bizarre. But we believe—we're not certain, but we believe that Abbajad goes by the code name '36' when being referenced in jihadi chatter online. We think it's unlikely that the baron will discuss anything about him openly by name. Listen for the number thirty-six if you are ever in a position to overhear his conversations. And listen for anything to do with dates, or any mention of the Syrian city of Latakia. That's not how it's pronounced in Arabic, but we don't believe the baron speaks Arabic. We have strong reason to believe that Abbajad will be leaving by boat from Latakia. You got all that?"

"Got it."

"Repeat it back to me." Mason did. "Okay, good. If any of that yields fruit it will be great. But all of it's a long shot. It's unlikely he'll leave his papers where you can see them. And it's unlikely he'll talk openly if he thinks anyone is in earshot. So now to the most critical thing we need from you." Spencer stopped walking. He set his briefcase on the railing of the building they were standing in front of and opened it. He very carefully removed an old-looking book with a brown leather cover, handed it to Mason, and said, "We know his office is in the library. We need you to put this book somewhere on a bookshelf in the library, within three meters of his desk."

"Is it a bug?"

"You could say that," Spencer replied. "It's a very special bug. It has a battery that will last for several years. It records any conversation above a whisper that is within its range. It also has a motion sensor in it. It stores the conversation and waits until thirty minutes after all motion within its view has ceased before transmitting its encrypted contents to us—just in case the subject has a transmitter detector and walks around sweeping the room to see if any transmissions are taking place. One way or the other, you've got to get into that library and plant this book without getting caught."

"Okay. To tell you the truth, none of that sounded as bad as I had feared," Mason said.

"Yeah, it always sounds easier than it is. Just take extra care to not get caught," Spencer replied.

"I will," Mason said, and after a short pause he continued, "Is that it?"

"That's it, mate. Please be sure to text my off-grid device when you have the dates fixed for the next time you'll be at the schloss. I think you guys are looking at next weekend, no?"

Mason shook his head with incredulity.

"Sorry to be intrusive—just doing my job. Also, be sure to check your luggage on the flight so your special little brown book doesn't get any scrutiny at security. And one last thing, if you are successful at planting the book, text me *only* the phrase 'Missing you.' If anyone happened to see your phone as you're texting, or your text history, anything, all they'll see is a completely innocuous phrase. If I don't get anything from you, I will assume you were not successful."

Mason nodded.

"Right. Let's recap. Check your bag when you fly. Treat the book like gold. Text me only if you succeed. Don't take any unnecessary chances that might get you caught, because you can try again later if you don't succeed on this trip. And one last thing: good luck and Godspeed. You're doing a great thing here, even though no one will ever know."

"Thanks," Mason said as Spencer shook his hand.

"Oh. And one final word of caution," said Spencer. "Remember, random bad luck is always your worst enemy."

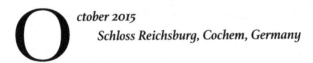

ctober 2015
    Schloss Reichsburg, Cochem, Germany

THE NEXT WEEKEND, as expected, Mason had to be in Frankfurt for a sales pitch with the parent company of a UK-based manufacturer that wanted to use SCI software. He had told Hans a few weeks before when the meeting was first set, and he called him again a few days before heading over to ask if he wanted to hang out in Frankfurt. As Mason hoped, Hans told him to just come to the schloss after his meeting. Hans wasn't a big fan of Frankfurt. He felt it had been taken over by English and American bankers and he often complained that it was too "new" for him—since much of the historic old Frankfurt was destroyed in the war.

Mason arrived that evening just a few minutes after Hans. It was a short commute home for Hans as he was now working at a private banking firm just down the road in Koblenz. Sabine was already making a dinner of sauerbraten and Karoffelpuffer for them, and the warm smells from the kitchen permeated throughout their entire wing of the schloss. Apparently, the baron was not home. Mason had had to gamble whether or not he would be there, not wanting to risk suspicion by asking in advance.

"It's too bad your uncle's not here. Be sure to give him my best," Mason said.

"Yes. Thank you. We are not sure where he is. Lately, he has been working a great deal," Hans replied. "He comes and goes at all hours, so we never know when we'll see him."

Mason and Hans feasted on Sabine's dinner and drank more Bitburger than they should have. They ended up sitting on the terrace overlooking the massive interior courtyard and the town of Cochem below until almost midnight, enjoying the last of the warm autumn weather and laughing and reminiscing about Paris. Finally, they both admitted that they were exhausted from the work week and headed up to their respective rooms to crash. Mason washed up and then set his iPhone alarm, on vibrate, for 3:30 a.m., put it under his pillow, and fell fast asleep.

He woke up what seemed like seconds later. He had decided that tonight was his best opportunity to plant the book in the library since the baron was not home. Wearing just his boxers, a T-shirt, and socks, he quietly made his way down the main stairs and to the wing that housed the library. It was hard to walk quietly, even when tip-toeing, given how the old wooden floors creaked with every step. The dead silence throughout the castle seemed to magnify the sounds.

As he feared, when he got to the library door, it was locked. But he had a plan B. He remembered that on his very first trip to the schloss, Hans had shown him a secret back staircase that descended from a closet on the second floor and came out into the library via a door on the back wall that was disguised as a bookcase. However, he wasn't sure he remembered in which closet the entrance to the staircase was hidden. He crept back upstairs as quietly as possible. And through a tedious trial and error of three closets, he found the entrance. He was certain that no one had been on that spiral staircase since Hans had first shown it to him, as it was covered in dust and spider webs. The smell of old, musty wood filled the stagnant air. Using the light on his iPhone he descended the stairs through the jungle of spider webs.

When he arrived at the bottom of the steps in front of the door, he was relieved to find that it only had a simple wooden handle—no special lock. He turned the handle and pushed. The door slowly swung open. No alarms, no surprises. He was in the library. He turned off the iPhone light. The full moon shining from across the Mosel River Valley was lighting up the room through the magnificent fourteen-foot-high windows across the left wall. The instant he took his first step into the library, his anxiety exploded from simple nervousness to profound dread. He was now past the point of no return. Being caught walking around the castle at night could be excused. But nothing could explain away being caught in the baron's private office. In Mason's mind, the betrayal of his friend was no longer conceptual. With this act it had now transpired.

He made his way over to the bookcase immediately behind the baron's desk and found an inconspicuous spot on the second to bottom shelf to slide the book into place. It fit perfectly among the scores of dusty, historic volumes that filled the six wall-to-wall shelves in the mahogany bookcase.

He scanned the baron's desk. It was neat and clean, with no random piles or loose papers of any kind. He tried opening the file drawers of the beautiful antique desk, but they were locked. He looked closer at the lock on the drawer to his left and realized that the old drawer sagged just enough that the lock mechanism barely fit into the strike plate above it in the desk frame. He took a letter opener from the top center drawer and pushed on the latch. With a short *snap* it gave way and the drawer opened exposing a drawer full of file folders.

Mason looked in the first few folders and found nothing of interest. But in the third folder was a series of financial spreadsheets and detailed notes, some typed, some handwritten. His Harvard Business School training kicked in and he was able to see immediately that the files revealed a series of cash inflows and outflows to and from banks all over Europe and the Middle East. Other folders had associated correspondence, much of which matched the bank transactions and dates. Some of the information was in German but most of the bank records and printouts were in English. For the next ten minutes, he pored over the documents and the spreadsheets. From what he could gather, every time there was a cash transaction coming in, presumably from one of the baron's ship captains for carrying jihadis, their weapons, or refugees, he would send a portion of that cash to a Swiss bank account. The memos for many of the transactions were identical: *zu Klug*. Mason knew that "zu" in German meant "to." The baron was working with someone who went by either a name or code name of Klug.

The other curious thing was that one file referenced, "MI6 using cable TV repairmen to try to bug the schloss." This info had "von Klug" written next to it—"von" meaning "from," indicating Klug was privy to MI6 intel on the baron. Mason could not tell much more than that, but his best guess was that the baron was getting inside info from Klug to protect him from being caught, and they were splitting the jihadi cash.

After a few more minutes of snooping, Mason realized that he should be taking photos of all of this with his iPhone. He spread out what he thought were the most critical documents on the desk and had just taken the first picture—with the flash on

—when he heard the main gate to the schloss compound opening in the distance. He initially froze with fear, but then, in an adrenaline-fueled rush of panic, he began a desperate scramble to put everything back in order and get back to bed. He closed the drawer and pushed the latch down again as hard as he could so that it slipped back up into the strike plate above and locked again. He then bounded across the library floor and waited for a few seconds to listen before going through the secret bookcase door. He had heard the gate open but had not heard anything else. He asked himself if he had mistaken some other sound for the gate and began to think it was a false alarm. Unable to resist the temptation, he crept over to the giant windows on the far wall of the library to peek out and see if anyone had driven up to the main wing of the schloss.

He had not been at the window for more than two seconds when the headlights of a car that had just come through the gate rounded the bend coming into the courtyard and illuminated him standing in his underwear smack dab in the middle of the giant library windows. Mason dove to the floor, almost certain that he had gotten out of view before whoever was driving the car could have noticed him standing there. He was confident he had moved instantly—but not positive. It all depended on where they were looking as the car flew around the curve. He bolted across the room in less than a second, closed the hidden door securely behind him, flew up the spiral staircase two steps at a time, secured the hidden door in the closet and the closet door to the hall, and bounded back down the hall to his room in leaping tip-toe steps that would have made Mikhail Baryshnikov proud. Quickly closing the door to his room, he dove back into his bed and faced the wall—his heart pounding at twice its normal pace—pulled up the covers, and pretended to be asleep.

Less than a second after his head hit the pillow, he heard the echo of the main door closing downstairs and someone coming up the steps at what could have been construed as faster than normal pace. He heard the door to Hans's room, next to his, open for about five seconds and then slowly close again. The footsteps came to a stop just outside his door followed by silence for what seemed like an eternity. Mason thought his heart would explode. After a brief pause, his door opened.

24

The next morning Hans and Mason were hanging in the kitchen. Mason looked a bit haggard from his lack of sleep the night before, but no one seemed to notice. Sabine was making wurst and scrambled eggs while they sat at the massive old oak table drinking Bloody Marys and talking. The smell of the meats cooking on the old stove, the fifteen-foot ceilings with exposed beams, the ancient stone tiles on the kitchen floor all helped fuel Mason's imagination as he daydreamed. *How many people over the centuries, speaking how many different languages, have sat in this kitchen, hungover, waiting for breakfast, while they discussed contemporary affairs of their era—affairs that were often of such a magnitude that we still study them in school today—wars, kings, plagues, assassinations?* Mason then shifted his thoughts to the events of the night before when he was interrupted by a question from Hans.

"So, how is the dating scene in London?" Hans asked. "Pam, the one we met at the beer garden, seemed quite nice. Are you and she seeing each other at all?"

"Not really. I'm just not rushing into anything yet with

anyone. Trying to stay active socially, but not seeing anyone seriously. Do you have any news from Véronique?"

"I think she is doing fine. She is presently dating the son of a marquis. He is a bit boring but a nice guy. Why do you ask? Do you have any regrets about her?"

"No. I still don't think we were meant to be together. And I can't say that I regret dating her for the short time we went out. I think she's a very cool young lady. I confess it was great to know that someone that rich and beautiful was willing to go out with a simple guy like me. But I don't think I'd say 'regret' is a word I would use with her. I'm hopeful that she doesn't dislike me."

"I know she does not dislike you. In fact, I have spoken with her, so I can say this with a strong degree of confidence." Hans continued with a playful look, "How about Kelly? I hear she just moved over to the UK office after finishing the training here in Berlin. How is that going to work out for you?"

"Ugh. That's gonna be hard for me, as you know. I still think about her a lot," Mason said when the baron walked into the room.

"*Onkel,* I did not know you were home!" Hans said. "Come join us for *Früstück.*"

"*Guten Morgen,* Herr Eiger," Mason said.

"*Ja,* I got home late last night. Tried not to wake you guys. *Hallo,* Mason. Nice to see you. I was wondering whose car that was in the courtyard. I peeked into the guest room as I came in last night to try to make out the figure in the bed, but I couldn't tell who it was," the baron replied, then turned to Sabine to ask for some breakfast too. "*Morgen, Sabine. Bitte machen sie noch eine platte für mich.*"

As far as Mason could tell, the baron did not behave as if anything was out of the ordinary or suspicious. He wondered: *Did he see me and he's just toying with me, or am I in the clear? If he*

*knows then he's a master at playing this game. Not knowing is
fucking killing me.*

The baron finished his meal in what seemed like three bites
and then headed up to his library to work. Mason and Hans
continued to talk at the breakfast table, and each had another
Bloody Mary, while Hans gave Mason the details on his budding
relationship with a young lady from Bonn who worked in his
office.

After breakfast Mason and Hans went to the gym in the
basement of the castle to work out for a while and continue
their talk. Mason steered the conversation back to women, as it
was a natural discussion for them and it kept his mind off the
stress of wondering if he had been busted by the baron last
night.

Looking over at the far side of the basement, Mason noticed
that a section of the stone foundation wall had been torn out.

"What happened over here?" he asked Hans. "It looks like
that section of foundation was dug out on purpose."

"Yes, unfortunately it appears my uncle was at it again. Once
or twice each year he—how do you say—'loses it' and digs,
either in the courtyard, out on the grounds somewhere, or here
in the house."

"Has he blown a gasket? What is he digging for? Don't tell
me he is looking for the lost gold. I thought you said it was most
likely a myth?"

"As far as anyone knows it *is* just a myth. But it seems to be
haunting my uncle and at times he cannot control himself. I
don't know what to do with him." They both shook their heads
in amazement.

Near the end of his workout, Mason heard the main door to
the schloss slam. He looked up through the small cellar window
and saw the baron get into his car and drive away.

"Hey, I'm all done. I'm going to hit the shower," said Mason.

"What do you want to do this afternoon? We could walk down the hill and hang at the Zum Kellerchen if you want. But I can't get too wrecked because I've got to fly back early tomorrow."

"I am easy. Zum Kellerchen is always good for me," Hans said.

Mason headed upstairs to shower. But before going up to the second floor, he couldn't help but wonder if the baron could have possibly left the library door unlocked. It was a stupid thought, because his main mission was accomplished—the bug was in the library near his desk, and he had been able to pull some significant intel out of the baron's financial documents. Plus, he had already dodged one bullet, or so he hoped. But he was all in on the mission and he held out hope that he might possibly get a chance to take some more quick pictures of the documents he'd seen the night before.

Mason very casually turned left after the main entrance hall, rather than going up the stairs, and headed down the dead-end passage that led to the library. Before he knew it, he was standing outside the library door. He listened carefully before proceeding. Sabine was in the kitchen washing dishes. Hans seemed to still be in the cellar. He placed his hand firmly on the doorknob to the giant library door and turned.

It was locked. But the instant he tried the knob, he heard the front door slam and the baron storm into the castle, cursing, "*Ich habe meinen Fickordner vergessen!*" Apparently, he had forgotten an important folder. In seconds he was up the four steps from the foyer to the main floor Mason was on and heading his way. Mason was trapped. There was nowhere to go. The baron was coming, and Mason was standing in the long drawing room just outside the baron's office in his private wing.

Mason was busted, and he knew it. He could feel his face flush and knew it would be obvious that he was guilty as hell. The least he could do was hustle over to the furthest point away from the library door in the drawing room and pretend to be looking up at the crown molding.

The baron could see him from ten meters away as he entered the drawing room. He immediately changed his demeanor from frustrated and hurried to very serious—the calm kind of serious that is beyond angry.

"Mason, what are you doing here...in my private wing?"

"Oh! Hello, Herr Eiger. I'm so sorry," Mason replied. "I was just on my way to take a shower after working out, and I couldn't resist just taking a peek at this beautiful wing. I find the entire schloss and its architecture so amazing." But Mason knew that he was doing a terrible job of hiding his red-faced guilt.

The baron stood in front of him speechless, with a cold and judgmental look on his face. Mason thought he was going to pull out a gun and blow his head off. He stood there waiting until finally, the baron spoke.

"Mason, I must ask that, as a guest in my house, you respect my wishes, which I have been very clear about. Please do not come into my private wing—ever."

"Yes, mein herr. Of course. I'm very sorry. I was just admiring, um, the house," Mason said as he hurried back to his room. As he walked away, he could feel the baron's eyes watching him until he was out of sight.

25

October 2015
London, England

MASON WENT through the bizarre text routine to arrange a debrief meeting with Spencer. They met at the Long Bar in the basement of the Royal Automobile Club, one of the nicest old-boy clubs in London, dating back to the grand era of the nine-teenth century when there was not much of a middle class in England; only haves and have-nots. The haves had gentlemen's clubs like the RAC where they could escape the burdens of family life with their wealthy friends. Each of these clubs is a members-only palace within the city where well-heeled, well-connected gentlemen, and now ladies and gentlemen, can pass the time enjoying racquet sports, fine food and wine, billiards, and swimming in regal splendor, in rooms with thirty-foot ceil-ings, marble floors and columns, and the finest amenities.

Spencer was a member, which is how he and Mason came to

be meeting at the Long Bar. Spencer lifted his beer and quietly said to Mason, "Here's to a successful mission. Our little book you donated to the baron's collection is already yielding valuable info for us. Everyone on my side is well-pleased."

"I'm glad to hear that. But more importantly, I'm hopeful that my betrayal of my friend's trust has made the world a safer place," Mason said. "Also, I have a few more details for you. I managed to get a look at some of the files in his desk, including cashflow spreadsheets and bank statements. In typical Germanic style, the baron keeps meticulous records. It shows payments to and from accounts in Europe and the Middle East. There's one curious Swiss account in particular; the name Klug appears in multiple documents as being a source of intel on jihadi movements as well as info on MI6 efforts to catch the baron. The thing that is most clear is that they are sharing the money from the jihadis. Every time the baron deposits a cash payment, which, if you guys are right is presumably from moving jihadis or their weapons, he sends a chunk of the money to Klug via a numbered Swiss account. One of the scariest things for me in reading all this is that it sure seems like Klug has info that could only come from the inside of some government organization. A handwritten note on one of the pages mentioned something about Klug referencing info he got from MI6 about you guys trying to bug the schloss using cable TV repairmen. I didn't get a chance to read it in detail but if my assumption is correct, then someone on the inside is working against you by giving the baron intel on your activities. Here's the only photo I managed to get of the docs before I had to run out."

Mason showed him the photo on his iPhone and Spencer zoomed in on the screen and studied it for a minute. Spencer was extremely concerned by this information and gave him an email address to send a high-resolution copy of the photo.

"I think you're right about the possibility of a leak. We've had other things, that I'm not at liberty to share, that have raised our suspicions that someone is either accessing our info or leaking it. Let's just say, none of us believes the baron is that good at this game. We've suspected for a while that he's had help eluding us for this long. Which is why no one other than me and my immediate boss knows that this listening device exists or that you planted it. We have intentionally kept this out of all reports and internal documents. If we do have a mole, we can't risk that he or she tips the baron off to the existence of this bug."

"That seems like a smart move. But I'm actually worried that the baron could already be suspicious of me," Mason said as he filled Spencer in on the details about possibly being silhouetted in the library window by the headlights, as well as getting caught in the baron's wing.

"Good Lord, mate, that is a problem. Possibly a big problem if he knows and is keeping it to himself. It opens up the prospect of him feeding us false intel to throw us off." Spencer paused for a minute and then continued, "Well. Not a lot we can do about it. For now, from everything we can tell, the bug is doing its job and we are capturing legitimate intel. But we'll weigh everything we hear against the possibility that he's gaming us."

"Are we good?" Mason said.

"Good? How so?"

"Are we good, as in, all done. Per our original deal, I'm hoping that my job is done and I'm out of it now."

"A deal's a deal. Yes. You're all good," Spencer said. "Don't lose my text number, in case you stumble across anything further that you think would be of service. But, beyond that, you're done. Thank you for your service. I know it wasn't easy. We are in your debt."

"One final question: Based on what you have now, what do you think will happen to the baron?"

"Hard to say. We cannot prove he has done anything illegal

until we catch a jihadist or weapons on one of his ships. Once we do that, he'll be going away for a long time. But we have to catch him in the act, or the rest of what we have is just gibberish that he can claim didn't mean a thing. But either way, you don't have to worry about any of it anymore."

26

L ate October 2015
London, England

OVER THE NEXT couple of weeks, Mason got back to life as normal, as he made the last few hires and sorted out final details so the UK office could become fully operational. He was also becoming disciplined about fitting in time to see Sally Seton-Wolfe, trying to stop by at least three times a month. He had come to enjoy hearing her stories from the war and sharing opinions about silver-screen stars from her era as well. Mason was a big fan of old black and white movies, especially film noir, and knew all the stars from the '40s and '50s. They shared movie trivia as much as war stories. He felt satisfaction knowing he was making a positive difference in her life—letting her know that someone cared about her. On the last Tuesday in October, just before leaving the office at the end of the day, Mason called Sally to confirm that he was planning to come visit her that Friday evening.

After his call, Mason locked up the office and left the building, turning right on Regent Street to head towards the Piccadilly Tube station. A sleek Jaguar with tinted rear windows pulled up alongside the curb next to him.

"Need a ride?" a voice asked out a sliver of the rear window.

"Actually, no. But something tells me you're going to insist that I do." Mason shook his head in resignation. Spencer got out and held the door open as Mason climbed in.

"How are things?" Mason asked.

"They are not good, my friend," Spencer replied, with a serious frown. "Not good at all."

"That sucks. I'm sorry to hear that."

"This is just a courtesy call between friends. You had my back when I asked for it. So, I'll always have yours. Here's the deal. Two nights ago, a von Eiger cargo ship loaded up in Latakia, Syria, with cargo headed for Italy. From everything we heard the baron talking about in his library, that ship was supposed to be carrying number thirty-six—Abbajad and his jihadis. We had two British naval destroyers intercept it in international waters in the middle of the night, before it made it as far as Cyprus. We searched every conceivable inch of it. We tore it apart. Nothing. Absolutely nothing. Not a single thing out of order. Not an article of cargo that wasn't legit and on the roster. No jihadis, no guns, no drugs. Nothing. Then, yesterday the bug you planted went dead. The general feeling at HQ is that we definitely have a leak somewhere that tipped him off that we were going to search this ship."

After a frustrated pause, he continued, "Now, none of us wants to overreact. But, as you pointed out, there is the possibility that he suspected you. There's also a possibility, though it kills me to think about it, that maybe he intentionally led us to believe that the jihadis would be on that ship, just to see if the ship would get stopped and searched. In other words, he might have purposefully said things to mislead us, as a test, just to see if he was being bugged. Once the ship was stopped, it confirmed it for him. He could have then torn the schloss apart to find it. Again, we don't know this for sure, but it's one possible explanation. So, we assume the reason it's no longer transmitting is because he found it and destroyed it. But we can't really know what has happened to it. And even if he found it, he can't know for sure who was behind it. Someone could have broken in and planted it. There's no reason to presume that he suspects you. Anyway, that's all I have. I just wanted you to know the latest."

Mason, rubbing his fingers across his forehead and looking down at the floor, finally said, "Wow. You weren't kidding. That is bad news. It's kind of the worst-case scenario, other than innocent people being killed. And what sucks even worse is that we didn't catch any jihadis...at least not yet."

"Yeah, we'll keep trying on that front. Unfortunately, the chatter we are picking up is that they are indeed on the move right now. That's why we were sure they were on the ship. But if they are on the move and they were not on the ship, then we don't know how they're traveling. Hence, the odds go up that they will make it into Europe. And once they're in, there are no borders to stop them. So, yeah, it's not good," Spencer replied.

"Okay. Thanks for telling me. I need to digest this and figure out what to do," Mason said, now scratching the back of his head and looking out the window.

"We are doing everything we can to track the baron's movements in case he comes into the UK. If he does, we'll let you know immediately. We're also going to have someone tail you for a while, for your own security, just in case he does suspect you and is pissed off about it. We don't have the manpower to do it 24/7 but they will be there on and off, to give you some protection, just in case."

"Yeah. Thanks for that. But you and I both know that if

someone wants to get to you bad enough, then it's going to be hard to prevent it, especially with a one-man security detail who is only there some of the time. But don't think I don't appreciate it. I do." Mason forced a polite but insincere smile. "Can you please stop the car? I think I'd prefer to walk home from here," Mason asked the driver in a quiet, melancholy tone of voice.

"I'm really sorry this has gone sideways," Spencer said to him.

"Hey, it's not your fault. We tried to do the right thing." Mason got out of the car and slowly made his way home.

As Spencer's car pulled away, Mason found himself instinctively looking over his shoulder to see if the car had been followed, or if anyone was walking behind him.

27

S pencer walked into the big conference room at MI6 headquarters. He knew that this meeting was going to be painful. Now that the operation had gone sideways, the rules of the bureaucracy, and CYA—cover your ass—had kicked into full gear. They were required to report the failure to a number of other people who had not been in the loop previously, to review what went wrong and, of course, look for people to blame.

Still, Spencer was hoping that this meeting would only have a few people in it. But he knew it was not a good sign that it was being held in the big conference room. When the meeting finally started, he counted no fewer than twelve people. The fact that the Royal Navy was dragged into it to search the von Eiger ship, in vain, was part of the reason it had become a larger affair. Either way, Spencer knew that for the next few months, half of his days or more would be consumed with bureaucratic finger-pointing.

His mood darkened further when he saw the man at the end of the table. Spencer leaned in to whisper to his colleague.

"Look down at the end of the table. Ed Pincus is here. He's

with the team from the internal security group. He's super smart but cold as a shark. If he starts digging into our department, we won't get anything done for a bloody year. We'll be up to our arses in paperwork requests from him and his team. I heard he spent two years chasing a mole in the Far East branch. In the end he came up empty but several of our best men retired just to be done with his harassment."

As the meeting got started, Spencer's boss, Director Seifert, made it clear that Pincus would personally be leading the investigation to find the source of any leaks from wherever they were coming—Spencer's department or elsewhere. As the meeting broke up, Spencer walked over to Pincus, shook his hand, and with a look on his face that was half frown, half grimace, said, "Pincus, nice to see you. Looking forward to working with you. How have you been?"

"Doing fine, thanks, Smyth. Our team has been focused mostly on Richardson's division lately. Been having some troubles with their team working on human traffic channels out of Albania. But looking forward to lending a hand here with what you gents have going."

"We could sure use it. Bit of an unfortunate cockup, not catching the jihadis on that von Eiger ship. They were supposed to be on it. We need to find out if someone leaked news of our plans to search that ship. Of course, it could just be a spot of bloody bad luck. Hard to know at this point until we all find out more. Anyway, I'll get the files over to you straight away, and maybe we can debrief in detail in a day or two once you've had a chance to review them. Sound good?"

"That will be fine. Sorry. I have another meeting to dash to. Gotta run. Cheers."

As Pincus walked away, Spencer turned to his colleague and said, "I just know this is going to be painful. Also—there is something about that guy that I've never trusted."

28

Just as Pincus started walking down the hall, his phone rang. He recognized the number right away.

"Hallo, Mum. How are you feeling today?"

"Not great, frankly. The arthritis in my feet and hands is acting up again and everything hurts all the time."

"I'm so sorry to hear that," Pincus replied. "Have you been taking your medicine?"

"Of course I have. But it doesn't seem to do any good anymore. I'm always in pain. When are you coming to see me? You haven't been up here in weeks. I can't even count how long ago it was."

"Stop it. You know I was just there two weeks ago. But it's a long drive to Birmingham, and things have been extremely busy here at work."

"I keep telling you to just take the train. We always took the train in my day. It's faster and more convenient, and you can do other things along the journey without having to always watch the road."

"Mum, we've had this conversation a hundred times. If I take the train, then I either have to hire a car or take an Uber to get out to your nursing home in the suburbs and it ends up costing a fortune."

"You didn't used to care more about money than you did about me when you were younger. You were always such a kind and generous lad."

"Mum, please stop. I will come see you again very soon. One day next week. Alright?"

"I want to change to a single room. I'm stuck in a bloody triple room and one of the other women in there just moans all the time, day and night. No one can sleep with her whining and groaning. I want to move to a single room."

"Mum, you know that's not possible right now. The NHS won't pay for a single room for you. We'll have to pay for it out of our own pockets, and it's just too expensive. I'm working on saving the money for that but I'm not quite there yet. Please be patient just a short while longer."

"I always found the money somehow when you needed it. It wasn't easy raising you as a single mum, you know. It was awfully hard at times, but I worked two jobs when I had to in order to give you what you needed."

"Let's not go through all this again. I promise to come see you next week. In the meantime, I'm working on saving enough money to get you a private room. Okay?"

"Okay. I gotta hang up now. An old lady in a wheelchair is giving me the stink eye because I'm talking too loudly on this strange new mobile phone you gave me."

By the time he hung up, Pincus was back in his own office. As he walked past his assistant Darcy's desk he said, "Spencer Hughes-Smyth is sending over a full case file from today's meeting. If you don't see it by the end of the day, chase it down. I want every detail of that investigation and I want it today."

Before going into his office, he turned around and said, "Also, please call Mangit, Director Seifert's assistant, and find a time in the next forty-eight hours when he can meet with me to discuss authorizing and coordinating the company-wide interviews I'll be conducting."

"Absolutely," Darcy replied. "Will he know what this is about?"

"He has tasked me with overseeing the internal investigation to uncover whether or not the leaks we've been experiencing are coming from within MI6. Over the next few weeks I intend to interview every agent and director who has a secret clearance or above. I want to get going on this without any bureaucratic delays and I need the full weight of his office behind me to ensure I don't get any resistance. I'm going to catch this bastard."

29

M ason looked out the window of his flat, hoping the beauty of Onslow Gardens would distract him. He'd been pacing back and forth in his living room for the last half hour. He couldn't stop worrying about what Spencer had told him in his car the day before, about the possibility that the baron might know he had planted the bug in his library. *If the baron did know, then would he want revenge?* He didn't want anything to affect his relationship with Hans. He knew there was no definitive evidence, and hoped he was over-reacting. Nevertheless, he took a different route to work for the next couple of days and was hyperalert everywhere he went. As he walked, he'd look at the reflection in shop windows to see if anyone behind him appeared suspicious. When he stepped out of the office to grab some lunch the next day, he spotted a well-dressed gentleman following him. He assumed it was the security detail that Spencer promised. On his way back from lunch he stopped for a few seconds and stared at the guy, who kept his distance back about fifteen feet at all times. Eventually the man looked him in the eye and nodded, confirming Mason's suspicion that he was from MI6.

Later that same evening, Mason was walking down Regent Street to get on the Piccadilly Tube to head home when he suddenly got the feeling, stronger than ever, that someone was following him. He almost ignored it, thinking it was just one of Spencer's men again. But the danger vibe he was getting was too strong. He stopped to peer in a shop window, while subtly looking in the reflection of the glass to see if the person had also stopped or made any sudden movements. Sure enough, a man with long hair and an unkempt beard stopped suddenly too. The man's tan pants did not look out of place, but he was wearing a loose-fitting shirt that resembled a Middle Eastern thawb, and a vague confused look on his face gave off the impression that he was unfamiliar with the area. Whomever he was, he wasn't great at tailing someone, because when Mason stopped the man stopped as well.

Mason had to find out if this was one of Spencer's men. While continuing to check in the reflection of passing windows to see if the guy was coming up from behind, he pulled out his phone and texted Spencer: "Urgent. Need to know RIGHT NOW if one of your guys is tailing me or not. Pls RSVP ASAP." It took longer than he had hoped to get a reply, but the response came through just as he was entering the Piccadilly Tube station: "2!" *No.*

Fuck. That is not good. He had to think fast.

As he descended the long escalator down to the platform, he decided to try a trick he had seen a dozen times in old movies. Rather than turn left to go to the train that headed towards South Ken, he instead turned right and went to the platform for the train headed in the opposite direction. He slowly kept his pace walking along the platform so he didn't have to stop and face the creepy guy. Every now and then he would pause, long enough to see that the guy was still following him, but Mason would never look directly at him. He pretended to be oblivious, looking at his phone. But the guy stayed with him and was becoming more and more bold with how close he was getting to him.

The next train pulled into the station and everyone stood back as a sea of humanity poured out onto the platform. Mason positioned himself so that he would be the very last person to step on the train. He acted like he was typing on his phone and pretended not to have noticed that his tail had also boarded the train into the very same car just one doorway down. He could tell from his peripheral vision that the guy was staring at him. Mason played it cool until the very last possible instant. The buzzer sounded and the doors began to close. But just as the doors next to Mason were about to touch, he put his foot between them so they would have to bounce partially back open for just an instant. He then lowered his left shoulder between the closing doors and put all his weight behind a full-body block of the right-hand door, which created about a one-foot gap for less than a second, just enough to slip through back out onto the platform. His tail saw the maneuver a split second too late. His door was closed and locked. However, Mason's maneuver had caused the guy to instinctively react, too late, to try to catch his own door. And Mason was looking right at him as he did. The guy knew he had been exposed. As the train began to slowly move out of the station, and knowing he was safe, Mason walked up close to the windows moving past and stared right at the guy as he went by in order to get a good look at him. As the train rolled into the tunnel, the guy stared right back at him through the glass—a cold, lifeless, menacing stare that sent a chill up Mason's spine. Mason no longer had any doubt that he was in danger.

30

S pencer was sufficiently spooked by Mason's encounter that he assigned full-time security to follow Mason starting that evening. The agent buzzed Mason at his flat when he arrived at about eight p.m. And the next morning when he left to go to work, sure enough, there was an agent in a jacket and tie waiting again. But it was still just one guy. Mason felt that there was no telling whether or not one guy could do much good in the event of an attempt to harm him. But it was better than nothing.

This all triggered a bit of a head game in Mason's mind. He knew that he needed to be worried about his safety. Although, he also tried to convince himself that maybe it was all in his imagination. After all, there are lots of Middle Eastern people in London. It could easily have been coincidence that the guy was getting on that subway train. But he kept coming back to the fact that the guy reacted, trying to prevent his own subway door from closing, as Mason slipped out of his.

It was Friday, and he had promised to visit Sally after work before meeting Ludo for dinner. He had to decide whether or not he was going to cancel on her at the last minute over his security concerns. He had never canceled a visit and was reluctant to do so. The more he thought about it the more he felt like he couldn't stop living his life and just hide. He decided he was just going to have to stay on his guard, count on Spencer's security guy, and hope for the best.

When Mason came out of work, he walked up the hill to catch the Central line to Notting Hill. He constantly looked around to be sure he wasn't being followed by anyone other than his security detail. He did the same thing again when he got off at the Notting Hill Gate Tube stop. All seemed clear. He made his way to Sally's flat, still looking over his shoulder regularly to verify that his security guy was still there.

SALLY HAD COME to count on his visits and they lifted her spirits. Getting to the door with her walker usually took about two minutes, given how little use she had of her legs. But it was worth the effort, since she rarely had visitors. Mason helped her get settled back in her large La-Z-Boy recliner.

"Lovely to see you, Mason. You look dapper as ever," Sally said. "You know, it's a joy for an old lady like me to see someone from the younger generation who knows how to dress. You always wear a proper blazer and nice dress shoes. I'll bet the one you're wearing cost a pretty penny. I wish I was fifty years younger, that I can tell you."

"Stop it, I know you're just trying to flatter me," Mason replied with a laugh.

"Well now. What shall we talk about?" Sally said with a huge sigh, after the substantial effort she expended getting across the room and back into her big chair.

"Oh, I don't know. What's been on your mind lately?"

Sally replied with a mischievous look on her face, "Funny you should ask. For some reason, I've been reminiscing a lot about my time as an actress and a dancer before the war."

"Now *this* sounds interesting. I want to hear the raciest story you dare tell, and it has to be true!"

Sally laughed and began to regale him with tales of the years leading up to the war. For a good thirty minutes she recounted how she and her girlfriends would meet, go drinking with soldiers, including Yanks, and how different the world was back then.

"And one night, a group of RAF boys came into the club, and there he was."

"There who was?"

"My Oliver. The man I would marry three months later. The love of my life."

Mason probed her for details of when she knew he was the one for her and how he proposed. She continued telling the story of their love affair and time together, without interruption, right up through when she received the telegram informing her that he had been shot down over Germany on a bombing mission and was presumed dead. It was only after the war that the wreckage was found, and his remains were identified. By the time she finished the story, both of them had tears in their eyes.

Towards the end of their visit, Mason got a text from Ludovico asking if he'd be on time, and he indicated that he might be five minutes late but no more. Eventually he explained to Sally that he needed to head out to meet a buddy for dinner.

"You go meet your friend. I know you have a lot going on. And I think it's lovely that you're living a full life out there in our beloved London. I'm just so grateful that you spare a little time for an old woman like me."

"The pleasure is all mine, Sally. I truly mean that."

As Mason got up, she added with an impish grin, "Just remember, whenever you have a date with any lady friends that may be in your life, I want all the details the next time you come to visit."

Mason leaned over Sally's chair and gave her a hug. "It's a deal. I promise to dish every detail on any dates I have with lady friends." He walked to the front door to let himself out. He turned to say goodbye as he opened the heavy outer door. A second after he turned the knob, someone on the outside of the door kicked it with the full weight of their body. Mason reflexively tried to jump out of the way, but his right shoulder caught the brunt of the force of the door, which knocked him back into the tiny foyer. Stepping assertively across the threshold was the Middle Eastern man from the Piccadilly Circus Tube station the day before, brandishing a hunting knife with a long blade.

Sally screamed at the intruder, "Here now! You get out of my flat this instant!"

Mason did not have time to think. In an instant he was in a fight for his life, as the man attacked him. Extending his left arm to block and his right arm to repeatedly stab or slash at his target, the man was clearly skilled with the weapon. Mason instinctively grabbed an old sweater from the hook on the wall and swung it in a panicked effort to block the knife thrusts. After deflecting one of the jabs, he punched the man hard, square on the nose. This halted the assault for two or three seconds, sufficient for the man to regain his composure. Now with tears streaming out of both eyes, he launched his attack anew, with increased ferocity.

Mason was able to avoid the blade and connect with a punch or two, even throwing some other articles from the coat rack on the wall at him, but he knew he wouldn't be able to avoid the blade forever. He was forced to leap backwards to avoid a slash and ended up off balance. He used his hands on the wall behind him to avoid falling down. As soon as he was stabilized, he pulled his hands back up in the air just in time to block a death-stab to the throat. In a test of strength, he held the assailant's arm with both hands, preventing him from stabbing his chest or neck with the knife.

Suddenly the sound of breaking glass filled the room, as fragments and shards flew past Mason's face. The attack was momentarily paused and the pressure on the knife aimed at his chest relaxed. The man moved backwards, in what was the beginning motions of a fall. Mason could now see that Sally had miraculously crossed the room and picked up a thick glass vase on the table by the door and smashed it square across the back of the man's head. He initially fell backwards, removing the knife from the edge of Mason's throat as he started to go down from the blow. But he regained his composure mid-fall, just enough to spin around—and plunge the knife into Sally's chest, burying the blade up to the handle square in her sternum. She let out a half-hearted scream and fell backwards like a falling tree. Her assailant followed her to the floor from his momentum. For a few precious seconds his lethal assault was suspended as he knelt over Sally's body to wrest the knife free from her chest.

Mason desperately looked for a weapon of his own. On the floor he saw several large chunks of glass from the broken vase. He grabbed the biggest chunk he could find and, quickly positioning it in his right hand, he lunged with all his weight at the kneeling assailant, driving the glass shard through the back of his neck, severing his spine. The pointed end of the glass came to rest protruding fully out the front of his throat. The man fell dead across Sally, who, Mason found out later, had also died almost instantly from the wound to her heart. He had never seen so much blood. It sprayed from the man's neck in three directions—pulsating with the final beats of his heart with the pressure of a fire hose—reaching clear across the room to where Sally had originally been sitting, showering the room in blood. Mason pushed the man's body off of Sally and tried to assess the extent of her injury to see if there was any hope of saving her. He called her name and shook her and put his fingers against the side of her throat to check for a pulse, but there was none.

He stumbled backwards and collapsed to the floor, with his back against the open door, in utter exhaustion, breathing so rapidly he thought his lungs would explode. In less than thirty seconds her peaceful old apartment had been converted into a scene from a horror film. *What the fuck was that? Did that just happen?* Two blood-soaked bodies lay tangled on the floor, a river of blood still draining profusely from the assassin's neck.

Mason started to shake uncontrollably. He pulled out his cell phone and, with great effort, dialed 999 and gave the police the address saying only that there had been a knife attack and two people were dead. As he hung up the phone to await their arrival, he noticed that the black plastic cover on the back of his phone was dented and had a cut in it. He checked his sport coat, and sure enough, there was a knife slit that had pierced his left lapel and gone into his left breast pocket, apparently hitting the plastic cover, and the metal backing, of his iPhone—denting it and leaving a cut in the metal. His attacker had gotten a full stab thrust in on his chest and he didn't even know it. Had it not been for his iPhone, Mason would be dead.

Reality started to sink in. Sally was dead. He had just killed a man with his bare hands and a chunk of glass. The memory of how he felt that night in Boston when he first heard that the man he punched had died came rushing back in his mind. He broke into a sweat. His stomach churned. Rushing outside, he vomited in the middle of the front porch, before he could make it to the railing. A bitter chill overtook his body. He sat down on the top step of the porch and hugged his legs close to his body, shaking back and forth. The sound of police sirens wailed in the distance. Mason stared blankly, wondering where his security guy was.

The dead man had no ID of any kind on him. The police were going to have a hard time identifying him. They questioned Mason at the scene for a while, but it was clear he was in a mild state of shock. They wrapped him in a blanket and put him in the back of one of the ambulances and continued questioning him as they rode with him to the hospital. Given that Mason had proper ID on him, and since he had been the one who summoned the police from his cell phone, they were not really suspicious of him, just being thorough. Mason thought to text Spencer, telling him what had happened. The reply came back—"3"—acknowledged. It didn't give him any info, but at least he knew that Spencer was in the loop.

Mason had not been at the hospital more than fifteen minutes when Spencer came walking through the curtain into his triage area. Mason showed Spencer the slit in his sport coat and the cut in the back of his iPhone case.

"I guess it was about as close a call as one can get and still be breathing," Mason said.

"Mason, I don't have the words to express how sorry I am to have gotten you mixed up in all this," Spencer said.

"No apology necessary. I'm a grown-up. I had a choice—well, kind of. Either way, I went in eyes wide open." Mason paused and said, "I can't believe poor, innocent Sally is dead. She died saving my life. That generation truly was 'the greatest generation.'" He began to tear up but worked hard to control it in front of Spencer. "Hey, by the way, what happened to my security guy?"

"Well, the good news is he's alive. But he's in pretty bad shape. We found him unconscious on the other side of a small wall, behind a bush, about a block away from Sally's flat. He has a severe concussion and has only just regained consciousness. The doctors think he'll pull through, but we won't know for sure the extent of any lasting damage he may have suffered for a few days yet."

"I'm sorry. Please give him my best," Mason said. "And if you feel like it, feel free to tell him in graphic detail how things turned out this evening for the motherfucker who hit him on the head."

"Just try to relax and clear your mind, my friend. Everything is fine now. There is nothing you need to worry or stress about." Spencer stared into Mason's eyes, as if willing him to believe it.

"I was supposed to meet a buddy of mine tonight," Mason said.

"What have you told him so far?"

"Nothing. I just texted him from the ambulance that I was sorry, that something had come up and that I couldn't talk right now but I had to cancel and would call him later."

"Good. Excellent. He can never know." Spencer looked relieved.

"How the hell do you expect me to pull that off?! It's going to be all over the morning news!"

"No, it's not, at least not what really happened. The news will say the man broke into Sally's flat to rob her, but she put up a fight, and both died from their injuries. Your name will not be mentioned."

"How is that possible? How can you be sure that none of the cops, and none of the ambulance people are going to talk?"

"The ambulance people don't know anything. Only the first cops on the scene, the ones that spoke to you at length, know exactly what happened. And we've got guys talking to them and their bosses right now. The official story will be that you came upon the scene immediately after it happened and found their bodies and were in a mild state of shock. That's what you need to tell your friend. You can never tell him the truth—the moment you do, the thread to the whole garment will unravel. The only way to cut the thread is to show that you were not the intended victim. It was a burglary gone wrong and you found them afterwards. Do you understand?"

"I get it. It will make my life a lot easier all around—with friends, co-workers, everyone—to not have to explain why some bad guy wanted to kill me," Mason replied.

"Come on. Let's get you out of here. I'll drop you at your flat." Spencer put his arm around him as they headed out.

THE NEXT MORNING Ed Pincus was finishing his third cup of coffee as he walked into the small conference room next to his office. He had his secretary book all the one-on-one interviews he was conducting with other MI6 execs in the tiny windowless room to minimize any distractions. It also afforded him the ability to scrutinize each person more closely, as he led the inquiry into the source of the leaks.

This meeting would be Pincus's third of eight he was conducting that day. The current interviewee was Duncan Cunningham, a no-nonsense former SAS officer and a fifteen-year veteran of MI6. He was one level below Pincus and they had worked together a number of times over the years, so they knew and respected each other. Nevertheless, in this setting Cunningham did not take their mutual respect for granted. He had heard the stories from some of the thirty or so other people that had already been through Pincus's interview—or interrogation—and he knew how serious this situation was. The highest levels of the British government were desperate to find out how top-secret information was being leaked from within one of its intelligence agencies. And given how long they had been searching for this mole, without success, everyone was out of patience.

When Pincus walked into the room, Duncan stood up to greet him, extending his hand. "Ed. Nice to see you."

"You too, Duncan. I wish it was not under these circumstances. Please, have a seat." After shuffling through some papers, Pincus continued, "Is it true that you have top-secret clearance?"

"Yes. It is."

"Right. And did you have any reason to see, or did you happen to discuss, any of the files pertaining to Baron Klaus von Eiger or the plans to stop one of his ships leaving Latakia, Syria, in October of 2015?"

"No, I did not."

"You did not see or discuss the baron at all, or you did not see or discuss information pertaining to the Royal Navy stopping his ship leaving Latakia?"

"No to both questions."

"Can you prove that?"

"Um, I don't know how I could prove it but if you check the files you will see that I have not had authorization to access any of the information on this case. I have none of the login credentials for the servers for that department and I have not had access to nor signed out on any of the physical files. You can check both of these things for yourself.

"Yes. I know. I've already done so. Tell me, do you know the code name of the mole we are trying to find?"

"No. No one does. Everyone is buzzing about the seriousness of this internal investigation. But you all have kept the details so secret I didn't even know for certain it was a mole-out until just now. And, again, no. The rest of us don't even know the name he or she is supposed to go by, or how you refer to them. Hell, we don't even know the name of this operation."

Pincus stared into his eyes to see if he could discern even a hint of dishonesty in his answer. Cunningham stared back at Pincus with the exact same distrust.

N*ovember 2015*
Barletta, Italy

IT WAS A RAW, overcast night on the Adriatic. A light drizzle came down, but the sea was as still as a sheet of glass. The thick clouds obscured the moon, making it ominously dark. A few minutes past two a.m., a small fishing boat that had not been painted in a decade quietly approached the main dock in the tiny seaside village of Barletta, Italy, ninety kilometers north of Brindisi. The captain cut his engines a hundred yards before approaching the dock, and coasted in.

"We are pulling up to the dock now," read a text message from one of the passengers' cell phones that alerted of a clunky delivery truck with Belgian license plates that had been parked on a side road on the outskirts of the village. Three minutes later the lights of his vehicle appeared at the beginning of the wharf, just as the small vessel arrived at the farthest tip extending out into the sea. The captain asked one of the men, a Saudi national, to jump over to the dock with the bow rope and to pull the boat up tight.

"Do not tie her off," he said. "I will not be staying."

The four other passengers, three Syrians and another Saudi, stepped from the boat onto the dock. None had any luggage. Their colleague holding the bow rope tossed it back to the captain and walked away with the others. No one thanked him or said goodbye. The captain turned over the ship's motor, and with a minimum of thrust and noise, turned the vessel around and headed out towards the open sea.

The men were arriving much later than originally planned, due to the slower speeds at which they traveled on different tiny fishing vessels. They had hugged the coastline of Turkey, then very slowly and carefully made their way through the Aegean Sea and around the southernmost tip of Greece, avoiding the Corinthian Canal, in an effort to make their journey as inconspicuous as possible.

As the men walked up to the old delivery truck they were greeted with hugs and salutations of brotherhood from its driver. Within seconds they were all on board and the vehicle quietly drove off through the deserted streets of the small town, out to the nearby highway, and headed north for Brussels.

A few minutes into their journey the lead man asked the driver, "What news of our brother Nassim? Has he returned from his assignment in London?" The driver looked at him from the rearview mirror with a pained look.

"I'm afraid the news from London is very bad. Nassim is with Allah in paradise. Somehow the target prevailed in a hand-to-hand knife fight with him. My contact says the target is alive, and Nassim was killed," the driver replied.

Everyone in the van gasped. Some shook their heads, others' mouths hung open in disbelief. Tears welled in the lead man's eyes and rage poured through his veins.

They rode on for a few more minutes in silence. Eventually the lead man took out his mobile phone to place a WhatsApp call. Speaking in Arabic he said, "Abdul, it's me. We arrived safely and were picked up as planned. We are on our way now."

"What news of Nassim?"

The man replied, "The news is very bad. There was a fight. Nassim is dead and the target is still alive. I am so sorry."

The man jerked the phone away from his ear as primal screams echoed through the receiver, followed by the sound of automatic gunfire. The man quietly wept as he waited for Abdul to regain his composure.

"No one touches the American! Only me," Abdul screamed into the phone, in a voice filled with venom. "I will kill him. Is that clear? Only me. If anyone else kills him, then I will kill that man. I, and *only* I, will avenge my brother!"

The line went dead.

ovember 2015
London, England and Paris, France

FOR YEARS, Mason had been in the habit of calling his parents every Sunday evening. After Sally's murder, he resolved to start calling his family more often, including his brother Joe Jr. and his sister Sandra. He had not yet shared the news of Sally's death with any of his family, as he didn't want them to worry. He also spent a lot of time talking on the phone with Hans, with whom he shared the story of Sally's murder, at least the version Spencer made him swear to.

He decided to take a few days off by himself. He took a train to Cumbria, in the north of England, to explore the Lake District and see Hadrian's Wall. Other than a check-in call from Spencer, Mason tried to take his mind off of all that had happened. Along his journey, he continued his pastime of stopping in ancient churches to pray alone in silence. He had always found peace and wisdom by doing this, and he needed guidance now more than ever.

By the second week in November he found himself ready to get back in the game. It had been ten days since the attack at Sally's flat and Mason knew the best way to get past it was to get on with life. He needed to go to HQ in Paris for a few days to help close a big pan-European client deal, and the trip just happened to coincide with a visit to Paris by his old Brazilian friend from HBS, Vicente Machado. So, he took the Eurostar over on Wednesday, planning to stay the rest of the week and return to London on the weekend, after having dinner with Vicente on Friday. He tried to get Hans to come down to Paris to join them, but he was too busy at work in Koblenz.

Friday night Mason and Vicente ate at one of his favorite restaurants in all of Paris, L'Entrecote, in the sixth arrondissement. Mason explained why it was so special: "You can only order one thing on the menu: steak frites. So when the waitress comes the only question to be answered is how you like it cooked. That's all they serve, other than drinks and desserts."

"How bizarre. I'm looking forward to trying it. You are not the only person who has told me of this place. Everyone says the sauce on the meat is what makes it so special."

"Exactly. No one knows the recipe for the sauce. It has been in the family for generations. Many people have tried to copy it but no one has succeeded. It's truly a trade secret. Anyway, tell me how you are and what you've been doing since you graduated."

"I am well, my friend. I am well. After graduating in June, I returned to Brazil for several months to complete the planning of our strategy with my father and his bank executives. Then, last month, we acquired our first group of regional banks in the southeastern US. My career for the next five years will be to acquire regional banks across the US until we eventually build a national position strong enough, we hope, to rival the giants such as Bank of America and Wells Fargo. So, it looks like I will be in the US for a while. My father has made me head of all US acquisitions and operations."

"That is so great, Vicente. What a perfect career that is for you."

Reaching across the tiny wooden table, Vicente put his hand on Mason's forearm and said, "My friend. I cannot let this night go by and not say something to you that is very important to me. I want to thank you once again for saving my life. I will never forget what you did for me in Boston, that terrible night."

"Don't be silly. It was nothing. You would have done the same for me."

"No. I mean it. I will never forget this. Had you not done this, I do not believe I would be sitting here tonight. Should you ever need anything from me or my family, you have only to ask and it will be yours, if it is in our power. I want you to know this and never forget it."

"Thank you, my friend. You know that I feel the same way."

"No. I really mean it. Especially the risk you were willing to take by punching him in that spot on his temple, knowing the likely outcome."

"Sorry? What do you mean?"

"I mean you knew that if you punched him in that spot, especially as hard as you did, that there was a good chance it would kill him. Yet you did it anyway to save me. To me it was as if you had a gun and you did not hesitate to shoot this man, knowing that there was a risk he would die, but you took this risk anyway. That is what makes your act of valor so profound in my mind."

"Sorry. But I believe you are giving me too much credit. I just swung wildly and happened to hit him there. It was pure chance that I happened to hit him where I did."

Vicente paused for a moment, his head slightly tilted in confusion.

"Mason, I was there that day—in the gym at Shad."

Mason just shook his head, confused.

Vicente said, "Just a few weeks after school started, when that Thai boxing champion gave the demonstration in the gym, and three or four of us stayed afterwards and asked him a bunch of questions. I was there. I didn't know you very well yet, but I was there as he showed us the three deadliest pressure points, and explained that they should only be used in a life or death situation, as they risked killing the recipient of such a blow. Did you really forget this, or are you bullshitting me?"

Mason looked off into the distance, and then took a long, slow sip from the half-empty glass of burgundy in front of him. When he looked back at Vicente the expression on his face had changed. It was a cold, emotionless look. All the smiling, arm patting, and diplomatic reassurances were gone.

Looking Vicente straight in the eye, Mason said, in a hushed but serious tone, "I saw that fucker's blade go into your gut. I had a split second to decide before he thrust again. I saw the open shot at his temple and I took it. *He* chose the life or death stakes, not me. And I would do it again."

Vicente's eyes bulged wide open, and neither of them spoke for a few seconds.

Finally, Mason said, "Let's, uh, let's agree to never discuss this again, with anyone—not even each other. Let's just put it behind us."

"I should not have reopened this painful wound. I'm sorry. You are right. We shall not speak of this again. I thought that this is what had happened, and I just wanted you to know how grateful I am."

. . .

AFTER DINNER they walked about twenty meters along the side street to Le Bonaparte café to have a nightcap. As they were about to enter, an unusually large number of sirens and emergency vehicles screamed by on Boulevard St. Germain, and they could hear others in the distance.

"Something must have happened," Mason said.

"Not to worry," Vicente replied. "This is just French first responders who are bored on a Friday night, so they all respond when there is a call."

They headed into Le Bonaparte, but only had a couple of drinks because Vicente had an early flight back to the US in the morning.

After they said goodbye, Mason hung back to use the men's room before he left. When he came out a few minutes later, he noticed that the place was dead silent and everyone had left their tables and was standing over at the bar, fixated on the small TV on the wall behind it.

He approached a man at the back of the crowd. "What's going on?" he asked.

"There has just been a terrorist attack here in Paris—in the fourth arrondissement, just north of the Place de la Bastille. There are many people shot on sidewalk cafés and apparently terrorists are still inside a nightclub called the Bataclan. No one knows what is happening to the people inside."

Mason knew exactly where this was. In fact, it was his old neighborhood where he had lived until moving to London. He watched the broadcast, his fists tightening by his side as he desperately hoped these were not the men he had tried, but failed, to help MI6 catch.

As the story continued to unfold on TV, the news reporter touched her hand to her earpiece and said, "We are starting to get reports on the identities of some of the attackers." Mason held his breath. But his prayers were not to be answered on this night.

The announcer named the ringleader as Abbajad. Mason's heart sank. He felt like someone had kicked his guts out of his body.

If only I had stayed away from the window that night in the schloss, maybe those people would still be alive. However, he didn't have time to chastise himself further, because the news broadcaster announced that reports from both German intelligence and the police in Brussels indicated that the terrorists had help from an unlikely source—an American, who was thought to still be in Paris. Apparently a piece of paper was found at the jihadi's apartment in Brussels, written in Arabic, that indicated the American was their driver. The scrap of paper had this man's name and mobile number written on it.

Nothing could have prepared Mason for what happened next. As the announcer continued the broadcast, a picture of the American came on the screen. Mason's face went stark white, his eyes squinted with incredulity, and his mouth dropped completely open. The photo being shown on the TV was his.

34

As Mason looked at the TV screen behind the bar at the Bonaparte his face contorted beyond recognition. He couldn't comprehend seeing his own picture on the news broadcast. It was his passport photo with his name written beneath it. *How is this possible?! Who could plant such an absurd story? And why would anyone do such a thing?*

He was trying to understand what was happening and think about self-preservation at the same time. Then he came to a chilling realization. *If someone has the ability to plant such a story, then who's to say that they haven't also planted false evidence?* He had to get somewhere safe so he could think. He felt like he was living a nightmare from a bad movie, only it was very real.

Fortunately, the passport photo was five or six years old and he had a high and tight haircut and was wearing a jacket and tie. His hair was currently longer than in the photo, he was sporting three-day stubble on his face, and was dressed in a rugby shirt and jeans. But he was definitely still recognizable. He needed something to disguise himself. Since he was at the back of the crowd, no one had turned around to look at him. He casually made his way over to the coat hooks on the wall and "borrowed" a black knit hat.

He had just used his credit card to pay for the drinks, and his cell phone was on. Both of these were like homing beacons for the authorities. The TV announcer said German intelligence *and* Brussels police had confirmed that he was involved. At this point Mason was suspicious of everyone. He wanted to believe that Spencer was legit, but right now he couldn't even be certain of that. *Given that I don't trust any of these fuckers right now, I sure as hell ain't sticking around to see who comes through that door.*

He walked past the bar and into the kitchen, strolling with purpose like he belonged there. The kitchen was empty, as everyone was out by the bar glued to the TV. It took him about three minutes before he found what he was looking for: aluminum foil. He tore off a big sheet and typed one last text message on his cell, to Monsieur Bourget, the CEO of SCI: "News reports about me are untrue. Someone has made a terrible mistake. Will get it sorted out right away. May be off-grid for a day or two while I do so. Will check back in with you as soon as it's cleared up."

He powered off his cell phone and wrapped it tightly in aluminum foil. He had read that cell phones can relay location, and ping towers, even when powered off. He wasn't positive if it was true, but he wasn't taking any chances. He then exited through the back door of the kitchen and walked off into the Parisian night. Exactly three minutes later the café was surrounded by French police in full combat gear.

Mason walked briskly down the street, desperately trying to understand why someone would do this—and then it dawned on him. *This isn't an accident or mix-up. This is another attempt on my life! I used to joke about it with my French friends. There are almost no jihadis in jail in France. Terrorists are always killed before they can surrender.*

Mason thought that theoretically there may be a scenario where he could turn himself in to clear this up, and he would survive. But he believed that it was more likely that as he tried to surrender, he would be riddled with bullets. He remained concerned about what fake information could have been concocted to make him look guilty. *Surely Spencer can vouch for me and help sort this out. But how many days will that take? And where the hell can I go or hide until the truth comes out?*

He decided that he needed to disappear for a minimum of three days, possibly as much as a week, until he knew the coast was clear and this was resolved. He would only surface once he saw newspaper headlines announcing his innocence. He couldn't check his phone or turn it on, or even unwrap it from the tin foil. He couldn't go back to his hotel. He couldn't put any of his French friends or business colleagues in danger, or their families' lives in jeopardy, by going to them for help. He couldn't use an ATM card to get cash. And sleeping on the street was not only going to be cold but it would maximize his risk of being recognized and shot by the cops. Most of all, he wanted to get back to England. Very few British cops carry firearms, whereas all French cops do. Moreover, the Brits have not historically been as trigger-happy as the French. And most of all, Spencer was in England and he was the key to clearing this up.

As Mason walked the backstreets of St. Germain des Pres in a daze, he began to feel hopeless under the weight of his situation. *Once again, my cavalier attitude about being able to do anything blows up in my face. I get into HBS and get chucked out. Then I land the best job in the world—in Paris, no less—and now I'm gonna get shot because of this James Bond bullshit. Even if I survive, it's a certainty I'm going to get fired. What the fuck was I thinking?*

Mason quickly decided that keeping his job at SCI was the least of his worries. First, he had to figure out a way to make it through the night.

35

Mason had an idea of where to go, and fortunately his destination was only three blocks away. He quickly walked over to Rue Princesse, the street on which Castel, a high-end nightclub he and Hans frequented when they both lived in Paris, was located. It was known as the place where the beautiful people went, especially pretty women. His problem was that he was low on cash and not particularly well-dressed. He was going to need to walk up to the door with a very attractive young lady, or ladies, to have any chance of getting in on a Friday night.

He waited at the northern end of the street in front of a café, pretending to be reading the menu on the outside of the window. He didn't have to wait long. Coming around the corner were three extremely good-looking French mesdemoiselles in their mid-twenties, all three of them dressed in very short skirts with low-cut tops. He had about eighty meters of runway between where they were passing him and the front door to Castel. Somehow, he needed to convince them to take him into Castel as part of their group.

He also needed to be on his game with his French tonight.

As far as anyone else in Paris was concerned, he was not an American wanted for terrorism. He was a Frenchman from a small village in Bourgogne, he decided. It would explain why his accent was a bit different than the Parisian accent. And he knew a fair bit about the wine that came from that region, so he at least had something to talk briefly about to authenticate his story. His gamble was that no one he was going to meet tonight was actually from Bourgogne.

Just as they passed where he was standing, he pretended to be heading out in the street on his own, without looking at them, and started walking in-step with them. After a few steps in sync, he looked up as if he had just noticed them. By the grace of God, the one walking closest to him looked back at him and smiled. He smiled back and continued to walk in stride as if he was with them, yet still ignoring them, saying nothing. He finally looked over again and they both started to laugh.

"*Vous allez chez Castel?*" Mason said.

"*Oui,*" she replied. After a few more steps, he was almost out of runway.

"*Bon, alors, on y va ensemble?*"

To which she replied, "*Pourquoi pas!?*"

No cheesy pickup line. He simply asked if they were going to Castel, and when she replied that they were, he suggested they go together. She agreed and that was it. Sometimes the best approach is the soft sell. The bouncer saw the ratio—three hot women, and one guy with them. The math worked. He was in.

Mason was trying to conserve what few euros he had left in his wallet. He had British pounds but only about eighty euro left, and no way to get more. He wasn't drinking much, because he couldn't afford to. It fit his cover well, since French people don't go out to drink themselves blind like many Brits and Americans do. He hung out with Olivia, the one who helped him get in, for the first hour or so. He told her his name was

Louis, but that his friends called him Lulu. However, he was careful not to talk exclusively to her throughout the night. If his plan was to work, he needed to create at least a bit of mystery. He made a point of chatting and dancing with a few other women as well—just enough to make himself appear normal to Olivia—but not so much as to make it appear that he had blown her off. By one a.m. he had circled his way back to her.

But the night would be cut short. As word of the terror attack spread, people were getting text messages on their cell phones inside the club. The cell signal inside Castel's is notoriously bad, which is the only reason everyone's phones weren't flooded with texts right away. But as word of the attacks, not just on the cafés in the fourth arrondissement, but at the Bataclan nightclub, reached a critical mass, people began leaving Castel's to go home. Mason was unsure if he had spent enough time with Olivia yet for his plan to work, but it was the only plan he had, so he had to play it to the end.

By 1:30 a.m. the mood in the club had changed sufficiently that Mason knew it was going to clear out soon. He turned to Olivia and said, "I'm not in the mood to dance anymore, with all that has happened tonight. I think I'm just going to go home."

"I was just about to say the same thing. I'm leaving too," she replied. They checked with her friends who said they were going to stay a bit longer.

"Where do you live?"

"On rue de Sèvres, near the Hotel Lutetia," said Olivia.

"I can walk you if you want—I live in that direction, but a bit further. I'm on Avenue Kleber in the sixteenth," Mason replied. She was happy to have him walk her, as the news of the terrorists had frightened her.

What they found outside neither of them had ever experienced before. The streets were not only filled with police, but heavily armed soldiers as well. It was like wartime. Soldiers were telling people to get home and to stay indoors. It was scary for both Mason and Olivia, but particularly for Mason. He was sure that someone would recognize him from the TV broadcast and start shooting. Poor Olivia was at risk of being mowed down with him. After a few blocks, she put her arm inside his and pulled in closely as they walked. Mason was very happy to see her do this, as it both helped his cover and increased the chance that his plan might still work.

Just about a hundred meters from her flat, a group of soldiers passing by on foot stopped them.

"What are you doing out and where are you going?" one soldier asked.

"We are just coming home from a club near St. Germain des Pres. I live just there at the corner," Olivia replied.

"Well go straight home—now! Get off the streets!" the lead soldier replied in a stern tone.

"Oui, monsieur," they both said and kept walking.

As they got to the door of her apartment building, Olivia said, "Are you sure you'll be alright to get the rest of the way home?"

Mason did not need to act. He had a sincere look of fear on his face. "I *think* I'll be okay. I'd be lying if I didn't say that all these soldiers are scaring the shit out of me." In reality, if he had to walk off alone it was almost surely a death sentence.

"You are welcome to stay here if you want."

His look of relief and gratitude was genuine, as he said, "Are you sure that would be alright? I mean, I would love to—for multiple reasons—not just my safety, but I didn't want to presume anything."

"It's okay. I want you too, as well—also for multiple reasons." She took him by the hand, typed in her code, and led him into the building.

. . .

MASON MADE love to Olivia twice that night. First, because the life and death game he found himself in made his blood run higher than it ever had in his life. But also because he wanted them to stay up as late as possible so that they would sleep until late in the afternoon.

She was beautiful, sexy, kind—and as he saw it, she was saving his life by giving him a safe, anonymous place to stay on what was unquestionably the most dangerous night of his life. The more time he could buy before discovery, the more likely it was that the false story about him helping the terrorists would have collapsed and it would be safe to come in.

Mason didn't wake up until almost three p.m. that afternoon. Olivia was still asleep. He quietly went into her kitchen to make them something to eat. He cobbled together a baguette, some jambon de bayonne, and café au lait, and brought it out as she was waking up.

They were silent for a good ten minutes while they devoured the simple meal, as they were both famished. They then talked about the extraordinary events of the night before for a few minutes, as she assessed whether or not this had been a one-night stand that would be awkward the next day, or if he was an interesting enough guy that they could relax and chat. Mason showed himself to be the latter—which led to him making love to her again, for the same reasons as before. He needed to stay as long as he could. And he was incredibly attracted to her physically. As genuinely frightened as he was for his safety, in a twisted way he had never felt more alive. Afterwards they just lay there in bed talking. He made a point of asking her a lot of questions about her life and her family and her dreams, hoping to minimize the number of questions about his background.

They finally got motivated to do something around six p.m. They showered and then went for a walk to go window shopping and enjoy the fresh air. The military presence was still everywhere, but without the ominous edge that had existed the night before when everyone was still wondering whether or not the multi-pronged attack was over. Mason was careful to put his knit hat back on and to hold Olivia close wherever they went. He knew that a French couple in love was not going to be suspicious. She asked what he was doing that evening and he replied, "Something with you, I hope."

"I have an idea! You made breakfast, why don't I make us dinner?"

Mason loved the idea. He was low on cash and wanted to minimize his time in public. They stopped by a corner boulangerie, and the boucherie next door to gather everything they needed for a nice meal. Better still, Olivia would not let him pay for any of the food. He bought a nice bottle of burgundy with his last euros.

They spent another wonderful evening together. Mason was acutely aware of the importance of this safe harbor and that the danger outside was still life or death for him. But he had burned up some critical time, while the authorities were turning Paris upside down looking for him. Hopefully, at least in England, some questions were already being raised and flying back and forth across the Channel.

Mason fell asleep Saturday night, knowing he would have to find a way to slip away the next day. It would look strange if another day came and went and he didn't have any desire to go back to his own apartment. What's more, it was only a matter of time before she would either catch him in a lie—about his past, or his family in Bourgogne, or his "job in Paris"—or his face would appear on the TV. Olivia's mom and a couple of different girlfriends had called and texted her with thoughts and news stories about the massacre, and she had turned on the TV Saturday evening for a few minutes while she and Mason sat there, stunned, in her apartment, mourning the senseless tragedy. The slaughter in the Bataclan had been so horrific that most of the coverage focused on that. Mason told her it all upset him so much that he would appreciate it if they didn't watch any more of it right then. She obliged and turned it off, miraculously before any pictures of him had come on the screen.

Mason felt incredibly lucky to have been able to find her and lay low as long as he had. But Sunday morning came and he knew he should not push his luck. He needed to move on. While she was showering after breakfast, he wrote her a tender, albeit vague, note.

"Dear Olivia, the last day and a half has been more special for me than you can ever know. I'm so sorry, I need to go take care of something urgently, but I promise I will see you again soon and explain everything when I do—including why I could not wait around to say goodbye properly. Thank you for this beautiful time together and for being such a beautiful person." He signed the note "Lulu," and quietly slipped out of her apartment.

As he walked down the stairs, he thought, *Man, this is a chickenshit way to leave such a lovely girl, who just saved my life. But I don't know how to tell her anything more without risking everything —definitely for me, and maybe even for her.*

One of the things that had been made clear on the news show he and Olivia had watched was that France considered itself in a state of war. The police and troop presence on the streets continued to be like nothing Mason had seen in his lifetime. He knew that every minute he was out on the streets he was in mortal danger. His plan for his next move was no less risky than meeting Olivia two nights before.

Mason came out of Olivia's apartment and turned left on rue de Sèvres, heading towards the Hotel Lutetia. He had not walked twenty yards before a policeman walking alone approached him from the opposite direction. As the man got closer, he looked hard at Mason's face as if he was trying to assess whether or not he recognized it. Mason couldn't help but instinctively look away. He knew his reaction was a dead giveaway.

"Excuse me, sir. Can I see some identification, please?" the policeman said to him in French, putting his hand up to stop him.

"I'm sorry, I left my ID in my apartment," Mason replied in flawless French.

The officer reached around behind Mason and patted him on the right back pocket, clearly feeling his wallet. "What, you don't keep it in your wallet?"

"Uh, normally I do but I don't have it today."

"Okay, then show me a credit card—anything with your name on it."

Mason stuttered and stammered for something to say, wondering how he was going to get out of this. Before he could answer, the cop became deadly serious and stepped up the pressure of his interrogation.

"Take off your hat so I can see your face more clearly," he commanded. Next he said, in English, "Speak English? Are you the American we're looking for? Speak English?" As he spoke, he reached for his gun.

Mason's desperate reaction was reflexive. He pretended as if he was going to put his hands in the air but instead, with lightning speed, he punched the policeman square in the nose, knocking him backwards onto the ground and causing both of the man's eyes to fill with tears from the blow. Mason knew that he had not hit him hard enough to really injure him. His goal was just to incapacitate him long enough so that he could run away, or at least get a head start. And he succeeded at that.

The policeman shrieked as Mason took off running. He hadn't even decided where yet. Within two seconds he heard the cop's whistle blowing and then heard him shouting into the microphone attached to his shirt. The officer could see where Mason was running through the tears streaming out of his eyes, but not well enough to dare run into the street after him. Two other policemen had been walking together about a hundred yards away and heard his screams and whistle. They sprinted in his direction and spotted Mason as he dashed across the intersection and into the Sèvres-Babylone Metro station. One officer stopped to check on the policeman. The other chased Mason, entering the Metro station just a few seconds behind him.

Mason flew into the station, jumped over a sleeping homeless man, almost knocking over his cart full of personal junk, hurdled the turnstile, and bounded down the stairs, fighting a mob of people coming up the stairs because a train was currently in the station. He darted onto the platform in hopes of catching the train, but with all the people coming out, he could not get there in time. The doors closed just as he arrived at the entrance to the last car on the train. He knew he could not go back up the stairs and that he was now in the situation he feared the most. This was when cops started shooting first and asking questions later.

Mason had no choice. As the train started moving out of the station, he ran along beside it, and just before the last car entered the tunnel, he jumped onto the back of it, grabbing one of the metal handles on either side of the doorway on the back of the train, his right foot landing on the little sliver of threshold that sticks out from under the door at the back. As he rode the back of the subway into the tunnel, holding on for dear life, he looked back and saw the policeman that had been chasing him run onto the platform and raise his pistol in his direction. The officer had the good sense not to fire, as he would almost certainly have hit innocent passengers inside the train car if he had missed Mason. Just before he was completely out of sight, Mason saw the officer run back up the stairs, yelling into his radio for all officers in the area to converge on every Metro stop on the number 12 line south of there.

Mason knew he had less than a minute to come up with a plan that the French police would not think of. After that, he believed, his fate would be sealed. The sheer number of police and soldiers on the street would overwhelm every Metro station on the line. And with their justifiable lust for revenge, he'd be in a body bag within minutes. He only had one idea. It was by no means a sure bet, but it was better than no plan at all. As the train was slowing down to stop at the next station, before the final train car, the back of which he was holding on to, emerged from the tunnel into the station, Mason let go, jumped down, and came to a running stop—still inside the tunnel. He then turned around and sprinted back in the direction from which he had just come, back to Sèvres-Babylone Metro station. It was the only place he could think of where hundreds of cops would not be right now. But he suspected it would not stay that way for long. Most Metro lines in Paris have large tunnels that are big enough to have the trains moving in both directions, so if a train came on the track he was running along, he could simply step out of the way. But he was at risk of being seen by a train chauffeur, who would alert police in seconds. He guessed that he had a very short window, measured in seconds, not minutes. Running as fast as he possibly could, he made it back in less than a minute, during which time no trains came in either direction. He jumped back on the platform and calmly walked back up the very same steps he had just sprinted down a few minutes before. He then walked up to the sleeping bum, who, as he suspected, was not asleep but passed out. He shook the man several times but got no response other than a grunt. Mason removed the man's long, raggedy overcoat, which reeked of urine and feces, and put it on. He then "borrowed" the unconscious man's little cart full of junk and rolled it slowly out of the Metro station onto the sidewalk.

He walked very slowly, completely hunched over, looking down and hopeless, as he made his way across the busy intersection at boulevard Raspail, taking care to cross with the green man so as not to draw any unnecessary attention to himself. Out of the corner of his eye he could see the policeman up the street whom he had punched in the nose talking with several other officers. Just as he made it across the boulevard, a truck full of troops screamed to a stop in front of the Metro station and poured down into it. The number 12 line was now sealed at every stop.

37

Slowly pushing the homeless man's shopping cart, Mason continued his creeping, methodical progression towards his original destination, the Hotel Lutetia. He discreetly watched the valet and waited for the precise moment. After careful deliberation, he pushed the cart off to the side, removed his putrid coat and placed it on top of the cart, and walked briskly into the hotel as if he belonged there.

He went to the first staircase he could find and instead of walking up to the guest rooms, he walked downstairs, into the service area. From there he navigated the labyrinth of laundry rooms and storage areas until he spotted the men's locker room. The only other person in there finished his business after only a couple of minutes and left. Mason scoured the lockers until he found what he was looking for: a valet's cap and jacket. It was comical since he wasn't wearing the right shoes or pants, but he donned the cap and a poorly fitting valet's coat, looking in the mirror to practice. He believed that if you stare someone in the eye and engage them in conversation, they rarely think to look at your pants or shoes.

Mason rolled up the coat with the hat inside and walked

back upstairs. He stopped at the hotel entrance with it casually tucked under his arm and peered out the window as if waiting for a friend. He waited for the valet to park the next car. Now came the hard part. The instant the valet was out of sight around the corner, Mason stepped outside and slid into the ill-fitting valet's jacket and cap. He prayed as he waited for the next car to arrive. If it arrived before the valet returned, he was in business; if the real valet came back before another patron arrived, he would be busted. With all the cops and troops gathered out front, right in front of him, Mason knew his life would be over in seconds if this went awry. He waited one minute, then another. Still no cars were in sight. He knew the real valet would return any second now and feared the end was near.

Then, a miracle arrived. A shiny black S-class Mercedes cruised into the hotel, driven by an elderly German lady, who made it clear she did not speak French.

Mason asked her, "Do you speak English?"

She did and was beyond pleased that he did as well.

"Are you checking in or returning?" asked Mason in his best valet voice.

"Returning," she said, and she pointed to the valet ticket already on the dashboard. He politely helped her out of the car.

"Will you be needing the car any further today? If so, I will keep it nearby, at the ready."

"No. Thank you, young man. I won't need it any further today."

"Very well, Madame."

She tipped him a five-euro note, and they bid each other good day. Mason drove off into the streets of Paris in the kind frau's shiny black Mercedes, passing dozens of police officers converging on the area as he casually drove away.

38

M ason was pleased to find that the car he had just borrowed had an automatic toll-paying device on the windshield behind the mirror. One, it would enable him to pay the tolls he would surely encounter; and two, it would help him throw the cops off his trail, once the car was reported stolen. He wanted to head north back to England, but he needed to divert attention from his real destination. So, he drove south out of Paris on the nearest interstate until he passed the first toll and then stopped at the next rest area. With a screwdriver he found in the trunk he removed the rear license plate and got back in the car.

Now, he needed two things: a black Mercedes to pull into the rest area, and the driver to leave it unlocked. He waited in the parking lot for twenty minutes. Two black Mercedes came in during this time. One driver left his female companion in the car while he went inside. The other locked his car.

Finally, after another fifteen minutes of waiting, a similar Mercedes to the one he was driving pulled in, and the driver failed to lock it. Mason pulled the automatic toll device in his car from its velcro attachment on the windshield and quickly walked over to the stranger's Mercedes that had just pulled in. He opened the door, leaned in, and swapped the toll device in the stranger's car with that of his own. He then swapped the license plate on the rear of the car with the plate from his own car in less than sixty seconds. When the stranger returned to his car, he would unknowingly continue on his journey south, through toll after toll, with the German lady's device on his windshield and license plate on the rear of his car. Mason meanwhile would be long gone headed northbound. By the time the police figured anything out, hopefully, Mason would be out of the country.

Mason maneuvered out of the rest area, did a U-turn at the next exit, and headed north. He was careful to stay within the speed limit and kept his black knit hat on. He listened carefully to the radio, soaking up any news he had missed over the past two days.

"Traffic is moving much slower than normal for all ships leaving Calais, as police and soldiers are thoroughly checking every person, vehicle, and container for any sign of the terrorists that remain at large," the radio announcer said.

Mason was mentioned only twice, whereas the real terrorists were mentioned dozens of times. He gathered that some uncertainty was growing about whether or not he was involved. The bad news was that one of the two times he was mentioned was an announcement that he had been fired from his job at SCI.

The blow was substantially lessened by the fact that at least he was still alive. That was the only thing he was focused on right now. He would deal with the pain of losing his job later.

After driving for a couple of hours, Mason was famished. He pulled off at a roadside gas station and spent the tip from the nice German lady to buy two bottles of water and a cold chicken sandwich. He devoured the sandwich and guzzled one bottle of water. He saved the other, knowing he'd need it.

He still couldn't take his phone out of the tin foil for risk of pinpointing his exact location for the authorities. But, as luck would have it, the new Mercedes he was driving had a GPS navigation system. He turned it on. *I need to find a small waterfront town in the north that is big enough to have a marina but small enough that it's not considered a point of entry or exit from France.*

Within seconds he'd spotted what he wanted—Boulogne-sur-Mer. He could see they had a small port in the old town right on the English Channel. And it was located across the shortest point of the Channel from England. By Mason's estimate, Dungeness Point was due northwest across the Channel only about thirty miles.

He drove to the outskirts of Boulogne-sur-Mer and parked the Benz in the lowest underground level of a three-story public garage. He knew that some expensive sedans had GPS trackers built in. When the frau noticed her car was gone, if she could even find a cop in Paris who had the bandwidth to fill out a police report, they would have trouble locating it on the lower level of the car park. This would hopefully buy him more time. He caught the local bus to the downtown with the few euro coins left in his pocket. He was twenty cents shy of the required fare, but the driver cut him a break and let him ride.

When Mason arrived at the old port, he walked along the quai examining the boats moored there. He chatted with one of the only boat owners on the dock and learned that no one was going out because a storm was approaching. But to Mason, this was the perfect cover. No one would expect anyone to be leaving, and most boat owners would be away from their boats.

Mason did not have experience sailing a full-sized boat. However, when he was a kid, he and his siblings had a fourteen-foot Sunfish that they sailed on the Chesapeake Bay, so he knew the basics. And of course, he needed something bigger than a little Sunfish if he was going to make it across the Channel. As luck would have it, there was a MacGregor 25 moored in the slip at the far end of the dock. It was secured by a wire that had a lock around it at one end. But it was not truly designed for security. The cleat it was locked to had only to be unscrewed in order to steal the whole thing.

Mason walked back down the dock and asked the gentlemen he had just spoken to if he could borrow a screwdriver, as he "had left his toolbox at home." The guy happily complied. Mason unscrewed the cleat about 95 percent of the way, so that he could pull it off with a swift jerk of his hand when he came back later. He then returned the screwdriver and walked around the downtown, eyeing the wharf area until dusk. As he suspected, no one else was out near the boats. He was starving again but had no euros left. He figured he could talk someone into taking the British pounds he had in his wallet if he had to, but he didn't want to do anything that would call attention to himself, not even a little bit. He had come this far; he wasn't going to blow it now over an empty stomach.

Once he saw the port area was deserted, and the last of the daylight was slipping away, he walked calmly, but with purpose, back out onto the quai, pulled off the cleat with the lock on it, pushed the boat as hard as he could away from the slip, hoisted the sail, and quietly headed out of the harbor. As he sailed past the eastern point of town, he waved at some kids leaning on the railing at the amusement park off on his right. They waved back. Mason then pointed the boat northwest, towards Dungeness, just thirty miles away. His sail filled with the wind of the open Channel, just as he heard the first rumblings of thunder from the approaching storm.

39

How hard could it be to sail a twenty-five-foot boat thirty miles? How bad could a storm be in the English Channel? It's not like it's the North Atlantic, Mason thought.

As he set out to cross the Channel, Mason figured he would average maybe five miles an hour, perhaps a little more with the storm wind. He estimated that he'd make it across to England before sunrise. It was the miscalculation of his life.

Within an hour of setting out, the winds were blowing at nearly thirty knots. It was all he could do to keep the boat pointed in a northwesterly direction, in the black of night. He couldn't see much at all in front of him since the engine wasn't on and thus, he had no power for lights. He focused on the swells that got bigger and bigger until they were crashing over the bow nonstop, soaking him to the bone. By the end of the second hour he had vomited three times, emptying his stomach of what little food he had. Worse, he could not get below deck to get a life jacket or look to see what they had on board that might keep him warm.

The storm tossed the boat, and Mason, like a rag doll, at times lifting him completely off the deck and crashing him back down. He eventually became so cold, exhausted, and battered that he curled up in the fetal position on the deck with the rudder handle in one hand and the main sheet in the other, holding on to both with all his might so as not to get swept away, as the boat was tossed about like a toy. His greatest worry was going overboard, which he knew meant certain death.

How could I have been so naïve? Is this really how I'm going to die? My God, no one will even know what happened to me.

He had purposefully disappeared from the world two days before. Now he was going to drown in a storm in the English Channel and his family would never know what became of him.

As he was starting to lose hope, he prayed for guidance and deliverance. The message came back loud and clear. *Fight!* He reminded himself of his Granddaddy Wright's words: "Your mama didn't raise no crybabies."

Mason screamed at the top of his lungs, "I'm not going to fucking die out here!" *I don't know how I'm getting out of this, but I am not going to die tonight. Not like this!*

With this newfound determination, he started to think more clearly. He knew the key to survival was getting below deck. Only a flimsy, locked, fiberglass door hatch stood between him and getting down there. He suspected he could put his foot through it if he tried hard enough. The problem was that he couldn't let go of the rudder, as he needed to steer the boat directly into the swells, or a broadside swell would capsize her. If that happened, he would freeze to death in the frigid water in a matter of minutes.

He used some extra main sheet rope to tie the old-fashioned stick rudder in a straight position so that it could not veer left or right. He then ran with all his might at the door hatch that led below deck and kicked it square in the center. On the first try, it cracked but didn't break. By the fifth attempt his foot went clean through the fiberglass, cutting and scratching his leg on both sides. What he did not want was to kick the door off its hinges completely, as this might cause the boat to take on water below deck. He reached his hand through the jagged hole and unlocked the door. Down below he found a life jacket and put it on. He also found several blankets on the bunk and wrapped himself in one, leaving two dry ones for later. A quick raid of the cupboard yielded a box of granola bars, an unopened case of bottled spring water, and some loose rope. Granola never looked or tasted so good in his life. His spirits improved. He had a blanket and a life jacket on, a couple snacks in his pocket, and a supply of fresh water. He was ready to fight.

Mason put his iPhone, still wrapped in foil, in the cupboard to keep it dry, and then headed back up on deck, untied the rudder, and took over at the helm. Settling into a sitting position to keep his center of gravity as low as possible, he proceeded to tie one end of the rope around himself and the other around the wire railing. At least if he went overboard, he could remain attached and climb his way back up onto the boat.

Within ten minutes of tethering himself to the rail, the boat was rocked so hard by a swell from starboard that she almost capsized, catapulting Mason through the air and into the sea. The rope jerked him to a stop, saving his life, just as he crashed headfirst into the water.

It took him over a minute to climb back on board the tossing vessel. In the process of doing so, the deck of the boat suddenly heaved and brutally smacked him on his left cheek just below his eye. For a long while after reboarding her he just lay there in the fetal position again, clinging to the rudder and the main sheet, as the sea mercilessly tossed him and the vessel back and forth, up and down, for what seemed an eternity. But he was determined to live. He would not let go. *The only way I'm fucking dying tonight is if this boat sinks. If it stays afloat then by God, I'm going to survive this night.* He spent the next eight hours enduring the greatest physical and mental challenge of his life.

Then, as suddenly as it began, the storm simply ended—just as the first light of the approaching sun began to peek above the horizon to the east. The smell of the ocean air, the noise of the seagulls overhead, and the sudden calm serenity of the sea itself, all seemed an impossible contrast to the horror of the previous night. Through eyes that were bloodshot and blurry from pure exhaustion, Mason could see the coast of England in the distance. His battle with the storm and the Channel was over, and he had won.

By his estimate land was still roughly ten miles away. He could see Dungeness far off to the East. He had been blown off course by at least twenty miles. But he counted himself lucky to not have ended up back on the coast of Normandy.

He was almost back on English soil. He was both humbled and grateful in the knowledge that he had been the beneficiary of at least three miracles that allowed him to get this far.

After the ordeal he had just endured, Mason did not have sufficient energy remaining to venture ashore. He was as exhausted as he had ever been in his life and desperately needed to sleep. The shredded skin on his hands hurt as much as the rest of his bruised and battered body. He sailed up to roughly a half mile from the jetty that marks the entrance to the Eastbourne marina and dropped his sail and as his anchor and went below deck. He devoured two more granola bars, chugged several bottles of water, curled up with his dry blankets on the spartan bunk in the bow of the boat, and fell asleep.

When Mason woke up the sun was just starting to set, which he knew meant it was approximately five p.m. He had to decide whether to go ashore now or tomorrow. If he went tonight, he would still have to find a way to get to London, probably by train, and then find a place to sleep once there. Or, he could go ashore in the morning, perhaps in the rush hour period to minimize the risk of discovery, and show up back in London by late morning, which would give him more options.

It was an easy decision. He was still exhausted and knew he was safe where he was. He decided to spend another night on the boat. As he lay there, drifting in and out of sleep, he thought of his family back home in Richmond. *Good Lord, they must all be going through hell! Surely this is global news. They must be sick with worry.* He prayed for them to find peace. But better for them to have to worry a few more days, and for him to live, than for him to break cover too soon and risk getting killed.

He drifted in and out of sleep. He thought fondly of Olivia. Her kindness had saved his life. But mostly he found his thoughts reverting back to Kelly. *I wonder if Hans has been right all along—that maybe there really is a natural fit with Kelly that I rejected without fair consideration. All I know is I think about her all the time.*

Mason had never believed more firmly in the old saying "life is short" than at that moment. Mostly he felt happy to be alive. Above all, he knew that if he kept his faith, then everything would work out as it was supposed to in the end.

His thoughts drifted back to his childhood when his family would spend weeks at a time during the summer at his grandparents' cabin on Lake Belleau in New Hampshire. He and his siblings would sit around the fire pit for hours as Granddaddy Wright told stories about World War II, and about right and wrong and good and bad.

He fell back to sleep and did not wake up until the sun was blazing through the boat's windows the next morning.

40

N ovember 2015
     Eastbourne, England

IT HAD BEEN three and a half days since the Bataclan massacre. There was a reasonable chance by now that Spencer, and the US embassy, had demanded evidence that Mason was involved, and had hopefully countered with evidence that he wasn't. But Mason resolved to stick to his plan of only surfacing when he saw newspapers declaring his innocence.

By his best estimate it was somewhere between eight and ten a.m. *Oh, how I miss just being able to push a button on my phone and see the time.* He still owned a fancy wristwatch, but it was back at his hotel in Paris, which had surely been raided by the French gendarmes.

He downed another bottle of water and went up on deck, sitting in silence for a long while, taking in the stunning morning view of the south coast of England. Finally, he raised the sail and the anchor and sailed into the marina at Eastbourne. He tied up at an open slip on the dock and nonchalantly walked away from the boat, saying hello to a man working on his much bigger boat as he walked past and out of the wharf.

With his black knit hat pulled down on his head, he stopped into a café about two blocks off the marina and ordered a full English breakfast. He used his best posh English accent to make the locals think he was British, and not a Yank, to avoid suspicion. He had plenty of pounds sterling in his wallet. Finally, money was not an issue. After stuffing himself with fried eggs, sausage, bacon, beans, and toast, he walked over to the nearest bus stop to see a map of the city, identifying the location of the train station, which unfortunately was about a mile and a half away. He could have hopped the bus, but decided he wanted to enjoy being back on solid ground, which he had desperately missed on his near-death voyage.

He walked along the coast to the train station. The timetable posted out front showed that the next train to London wasn't leaving for a half hour. Mason bought *The Times* at the newsstand and sat on a bench with his face buried in it while he waited. He read everything he could find about the attack in France. He noticed that he was only mentioned in one article and that there were indeed suspicions already being pushed from the UK that the original story about him was in error. This was a good start, but not the full declaration he was waiting for. He bought his ticket and took a walk, returning to board the train just seconds before it departed.

The train he was taking was the local, not the express, so he ended up arriving in London in the early afternoon. He still wanted to minimize interaction with others, so rather than take a cab he walked from Victoria Station back to South Ken. He took his time, winding through beautiful Belgravia on the way.

By three p.m. he found himself in front of a small café in South Ken and bought a sandwich and crisps. He then walked the few blocks up to Cromwell Road and spent the rest of the afternoon wandering around in the Victoria and Albert Museum. He surprised himself by how much he enjoyed looking at Albert Saxe Coburg Gotha's nineteenth-century eveningwear, and famous dresses worn by Princess Diana. By six p.m. he decided it was time to head over to his destination to get in position.

He knew he couldn't go home to his flat. It was surely being watched 24/7. So, he meandered west on backstreets until he found himself in front of Kelly's flat. Since they never hung out together, it was unlikely that the London authorities would have decided to watch her flat, especially since they thought he was somewhere in France, or dead.

He knew she took the Piccadilly line to and from work and that Earl's Court Tube station was her closest stop. What he didn't know was if she had a date that night or was hanging with friends or doing something that would bring her home late. He was hoping that on a Tuesday night, with all this craziness going on, not the least of which was his disappearance, she would come straight home from work. He couldn't risk suspicion by pacing up and down her street right in front of her flat. So, he crisscrossed different streets and different blocks that still gave him a view of the route she would have to take from the Tube station home, while pretending to read his newspaper.

He had been at this scheme for about forty-five minutes when he saw her emerge from the Tube. He could tell it was her by the sexy way she walked and the svelte outline of her incredible body—both of which he had subconsciously memorized. He waited for her near the corner of the last cross street she would have to traverse before arriving at her door. As she came to the street, she looked both ways before crossing and saw him standing there about twenty feet off to the right. He had not shaved in a full week at this point and he was wearing the black knit hat, but she recognized his big, kind hazel eyes in an instant. She turned, squinting to see if it was really him, and started walking towards him. He looked down with a shy grin and started walking slowly towards her. She broke into a run and jumped the last three feet into his arms, hugging him so hard he thought she would break him.

"Oh my God, everyone said you were dead! I thought you were dead! But you're not. You're alive! And you're here! Oh my God, you're alive! Thank God! And you're here! I can't believe it!" Kelly said, choking back tears. She stopped talking and gave into her intense relief, sobbing uncontrollably into his chest. He gently stroked her hair and her back until she gathered her composure. As he embraced her, the extraordinary trials of the past four days caught up with him. Mason was so touched by her genuine emotional response at seeing him alive that he let his guard down and began to weep as well.

In a totally unexpected reaction, their instinctive emotion at seeing each other, under these extreme circumstances, broke down any façade of propriety that had existed. Everything about what one can and cannot do was reduced to triviality by the seriousness of the situation, and the fact that she had thought he was dead. He was caught off guard at that instant by the unlocking of what must have been a subconscious emotion he felt for her, and she clearly felt for him. Somehow each of them felt safe in letting these private emotions flow freely. They stayed there hugging each other with all their might for at least another minute, maybe two, without saying a word. Mason had not anticipated any of this. He didn't realize how fragile he was behind the toughness he had had to find in himself over the past few days. He also knew he had to snap out of it because his ordeal wasn't over.

Finally, Mason spoke, in a voice that was no more than a whisper in her ear. "I need you to listen to me very carefully.

And please know there is no right or wrong answer to this question. I need to know if you have any doubt, whatsoever, that I could have been involved with those terrorists. If you have any doubt at all, please tell me, and I will leave you alone and not bother you at all."

"No. I have zero doubt. No one we know has any doubt. Everyone knows it's a lie. We don't know how or why the authorities could have thought that, but no one believes it, least of all me. Thank God, even the news just today was saying that MI6 was going to issue a formal statement very soon saying that there had been a mistake." Just then she noticed the black bruise under his left eye. "Oh my God, were you in a fight? You're hurt!"

He winced from the pain as she tried to gently touch the shiner on his cheek.

"It's nothing. I got into a fight with a sailboat and lost. It's a long story. But that's great to hear about MI6. I still don't trust that it's safe to surface. I need a place to hide for maybe a couple more days until I know that this isn't some trick to get me to come out of hiding, if I'm still alive. By the way, you and I are literally the only two people on the planet who know that I am. Would it be too much of an imposition if I were to crash on your sofa for a day or two?"

Kelly didn't even answer his question. She just grabbed his hand and started marching him towards her flat. As she did he made a subtle grunt in pain, causing her to stop and look at his chapped and lacerated hand. First one, and then the other.

"Oh my God, what happened to your hands?"

"Like I said, it's a long story. It involves a boat and a storm."

41

As Mason stepped into Kelly's flat, he was incredibly conflicted. Their embrace on the street a few minutes before validated what he had suspected for some time, that she liked him, maybe even a lot. It had also forced him to admit to himself what he felt for her. Given what he had been through, and how incredibly attractive he found her, he had never had a greater urge to make love to a woman in his life. On the other hand, he knew he was in an extremely compromised physical and emotional state. The only thing that superseded his passion for her right then was his relief at feeling safe for the first time in four days.

What the hell do I do here? I desperately want to tear her clothes off right here in the living room, and I think she may, in fact, want me to do that. But if her reaction outside was just based in friendship, and I make a play for her, then I risk fucking up my chances with her, or worse—being back on the street tonight without a place to sleep again.

He decided he didn't have the energy to risk the drama if he was reading it wrong.

"Have a seat. You want something to drink?" Kelly said, as

she walked straight into the kitchen, gesturing for Mason to sit in the living room.

"Sure. What kind of beer do you have?"

"I only have French beer. Kronenbourg, Seize soixante-quatre."

"That's perfect. I love that beer. Thanks."

Kelly lived in a one-bedroom, one-bathroom flat. The kitchen was just off the small living room, and just off the kitchen was a hall to a large bedroom with en suite bathroom that also had a door allowing access to it from the hall. The flat had come partially furnished with classic nineteenth-century replica antique furniture. The living room had a small sofa and a single large matching chair, as well as a mid-sized flat-screen TV on the wall.

Mason chose to sit in the single chair. She came bounding back into the room with their beers, still full of energy. If she was disappointed by his choice of seats, she didn't show it. Handing him his beer, she plopped down on the sofa, curled her legs up, and said with the excitement of a teenage girl talking to her best friend, "So tell me everything. What the hell is going on!?" She launched a dozen questions at him. "How did they confuse you with a terrorist? Where have you been? And how did you get back to England without getting caught, with the whole world looking for you?"

Mason's mind raced. He knew he had to answer her questions, at least to some degree. But he also couldn't tell her he had been helping MI6 spy on the uncle of their dear friend Hans. *How the hell did I not think this through already? I need a little time to come up with a clean story for her.*

"I promise to answer all your questions, to the extent I know the answers myself. But first, please give me a few minutes to drink this beer, and then take a shower. After that, my time and my fried brain are yours."

"Of course. I'm sure you're exhausted from all you've been through—every detail of which you will shortly tell me! And, yeah, I wasn't going to say anything, but oh my God do you stink." They both laughed.

"Yeah, I don't even have my trusty New England Patriots hangover cap to wear to hide my greasy hair."

As he drank his beer, Mason got Kelly to fill him in on the mood and the stories at the office, how many government agents had come to interview everyone, what people were saying or speculating, and what news they had received from HQ in Paris.

"One thing is for sure, it hasn't been dull," Kelly said.

When he excused himself to go shower, Kelly pointed out that he didn't have anything clean to change into afterwards.

"I'll wash those smelly clothes for you and give you some baggy sweats to put on until they dry."

Mason thanked her and headed to the bathroom. He took a long, hot shower, savoring the luxury of just being able to wash up, as well as feeling safe. This, combined with the beer he had just pounded, suddenly made him very sleepy. While drying off and getting dressed, he spent some time deciding what he should and should not disclose to her. *I need to tell her the truth, but somehow I have to refrain from telling her the whole truth. Besides, as sweet and innocent and kind as she is, I'm sure this cloak and dagger shit is so far out of her world that it will likely scare the hell out of her.*

When he returned from the shower in her sweats, Kelly looked up and saw him, and then looked right back down as she tried desperately to refrain from laughing. Seeing this, Mason began nodding his head, with a look of feigned humiliation on his face.

"Okay. Alright. Go ahead and have your laugh now, at my expense." Kelly erupted with laughter, causing him to immediately do the same. He then proceeded to parade back and forth in front of her as if he were a runway model in a fashion show, which only added to the hilarity of the moment.

Eventually, they settled down and he dropped back down in the chair to submit to her questions.

"I honestly don't know who planted the fake story about me being part of this horrible terrorist attack. The only thing I can think of is that I had recently, through some personal connections of mine, tried to help some people—good guys—try to uncover information about the movement of some very bad guys. That's all I can tell you without betraying their confidence. But I assure you it was basic, vanilla stuff. And the next thing I know I'm on INTERPOL's most wanted list as a terrorist. I was just finishing dinner in St. Germain des Pres last Friday night, the night of the massacre, and all of a sudden my face comes on the TV behind the bar as being connected with the jihadis. I couldn't believe it!"

As Mason told the story, Kelly's eyes were glued to him. "What did you do!? Did you go to the police to try to explain it was a mistake?"

"No. I was too worried that whoever had made up the story could have possibly planted bogus evidence to back it up too. Besides, you know as well as I do that the French police tend to shoot first and ask questions later when it comes to terrorists. I just looked for a place to hide."

As he said this it was clear he was fading. He was fighting to keep his eyes open.

"You can't fall asleep yet," Kelly said. "You have to at least tell me how you got back."

"Sorry, uh, yeah," Mason apologized. "I went to Castel for a while and made some new friends and then hid out in one of their apartments near the Hotel Lutetia for a couple of nights. I then stole a car, drove to the small coastal town of Boulogne-sur-Mer, where I stole a sailboat and sailed across the Channel by myself night before last, in a fucking storm that nearly killed me. I was trying to sail to Dungeness, but ended up being blown off course to Eastbourne. Anyway, I caught a train from there this morning, walked here from Victoria Station, and here I am." As he finished, a childlike look of humility came across his face and he shrugged his shoulders.

Kelly was still staring at him, dumbstruck, her head shaking side to side. Finally she said, "That has to be the most insane story I've ever heard in my life. Stealing a car? Then stealing a boat? It's like you woke up one day and decided to become an MI6 agent. Who does that?! Oh my God! And it sounds like there are at least four other stories within that story. I'm going on record as saying that I want to hear all the details—at least all the ones you can share—of each of those stories. But I see that you're literally falling asleep, so I can wait until tomorrow."

"Why would you use the expression 'MI6 agent'?"

"Oh. I don't know. It was just a figure of speech. You know, like in the spy movies, everyone is an MI6 agent."

Mason, still a bit confused from his fatigue, replied, "Okay. Anyway, to your point about sleep, I don't have to crash just yet. I'd be happy to get a bite to eat before crashing, if you'd like. Are you hungry at all?"

"I am. Do you want to order takeaway from the pub on the corner? They make an amazing curry."

"Sure. That would be perfect. I'll make you a deal: I'll buy if you don't mind picking it up. That work?" Mason pulled a couple twenty-pound notes from his wallet.

"It's a deal," Kelly said enthusiastically. "Besides, I'm looking forward to running to get it. I feel like a Bond girl in a movie now."

. . .

THEY DEVOURED the curry and polished off the rest of her Kronenbourg, as they spent the next two hours sharing details of their backgrounds. Mason told her about his family, his life after college, and the full story of why he was thrown out of HBS. Kelly shared her love of having grown up in Galway, and the challenges she faced having to move to France, learn a new language, and find a new set of friends, at the tender age of ten years old.

"My parents didn't have a great deal of money and so they were excited to find a nice apartment in Paris that we could afford. The downside was that it was on the border of a slightly sketchy neighborhood, next to the Gare du Nord area in the tenth. So my brother and I had to learn how to handle big-city life at a pretty young age."

They even shared their impressions of each other when Mason first joined SCI. Kelly said, "I thought you were really good looking, and interesting. But you seemed to spend all your time with Hans and Annabelle, so I never got to know you as well as I had hoped to."

Mason, the beer having gone straight to his head, confessed, "Yeah. I thought, and still think, that you may be the most beautiful woman I've ever met. And I guess I was just a bit threatened, or overwhelmed, or hell, I don't know." He looked away and started shaking his head back and forth with embarrassment.

This caused Kelly to reply with a huge grin, "No. No. Don't stop there. Keep going. You have my undivided attention."

A SHORT TIME LATER, Kelly was helping Mason put sheets, a pillow, and some covers on the living room sofa. When they were done, she turned to say goodnight. Without any hesitation she gave him a long hug, burying the side of her head in his chest. Mason, hugging her back and resting his cheek on the top of her head, softly said, "I can't thank you enough for letting me crash here. You are truly a life saver."

"You're very welcome. And thanks for knowing you could trust me. It means a lot to me."

With their arms still around each other, she pulled her head back from his chest and looked him in the eyes. Their faces, and their lips, were just inches apart. Yet neither of them was nervous or uncomfortable at all. After a few more seconds of looking and smiling at each other, Kelly gave him the classic French parting salutation, a light kiss on each cheek, and turned and walked into her bedroom.

42

The next morning when Mason woke up, Kelly had already gone to work. He had slept for twelve hours and felt fantastic. After a few minutes of stretching and savoring the safety of a warm apartment, he got up and wandered into the kitchen. Kelly had left a note on the table right next to Mason's neatly folded clean clothes.

"Fridge is pretty well stocked. Make yourself at home. Feel free to eat any and everything. Will leave work early to pick up dinner and wine on the way home. Should be back by 6ish. Try not to kill any of the neighbors while I'm gone. LOL." The note was simply signed "K" with a happy face drawn next to it.

Mason's entire being filled with joy as he read it. He couldn't remember the last time he felt this alive. His excitement was partially due to his happiness of having survived his ordeal, but also because he could no longer hide from himself the fact that he was in love. Like a switch had been thrown, he went from burying and denying it to wanting to jump and scream and run around the room. He loved every single thing about this woman. He loved her beautiful face. He loved her kindness. He loved her incredibly beautiful body. He loved her long hair. He loved that they both shared the experience of being bilingual and drawn to France and French culture. He loved that she was confident, and smart, and independent, and playful.

But, totally out of character for him, he was suddenly nervous about ensuring that he did everything just right so as not to blow his chances with her. Rather than his traditional approach of being carefree and confident about making a move, he began to overthink how to not mess it up.

Being trapped in her apartment alone for the whole afternoon just gave him more time to think himself into a knot. *What if I'm just imagining this? What if she's only being nice because she knows I'm in a jam? I guess I'll know by how she behaves when she comes home. No need to risk blowing this or looking like a chump by rushing it.*

Around 3:30 p.m. he finally was able to put the subject out of his mind and regain some sanity. He watched an hour of Sky News, looking for any mention of his name. There was a brief bulletin that he had not been heard from or found, but that authorities on both sides of the Channel were admitting it appeared there was misinformation or some kind of mix-up and that his involvement was doubtful, but that they'd still like to talk to him. The newscaster relayed an appeal for him to contact authorities. This was followed by repeated coverage of all those poor souls massacred in the Bataclan nightclub. Just the mention of it filled him with guilt for not having succeeded in helping Spencer and his team catch the jihadi fanatics before they made it to Paris.

Finally, he heard her on the stairs and her key in the latch. He found himself strangely more excited to see her than he had anticipated. He noticed the emotion right away. *What is up with you, dude? You're like a teenager with a crush all of a sudden. Get ahold of yourself!*

He met her at the door, took the groceries from her, and

carried them into the kitchen. She had also bought a copy of the *Evenings Standard* to show Mason the article stating that multiple anonymous sources in the British government had confirmed that Mason was not a suspect and that the tips were misinformation.

"This is reassuring. In fact, it's exactly as I had hoped this would play out. My guess is that within the next day, maybe two, we'll get the official confirmation that I was framed, which they alluded to yesterday. If it's alright with you, I'd still like to hang here until it's official."

"Absolutely, you are welcome to stay as long as you need to," Kelly replied.

That evening they made spaghetti Bolognese together and polished off two bottles of a lovely white Orvieto Classico. Kelly boiled the spaghetti and made a salad while Mason made the sauce, which he proudly declared would warrant a Michelin star if he were a chef.

As they talked over dinner, and drank the rest of the wine afterwards, they each shared more details of their lives.

"Prior to coming to SCI, I worked for several years at a Paris-based charity dedicated to helping survivors of human trafficking. In fact, I spent a year working at a refugee center in Samos, Greece—in the eastern Aegean, very close to Turkey. My main job was helping people get the required paperwork to enter the European Union. But of course, in these places one ends up doing a great deal of counseling as well. Those people have been through so much. The children have seen things that no child should ever have to see. And so many of the women and teenage girls are lured into human trafficking by the promise of faster passage into Europe, only to find out, when it's too late, that they've been duped. By then they've been forcibly hooked on drugs and sold into prostitution.

"While I was there I fell in love with a freelance photojournalist named Don Kennedy, who was investigating the criminal and terrorist organizations behind the traffickers. He was a really special guy, and he cared as much as I do about the refugees. Unfortunately, he got too close to the truth and was murdered. His body was found next to a roadside, badly beaten and shot in the head. I came back from Greece right after that, because it had become too dangerous. But I returned more determined than ever to keep working to help those people—albeit in different ways now."

Kelly fell silent while she gently wiped the tears from her eyes with a napkin and regained her composure. Mason, also with tears welling in his eyes, reached across the table and placed his hand tenderly on top of hers.

"I'm going to stop talking for a few minutes," Kelly said. "It's your turn now."

Mason recounted the details of the different components of his escape from France—even sharing that he stayed at Olivia's after meeting her at Castel.

"As I was walking her home, it was literally one of the most frightening moments of my life. There were police and soldiers everywhere, and I knew they were looking for me—specifically to kill me. I also knew, with each step closer to her door, that if she did not ask me to come inside, if she left me alone on the street, I was going to be shot within the next two minutes. I think she could literally see the fear on my face. I wasn't pretending to be scared. It was the real deal. Thank God she felt sorry for me and invited me in."

Mason's sincerity in recounting this very raw, recent memory was evident, and both he and Kelly teared up again as he was telling it. He continued, "But look at me. You see how I could never really be an MI6 agent. Here I am spilling my guts and giving away all my trade secrets after just a few glasses of wine."

He suspected, accurately, that Kelly didn't like hearing the part of the story about Olivia. *If she likes me then she's surely bummed that this happened less than a week ago. But there isn't much I can do about it. At least she knows how sincerely desperate I was that night.*

Later on, they went through the same routine of making up his bed on the sofa. Only tonight both of them were more relaxed and a little more flirty. At one point, as they were tucking the sheets in around the cushions, Mason purposefully swung his hip over and bumped hers, knocking her off balance. Kelly came right back and butt-bumped him in return, as they both started laughing.

A few minutes later the time came to say good night. Kelly turned to hug him again as she had done the night before. Only tonight the hug lasted just a few seconds longer, with no words exchanged. When she pulled her head away to look him in the eyes, Mason again looked back at her calmly and lovingly. But something would not let him lean in just those two inches to kiss her lips. He was ninety-nine percent sure that he should. But he was so hopelessly in love with her that even that one percent was suddenly too much risk. *I'm willing to sail the fucking English Channel in a storm, but I'm too big of a pussy to kiss this beautiful woman! God, I'm an embarrassment to mankind.*

But he didn't have much time to chastise himself, because at that instant, Kelly leaned in and kissed him on the lips. He pressed his lips back against hers for what felt like both a millisecond and an eternity. She gave him a last look—a gentle, loving smile—before looking down, turning, and shuffling delicately back to her bedroom.

For Mason it was as if a thermonuclear blast had gone off. He was soaring above the earth in the clouds. He couldn't recall a time in his life when he felt so happy. Not even being accepted at Harvard had made him feel this way. *Should I follow her into the bedroom? Fuck it. At this point, it doesn't matter. I can wait one more day. Hell, I could wait a thousand years, just hanging on the knowledge that she likes me back.* He was content to just lay down on the sofa and try to go to sleep—which he knew was going to take a while given how fast his heart was racing.

43

Mason heard the shower running and slowly began to stir awake. He had just spent his second night on Kelly's sofa, and the memory of her kiss the night before leapt into his mind, instantly energizing him with hope and excitement. He sprang off the sofa, wide awake, scurried to the bathroom door, and gently knocked.

"Hey, beautiful, do you want me to make you an English breakfast?"

"Thanks, that's sweet. But no, I have a call I have to be at the office for. I'll just get a coffee and a croissant at Prêt a Manger on my way in. But feel free to make one for yourself."

As he was at the stove firing up the fried eggs and rasher of ham, she hurried through the kitchen on her way out. She stopped long enough to kiss him on the lips goodbye.

"My afternoon is not too busy. I should be able to be home by five-thirty or so. Try not to go stir crazy, locked up here in jail."

"As long as you're trapped in my cell with me, I don't mind this jail." His eyes followed every contour of her body as she walked across the living room and out the door. *Good Lord, that woman is as fine as they come. Even the way she walks drives me crazy.*

After breakfast, knowing he still couldn't turn on his phone, Mason settled in to binge on some bad daytime TV. He watched Sky News for a while to get the latest on the attack. Finally, he saw what he had been waiting for. The British government released a joint statement from MI5, MI6, and the home office fully clearing him. The statement also alluded to the fact that the government was concerned for his well-being and was unsure what had happened to him, as there had been no veri- fied contact or sighting of him since the prior Friday night. He switched the channel to France2 and saw a similar statement from the French authorities.

The French and the English couldn't coordinate a story if their lives depended on it, he thought. *Today is Thursday, so tomorrow it will be a full week. I guess it's safe to come out. But just for good measure, I'll wait until tomorrow.*

LATER THAT AFTERNOON HE WALKED, without his hat, down to the local market where he bought a razor, deodorant, shaving cream, and a toothbrush, so he didn't have to keep using Kelly's. He also bought a case of Kronenbourg 1664. He wanted to replace all he had drank of Kelly's and have plenty for that evening as well. He knew it was risky to go out; if he got busted it would ruin his evening plans with Kelly. But he also knew there was little serious danger any longer. *I'm going to try to see Spencer tomorrow anyway. And none of the photos out there show me with this beard I'm sporting now.*

Nevertheless, as he was paying cash at the register, the clerk said, "You look familiar. Do I know you from somewhere? Are you an actor maybe?"

"I get that a lot." Mason grinned and left the clerk guessing.

He finished showering and shaving just a few minutes before Kelly got home, leaving just enough time to pour them each a cold beer. He was past his overthinking phase now. Her kiss the night before had finally convinced him that he could be himself. Their feelings were mutual. As she came through the door, he met her halfway across the living room and gave her a big hug and a long kiss, both of which she fully reciprocated.

"Wow! Clean shaven. How on earth did you manage to do that?" Kelly rubbed his smooth face.

"I have a confession to make. I went rogue today and broke out of jail. Went down to the local market and loaded up on toiletries and a case of 1664."

"Are you crazy? What if you'd gotten caught?"

"I know, I know. But I think the danger is pretty much over. I saw the home office spokesperson on TV today essentially proclaim my innocence. I think I need to go talk to the government folks tomorrow and put this behind me. But as for tonight, I was thinking that maybe we order a Grubhub delivery from La Famiglia in Chelsea."

UNLIKE PRIOR EVENINGS when they sat across from each other at the small kitchen table, tonight Kelly set their places side by side on the corner. Mason found himself spontaneously touching her hand sometimes as she would talk, or just lightly touching her back, or putting his arm around her waist if she was doing something at the counter.

Just like the prior two evenings, time flew by. Hours felt like minutes as they talked, learning more and more about each other, and as they tried to finish the huge portions of risotto and the delicious branzino they had ordered. Tonight's conversation focused more on future dreams than the past: where did each see themselves in ten years, geographically, married or not, how many kids, professionally—the conversation ran the gamut.

At one point Kelly said, "It's funny, I have family in Ireland; I have family in the US and friends from Purdue there; and of course I have friends and family in Paris; I even have friends still working in the refugee camps in Greece. But somehow with all the moving around between different cultures and countries, I have always felt a bit lost—like I'm not sure where I fit in or really belong."

A look of incredulity appeared on Mason's face as he stared directly into her eyes, unable to find the words to relay the myriad of emotions sweeping over him at that moment.

As the evening was winding down and it was clearly time for bed, Kelly excused herself while Mason was putting the leftovers away and washing the few dishes they had used. He thought she may have been going to get his sheets and pillow for the sofa, but when she came back out of the bedroom, she was empty-handed, and had changed into her pajamas. He dried his hands after washing the last dish and shot his best naughty look her way.

"Oh my. Miss O'Callaghan, whatever am I to do if I don't have sheets to sleep on my sofa tonight?" he said in an exaggerated southern accent.

"I think we both know you've spent your last night on that sofa," she replied with a knowing grin.

"I was hoping you were going to say that." He kissed her, ever so gently on the lips, once, twice, then a third time, as she put her arms around his neck. He pulled his head back slightly so he could see what he was doing as he began to unbutton the front of her pajama top. With the two sides now hanging open, exposing the contour of her beautiful breasts, he slowly eased his hands around her waist, and then around her back, gently pulling her in to kiss her some more. Next, he slid his hands around to the front and gently caressed both of her breasts, ever so lightly letting his palms brush across her nipples.

Kelly was feeling as if every nerve on every square inch of her body was about to explode in erogenous excitement. She had never had someone take such care to gently ease into love-making, especially given how much they wanted each other. The anticipation was overwhelming her. With her arms still around his neck she climbed on him with her legs wrapped around his waist. Mason slowly walked them into the bedroom and laid her on the bed, removing her PJ bottoms yet leaving her PJ top on, spread open.

He took off his shirt and pants, leaving only his boxers on. As Kelly tried to take his boxers off for him, he stopped her and gently laid her head back on the pillow saying, between long, slow kisses, "There will be plenty of time to take care of me. I'm going to take care of you first. I just want you to lay there and enjoy this. Is that okay?"

She looked him in the eyes, unknowingly biting her lip in anticipation, saying nothing, and just nodded. Mason proceeded to massage, caress, and stroke every part of her body—with his hands, his fingers, and his tongue, for the next half hour— bringing her to climax twice.

After a few minutes of rest, she said, "Now it's your turn," as she removed his boxers.

"I've never been this comfortable being naked with someone in my life," he said. "It's like I've known you forever. And yet, this whole experience is so impossibly exciting I feel like it's my very first time."

"That's *exactly* the way I feel," Kelly said. She then proceeded to return the same passionate oral pleasures on him that she had just received, bringing him to an earthshaking climax that may have woken the neighbors as he yelled. They both laughed uncontrollably and collapsed together back on the pillows at the head of the bed. Then they just lay there tangled up in each other's naked bodies, talking, neither of them having any concept of time.

At some point Kelly felt something hard under her leg draped across Mason's body. "Something's happening down there." As she moved her leg and felt with her hand, she said with a mischievous look, "It looks like your friend wants to come out and play some more. I was hoping he wasn't going in for the night."

"You are literally too good to be true," Mason replied, shaking his head.

Mason and Kelly made love for the next half hour, with greater passion and fervor than at any point in the night, maybe in their lives, until Kelly came for the third time, which Mason found so erotic that it caused him to climax again at the exact same time. They collapsed back on the pillows, utterly exhausted. In less than a minute they were both sound asleep.

44

"Wake up, sleepyhead."

Mason woke up to find Kelly kneeling down to talk to him as he lay in bed. She was already showered and dressed and ready to leave for work. As she saw his eyes open and finally register where he was, she whispered to him, "Yeah, uh, I just feel compelled to tell you that last night was, uh, I don't have the words. Let's just say if I live to be one hundred years old, I will never forget it. I don't think anything will ever top that experience."

"Well, look at what you've done now. You've laid down a challenge for me to try to exceed that performance," Mason said, as he raised his eyebrows.

She laughed, and gave him a quick kiss. "I'm going to be late if I don't dash. Do you think you might come into the office today?"

"I just might." Mason sat up in bed and thought for a second. "But I'm not sure just yet. Let's see how the day unfolds. Until I know for sure, please don't tell anyone anything."

"Of course. Call me later?"

He nodded as she turned and walked away.

At about ten-thirty a.m. he walked down to Earl's Court Road to flag a passing cab. He told the cabbie to head into town and unwrapped his foil-wrapped iPhone and powered it on. He had twenty percent battery left. That would be enough. The first thing he did was text Spencer's private number.

"Can you meet me in thirty minutes at the same place where you and your Virginia friend first met me?"

The response came back within seconds: "1." That's what he had hoped. Mason would finally get to see Spencer face to face and hopefully get some answers about what the hell had happened, and what the hell he should do. Next, he told the cabbie to drive around for a few more minutes as that would give him enough time to call his folks.

It was 5:45 a.m. when the phone rang at the modest home just off Grove Avenue in Richmond, Virginia. Mason knew that his dad would already be up making breakfast but his mom would just be stirring—although, given all that had been going on, who knew what their sleep habits would be. Mason called his mom's cell via WhatsApp from his own iPhone so she would recognize the caller ID. She answered on the second ring with the loudest "Hello!?" he had ever heard her utter.

All he had time to say was, "Mom?" before the voice on the other end exploded with joy. "Oh, my sweet boy, it's you! You're alive! Praise the Lord! Joe, Joe, it's Mason on the phone. Come quick."

Joe Sr. bounded up the stairs in two leaps, making it from the kitchen to her bedside in less than three seconds. Mason's sister Sandra was there too; she and Joe Jr. had been staying with their parents all week, but Joe Jr. had gone back home the night before.

"I'm going to put you on speaker, honey, so your dad and

Sandra can hear, too," his mom said. "Where are you? Are you okay? Tell me you're okay."

"I'm fine, Mom. Totally fine. God has been watching over me. I'm back in London and in a cab on my way to meet some government people to clear all this madness up." His family let out simultaneous exclamations of relief.

His dad yelled into the speaker, "Where the hell have you been?! The whole world has been worried sick about you. Were you kidnapped? And why do they think you're connected to these terrorists?!"

"I wish I had all the answers, Dad. I really do. But the short story is that of course I had absolutely nothing to do with the terrorists, as you well know. And I have no clue how my name got confused with these guys. But it's clear someone was trying to set me up. Regarding where I've been: I've been hiding. I know I put you all through hell, and I'm so sorry for that, but I could not surface to call, or even get a note to you, or I would have been risking my life. I figured it was better to stay alive and let you worry than it was to put your mind at ease and risk getting shot. As you may or may not know, there is a reasonable chance that your phones are bugged and that the boys in Langley or in Maryland are listening to us right now. But I thought it was safe to come out now that the news is reporting that this whole thing was a misunderstanding."

They talked for a few more minutes and his family reiterated how much they loved him. He promised he'd call again later that day once he'd had his meeting, and they hung up just as the cab pulled up in front of the Grenadier.

45

Spencer was five minutes early. Since it was still before noon the Grenadier was almost empty. He walked up to Mason like a long-lost brother and gave him a bear hug.

"I've been on cloud nine since I got your text. You don't know how I worried that we had lost you. I was never going to forgive myself if something had happened to you. Thank God you're safe. By the way, nice hat." They both laughed, and then let out a long, slow exhale. Spencer continued, "We're drinking and I'm buying, and you're going to tell me everything."

"I'll have a Fuller's ESB—and I'm hoping that it's you who will tell me everything," Mason replied.

Spencer returned with the beers and smacked them down on the table, and then reached across and pulled Mason's black knit hat off and messed up his hair, as they both smiled.

"Where the fuck have you been, mate?" Spencer teared up as he spoke. "And how the hell did you get back to London? We've had every possible means of transportation bottled up with agents for the last week. We even have a diplomatic row going on behind the scenes with the bloody Frogs because we dumped so many of our own boys into France trying to find you and extract you before their trigger-happy police could gun you down—which is what they have done to every terrorist they've caught since the attack."

"Yeah, I've spent enough time in France to know what was in store for me if they caught me," Mason said. "When I saw my name on the news, I knew I had to go underground."

"By God, I can pick 'em, can't I? You did a better job than a trained agent! We found out later on the security camera that the French police missed you by two minutes at the Bonaparte. After the first day we thought that maybe you had gotten lucky. After two days we thought maybe you were super lucky. On the third day they claimed they chased you into a Metro, but no one was sure it was you. Was that you?"

Mason nodded. "But tell the French it wasn't me. I don't want them trying to charge me with assaulting a policeman. I don't think I really hurt him."

"Yeah, he's fine. And they weren't sure it was you anyway. After four or five days, we thought for sure you were dead. No cell ping. No credit card. No hotel. No sleeping on the street or in the parks. No showing up at any friend's apartment, or train station, or car rental, or bus station, or airport. Hell, as someone trained in this craft, I'm dying to know how you managed to vanish so completely."

They talked over beers for the next two hours. Mason told him every detail. Spencer was particularly incredulous about the stolen sailboat.

"What bloody nutter tries to sail the English Channel in a storm, in November, with no supplies, in a small sailboat—alone!? I knew you had a tolerance for risk but hell, man, you're into the realm of statistical anomaly, or just lunacy on this one."

Looking away modestly, Mason said, "I just saw it more as desperation than any exceptional tolerance for risk."

Mason asked Spencer to explain what he knew about all that

had happened. "I understand how German intelligence could have received the false story and given it to the French authorities. But I'm still wondering how the terrorists got my mobile number to leave it in their apartment. I believe it was that second source of validation that gave it sufficient credibility for the media to put it on the air."

"We chased down every source and every contact we have trying to figure out the answer to that question," Spencer said. "The only answer we keep coming up with is that it must have been the baron. He could have gotten your mobile phone number from Hans and given it to his jihadi contacts, suggesting they leave the paper behind in their apartment as a way to get you back for having killed their jihadi brother in Sally's flat."

"That avenue seems suspect to me, unless there is some way he got my number from Hans's address book or cell phone without him knowing. Because there is no way Hans would have given my number to his uncle without asking what he wanted it for."

"We agree. Clearly don't have that fully figured out yet. Either way, we've been telling the French since it first appeared that it was bogus intel and that you had been set up. It still took the buggers three days to start printing the retraction, half-heartedly at first then finally all the way. We have also been tearing the place apart here to try and find this 'Klug' mole you suspect exists. The information about our efforts to catch the baron was only known by a very small handful of people. Either one of them is a traitor or someone is getting access to our reports. The good news is that I know the guy who is heading up the investigation to try to uncover Klug's identity. His name is Ed Pincus. I've worked with him a number of times in the past and he's a first-class asshole. But he usually gets results. So I'd wager we catch this Klug guy sooner rather than later."

"I'm glad you're confident about it all turning out well. But for me, I just want to be out of it—as in really, truly done and out of it."

"Mate, as far as I'm concerned you *are* out of it. I've been straight with you on that. Of course, I can only control what's in my power. But I promise to do everything I possibly can to find the guys who've tried twice to burn you now. Hell, I feel more terrible than you'll ever know about what you've already been through. If there is anything you need, anything I can do to put this right, just say the word."

"The biggest thing on my mind right now is the press," Mason replied. "I have to believe that as soon as it's announced that I'm alive every journalist in London will stalk me night and day to get a quote or an interview. I can't handle that. So, just thinking out loud, here's my ask: promise me that MI6 will hold a press conference—without me—to tell the press some story, like maybe the mix-up came from some fake evidence that the terrorist planted to throw you off their trail. And you guys get to be the heroes by having discovered that the evidence was bogus. And maybe say that I was camping with friends in the French Alps the entire time and had missed the whole thing. In other words, no drama, no hiding, no sailing the Channel in a storm, just a fake story that got exposed, about a boring businessman who knew nothing about any of it and only found out when he came home; a non-story from start to finish. Nothing to see here."

"I will do my best to deliver that story, or something directionally similar to get you off the hook with the press," Spencer replied.

"Thank you. Just a few more minor things. Please get the French police to send over all my things that I'm sure they confiscated from my hotel room over there, including my passport. And I need you to either call my boss in Paris, today if possible, or have someone stop by his office and explain what's going on. I know you're worried about keeping everything quiet, but he's a former top cabinet minister from Chirac's time, and a former bird colonel in the French special forces, so I'm certain he knows how to keep things quiet. Basically, I'm hoping you can help me get my job back—and hoping that he'll listen to reason, now that you guys are going to announce it was all a mix-up."

"I actually know your boss," Spencer said. "I worked with him on a project a long time ago in Lebanon when he was still in the military. In fact, he has quite an impressive resume when it comes to off-the-record operations. I have no problem giving him a call. It will be a pleasure to catch up with him. And, yes, we'll get the gendarmes to send your stuff back from your hotel room."

Mason smiled and nodded.

Spencer added, "I do have one last favor to ask of you."

"What's that?"

"Even though you are indeed completely out of all this madness, I would sleep a lot better at night if I knew you had gone through our basic self-defense and weapons training. It doesn't have to be formal, just a few evenings a week for the next month or two. I'll understand if you want nothing to do with us at all. But just in case something, or someone else were to pop up by surprise, you'd at least know the basics in an emergency."

"It's not a crazy idea. Let me think about it. Thank you for the offer."

By the time he and Spencer finished their meeting at the pub, Mason was buzzed, exhausted, and wanted to go back to his flat. He didn't have the energy for another reunion today, so he skipped going to the office. Also, he thought it would be easier to have Spencer's press conference happen before going back to the office. He went back to his flat, the keys to which had been in his left front jeans pocket for the past week, and spent the rest of the afternoon calling friends and family: a few of his friends in Paris, his brother and sister, and his parents again. He also called Kelly just as she was about to leave the office.

"It's nice to see your caller ID pop up on my phone," she said. "How did your meeting go today?"

"It went fine. We've devised a half-assed way to try to make it look like I was in the Alps the whole time and out of mobile coverage range and knew nothing about any of it. Who knows if it will fly? But they've promised to do everything in their power to keep me out of all their madness from here on out. I sure hope they can deliver on that. Hey, I'm back at my flat now, and I have a bunch of calls I have to make to tell the world I'm alive, including calling Bourget about getting my job back. But I just wanted to say that I'd like to see you again, like a lot."

She replied with a huge grin, "Yes, I'd like that very much. And for the record, if that wasn't the case then the French police would be the least of your worries."

"We haven't talked about this, but maybe we keep the fact that we're seeing each other just between us."

"For sure. I was going to mention that. The last thing I want people thinking is that I'm dating the boss. Let's have a rule that we never discuss anything at work but work and when we get together it's only outside of work."

"Perfect. It's a deal. Okay, I'm going to get to my calls and then crash early. I was up kind of late last night, doing a very special performance review of a star employee, and I'm exhausted today. How about dinner tomorrow night? Maybe Le Boudin Blanc in Shepherds Market? After which we can do another deep-dive performance review at my place."

"It's a date," Kelly said with an ear-to-ear smile.

"Great. Have a good evening, beautiful. And thanks again for bringing me back from the dead."

.   .   .

Mason waited until about nine p.m., hoping Spencer had come through with his promised call, before he dialed Monsieur Bourget on his personal mobile phone. Bourget answered after one ring.

"Hello, Mason, I'm so glad you're alright. You had everyone worried, as well as confused," Bourget said in his thick French accent.

"I'm so sorry that I couldn't call sooner and explain everything. I was able to keep up with the news a bit and I read that you guys had made a statement that I had been let go from the company. I'm hoping I can convince you to reconsider."

"Don't worry. I had a call this afternoon from your friend, Spencer Hughes-Smyth, who I know from a former life. It was great to catch up with him. He told me everything," Bourget replied. "And you don't need to be concerned about my discretion. Your 'extracurricular' activities are safe with me. I spoke with Le Lidec just an hour ago. He and I are in agreement. Your job is perfectly secure. On behalf of the people of France, thank you for what you did to try and help us. The next time you're back over here, you and I and Le Lidec are going out for a long dinner and a lot of wine. We'll take you to Maxim's."

They spoke for a few more minutes and Mason shared most of the details of how he had escaped. After he hung up the phone, a strange sensation came over him. He suddenly felt a wave of optimism that he had not felt in a long time. *Maybe history is not going to repeat itself this time. I'm not going to have to start over again. Maybe I can finally feel part of something permanent, a full member of the club—not just someone passing through.*

46

M ason waited until the next morning to call Hans on WhatsApp. By then the news had broken everywhere that Mason was back in London and it was official—that it had all been a mix-up.

"Mason!" Hans said.

"Yep. Still here," Mason replied. "Who was it that said, 'The reports of my death are greatly exaggerated'?"

"Mein bruder, you do not know how happy I am to hear your voice! It has been so long without any sign of you, I was sure you were dead. I could not believe the good news when I read it this morning! Where have you been?"

"Yeah, it's a really long story..."

Hans interrupted, "And what is this story about you camping in the Alps? You were in Paris the night of the attack. I know because you asked me to come to Paris to meet you for dinner. Why do the papers have this story?"

Mason knew before he called that he was going to have to come clean with Hans.

"Yeah, that story is not accurate. I was planning on telling you the straight scoop about what's happened, but I need you to swear to me that it will stay between us forever."

"You know that you can completely trust me," Hans replied.

Mason began. "A few months ago I was approached, totally by surprise, by the uncle of my friend Pam, both of whom you met that day in the beer garden here in London. I know she joked about it, but apparently he really is some kind of spy over here. He works for MI6. They convinced me, with a bunch of evidence, that someone I know has been working with terrorists and they needed my help to try to get information on movements of these jihadis so they could try to prevent the attack that just happened in Paris. I tried to help. Then a few days later some Middle Eastern psychopath starts following me here in London, and then tries to kill me with a big-ass knife as I'm leaving Sally's flat in London. I'm sorry I lied to you about what really happened there, but they swore me to secrecy. The truth is, I did not find them dead after it happened. I fought the fucker, and with Sally's help, I killed him by driving a big glass shard through his neck. Unfortunately, as you know, Sally did not survive the fight."

"What the hell! You killed that man?! I cannot believe that. Good Lord. I'm so sorry, my friend. Tell me what really happened."

Mason recounted all the details of the fight and the deaths of Sally and Nassim, and then continued with his story about the night of the massacre.

"Then last Friday, when I was in Paris on the night of the Bataclan attack, I saw my face on the TV as being someone involved with the terrorists—that I had been their driver! I couldn't believe it. It turns out that this fake story was just another attempt on my life, trying to get the French police to kill me. We know that the story was planted from Berlin and that someone must have had direct contact with the jihadis to give them my mobile number so they could leave it in the flat in Brussels. It's pretty fucked up that someone wanted me dead bad enough to try again. But either way, I've clearly pissed off some very well-connected people."

Mason went on for the next twenty minutes telling Hans how he escaped from Paris. When he was finally done, he said, "So now you know the full story. I'm so sorry I couldn't tell you everything before."

"And have you told me everything now?" Hans asked.

Mason paused, recognizing that Hans was clearly baiting him, but it didn't matter. If he was baiting him it meant he already knew anyway.

"Everything except one final piece of information: the person they asked me to help them eavesdrop on to try to catch the terrorists. It was your uncle. In fact, everyone thinks that he's the one who has been trying to have me killed, because I planted a listening device in his library and he found it."

Hans waited a long time before speaking. "Thank you for finally being honest with me. I know my uncle is not a saint. I do not know about his business dealings, but I do not believe for an instant that he has agreed to transport jihadis or humans being trafficked. It's possible some of his ship captains have agreed to take contraband, but there is simply no way he would take people or terrorists. And you are certainly mistaken if you think he tried to kill you because you planted a bug in his library."

"How can you know what he's capable of? We know he found it and destroyed it, so he's bound to be out for revenge."

"You have it all wrong. My uncle doesn't even know about the bug. He didn't find it and destroy it. I did."

Mason went silent in disbelief. Neither spoke for what seemed like an eternity.

"So how long have you known?" Mason finally said.

"I could not know for sure that it was you until just now,"

Hans replied. "I did not want to believe it. But a few days after you left, my uncle asked me how well I knew you. I told him I trusted you with my life. He warned me to be careful with that kind of trust."

"Thank you. I hope you know I also feel the same way about you."

"Then he said the last time you were there, when we had been working out in the cellar, that he had left the schloss and then remembered he had forgotten something. When he came back in, he said he caught you acting suspiciously in his wing by the library. I told him he was imagining things. But I then thought about what he said. And, I thought back to the night before. Just before he came home that night, I could have sworn I heard someone running down the hall outside my door. There is no chance Sabine was up on our floor or running like that. I did not know if I had dreamt it or not but could not get it out of my mind. I did not want to even consider it. But finally I had to put my mind at rest.

"The next day, when my uncle was not home, I went to the back staircase that leads to the secret entrance to the library. I remembered I had shown it to you on your first trip to the schloss. No one has been on it since then, so the steps are covered in dust. I turned on my iPhone flashlight and sure enough, I saw big footprints on the steps, going all the way down to the hidden door, and coming back out. Now I know you are not a thief so the only other thing I could think of was, if you were not taking something out of there, you must have been snooping. But his library is always spotless. I could not figure any way you could have gotten any information from just looking around. So I thought about it some more. And then the idea came to me. Why would you care about his business? You would not, unless you were helping someone else. This is when the idea of a listening device came to me. I spent two hours going over everything in there, looking for anything that seemed out of place, until I found that strange book with some kind of device inside."

"What did you do with it?" Mason asked.

"I took it to a bridge near the schloss, smashed it to bits against the cobblestones, and threw it in the river," Hans replied.

"Why would you do that?"

"To protect you. You are right about one thing, my uncle would have gone, how do you say—'fucking crazy' on you if he thought you had planted a device to listen to his private conversations in his own office. I did not know what he would do, but I did not want to find out. I also did not want to have him reminding me over and over for years about what a bad judge of character I am for having invited someone into our home who would betray us like that. Anyway, I believe you are wrong about him. Something about what these spy people are telling you doesn't add up. If my uncle is innocent, and I believe he is, then someone is setting him up."

"You have given me a lot to think about. I will pass on your concern, although I won't personally be looking into anything. I never wanted to be part of this and I'm done with it now—forever. And just for the record, I'd like to say that I don't have words to express how sorry I am to have betrayed you. I won't even ask for you to forgive me because I suspect the betrayal is too great. But if it's any consolation, I also think of you as a brother and I would die for you. I suffered over the decision before deciding to participate in this. At the end of the day, I knew that I might be sacrificing our friendship by doing so, but the truth is, I would do it again. It's bigger than me, and it's bigger than you, and it's bigger than our friendship. We were trying to save lives, a lot of lives. We failed at that. It looks like I failed all around. But that doesn't mean it was wrong to have tried. I'm so sorry if I've lost your friendship. I'm so sorry to have betrayed your trust. If there is any way you could ever see my perspective on this, and still be my friend, I'll be the happiest man alive. If not, I will understand."

"It's a lot to ask. I don't know what I should or will do about it. I need some time to think about it all. I'm glad you are alive, I know that. I'll reach out if and when I feel like talking about it some more," Hans said. "Thank you for finally telling me the truth. As upsetting as it is, I will still keep it just between us, as you asked."

"Thank you, my friend. I hope you feel like speaking again soon. *Tschüss.*"

Mason hung up the phone, more confused than ever. *If the baron never knew about the bug, and only has a vague suspicion of me, then who the hell is trying to kill me?*

47

D ecember 2015
London, England

EVEN WITH THE press conference declaring that the release of Mason's name was just a mix-up, reporters still tried to track him down. A number of them came by the office but the receptionist turned them away. Mason kept an ultra-low profile for the next several weeks, declining all efforts by the media to interview him. He tried to stay away from the office altogether for the first couple of weeks, working from his flat some days, and Kelly's flat others. He even disguised how he looked when he started going back into the office. And then one day, enough time had passed, and enough other new stories dominated the headlines, that the requests for interviews stopped. He had become yesterday's news.

Much to Mason's relief, about a month after their phone call, Hans called to tell him that he understood what Mason had done and he respected him for what he tried to achieve. It looked like their friendship was going to survive, even if it might take a while to get back to where it once was. Finally, it appeared as if he would be able to put this whole nightmare behind him and move on to a happier phase of life. Best of all, Kelly convinced Bourget to let her work out of the UK office permanently.

THROUGHOUT THE NEXT YEAR, Mason and Kelly enjoyed one of the happiest periods of their lives. They loved their jobs, and enjoyed the thrill of keeping their romance a secret. They were making great money as they helped grow the UK office with success after success, and together they had a healthy disposable income. They ate in some of London's nicest restaurants every week, and the most romantic cities in Europe were just a short flight away. They jaunted to Prague, Venice, Rome, Lisbon, and Copenhagen for three-day weekends. And of course, they regularly visited Paris, which was still their favorite city.

One Thursday evening in May, Mason was looking at the dreary weather forecast for London for the weekend. He happened to glance over at the weather forecast for Paris, as well.

"How busy is your afternoon tomorrow?" Mason asked Kelly.

"Not too bad, why?"

"The weather is supposed to be overcast again here in London—but Paris is showing sunny and 24 degrees centigrade for the whole weekend. What do you say we take off at lunchtime and spend the weekend in Paris?"

With a gigantic grin Kelly replied, "Done."

.   .   .

SATURDAY AFTERNOON they strolled arm in arm past the eighteenth-century church, St. Sulpice.

"I feel like an afternoon drink. Let's sit out on the sidewalk over at Café de Flore for a while," Mason said.

Two hours later they were just finishing their third drink at Flore and looking for the waiter to pay the bill, when suddenly, Kelly said, "Oh my God. Look who it is!"

To their amazement, there was Hans! He was walking up with a young woman with short brown hair. Mason and Kelly both yelled and waved for them to come sit at their table. Hans looked a bit startled but nodded rapidly and complied with their request.

Hugging him as he arrived, Mason asked, "What are you doing in Paris? We would have called you if we had known you were coming in from Reichsburg."

"I was going to ask you this same question. Mason, Kelly, this is Kristen."

They all exchanged salutations and hugs and settled in to have a few drinks together. Kelly and Mason soon realized that this was the young English student attending Beaux-Arts that Hans had been seeing.

"Kristen, I can't tell you how nice it is to finally meet you," Mason said. "We've been hearing about you from Hans for the last couple of years, but somehow our paths never managed to cross."

Kristen glanced shyly at them through her thick glasses, as if making conversation was a bit of an effort for her, and replied, "Yes. It seems Hans is often busy, or often I am the one doing things with my friends at Beaux-Arts, and somehow we never managed to all get together. I hear about some of the glamorous parties that you and Hans have been to. One of these days I'm hoping he'll take me along to one with you guys."

"There haven't been too many parties happening lately,"

Hans said. "With Mason off in London, me living in Koblenz now, and everyone else moving on with their lives, it seems like our party crowd is slowing down a bit."

At one point, Kelly took out her phone and took an unannounced group selfie, to capture the memory. Hans had not realized what she was doing until the last second and instinctively said, "Oh. No. You don't need to take a photo."

"Oh, come on now. We want to remember our good fortune at having bumped into you," Kelly replied, although she registered the slight grimace that came across Hans's face.

After just two drinks Hans and Kristen explained that they had another event to go to, and made a polite exit. Once they had departed, Mason and Kelly both noted that something seemed slightly amiss.

"What did you make of that? Kristen seems perfectly nice, but she sure seemed less dynamic and a lot less chic than the women I'm used to seeing Hans with at the chateau parties we've been to."

"Yeah. That was indeed a bit confusing. I didn't get much of a sense of chemistry between the two of them. And why do you think he was so edgy about my taking a simple selfie of us all?"

"I don't know. He's always been a bit guarded about his relationship with her. Hell, we are best friends and it's the first time I've ever met her. Oh well. I'm sure he has his reasons."

THROUGHOUT THE SUMMER and early autumn of 2016 Mason and Kelly continued to develop their relationship, and traveled around Europe on romantic getaway weekends and holidays. And even though Mason had never been more in love, he still was not consciously thinking about marriage. That is, until one day in October of 2016.

Mason needed to go to the German office for two days,

followed by three days at HQ in Paris. Being away from Kelly for a week was longer than they had been apart since they started dating.

While he was gone, he called her twice a day, every day. He assumed he would miss her, but he was caught off guard by just how much. By the end of the week, he was almost physically ill from being away from her. He couldn't stop thinking about her.

On the Eurostar ride home, sitting alone in his seat, he started laughing out loud like a crazy man. It finally hit him. *This is the one. I don't know why I didn't see it sooner. This is what everyone means when they say, "Trust me. When you meet the one, you'll know it."* And man did he know it now. He felt like he had undergone a metamorphosis. He wanted to race home from the train station and propose to her immediately. But he knew that was not the way to go about it.

48

November 2016
    London, England

ONE NIGHT, a few weeks after coming back from the continent
and just a few days after Donald Trump's surprise election
victory in the US, Mason and Kelly were out to dinner in South
Ken when his mobile phone rang. He saw that it was Corrine, a
French woman he had dated briefly when he lived in Paris. He
had originally met her at one of the fancy parties he attended
with Hans. She was coming to London and wanted to get
together. He politely declined, spoke for just a minute, and said
goodbye.

Since Kelly also spoke fluent French, she understood the
whole conversation and couldn't help but feel a little bit jealous
that women she knew nothing about were still calling Mason.
She wondered how often it was happening, and of course,
whether or not he ever saw any of them. She busied herself

arranging and rearranging her silverware throughout the duration of his call.

"Who was that?" Kelly asked, her voice calm and steady.

"Oh, just a woman that I dated a little bit last year before all the crazy MI6 shit happened."

Kelly was quiet for a minute. "Was it the woman from Castel's who you stayed with the weekend of the Bataclan attack?"

"Good Lord, no," Mason said. "She doesn't know my number. I've never contacted her since that weekend. But I do owe her an explanation. I feel like I need to reach out to her at some point to explain."

Kelly knew a bit of the story from when Mason had first returned after the attacks, but she didn't know any details. She had always wondered about the specifics of that night but never felt like she had a right to ask. At this point they had both had enough to drink that they should have saved this conversation for another time. But, as it often does, alcohol elicited the opposite behavior.

"You never told me the full details of that night," Kelly said, continuing her line of questioning.

"Yeah, well, it's not a night I like to remember."

"What was the girl's name you stayed with?"

"Olivia," Mason replied, not liking where this was going.

"Did you make love to her?" Kelly asked, then took a big gulp of wine.

Mason stopped eating, put his fork down, and looked directly at Kelly.

"What are you doing? There is nothing happy at the end of this path. Do we need to do this?"

Kelly, fearing that she would never have the courage to bring up this topic again, persisted.

"I just feel like we should always be honest with each other. We shouldn't have any secrets."

"It's not a secret," Mason said. "I told you about it the night after I got back. I just don't see what is served by doing a deep dive on a difficult issue that's ancient history—and that happened *before* we were dating."

But the alcohol was going to have its way. Kelly was quiet for a minute before asking again, "Well? Did you make love to her?"

Mason, clearly annoyed now, looked her calmly in the eyes and said, "Yes. I did. Now can we please put this subject behind us?"

"How many times?"

Mason's instinct told him not to answer, but her persistence had upset him.

"Four times."

"Four times!" Kelly slammed a hand on the table. "I thought you were only there for one night!"

"Actually, I was only there for one day, but two nights." And, because he too had had one too many drinks and so was not thinking clearly, he let his annoyance with her get the better of him, allowing an ever-so-subtle grin to creep across his face as he said it.

Kelly's mind raced. The combination of her own worries, the phone call, and the revelation about Olivia was too much for her to take, particularly after four drinks.

"This is never going to work," she muttered under her breath. She got up, grabbed her purse, and stormed out. Before Mason could catch her, she was in a cab and headed off down Fulham Road.

What the fuck just happened?! Mason thought to himself. *I didn't do a damn thing wrong and I just lost the love of my life.* He went back inside and paid the bill and then headed home, depressed and confused, wondering if his perceived "curse" was still haunting him after all. He walked past a newsstand and glanced at the headlines.

"President-elect Donald Trump vows to wipe out ISIS in a matter of weeks once he takes office in January."

49

D*ecember 2016*
Raqqa, Syria

THE SCALE of the Paris massacre in November of 2015, and the international attention it received, was a big morale boost for ISIS. A few months later, Abdul bin Hakam began making it clear that he felt it was time to make his own mark with some form of high-profile attack in the West as well. Having proven himself as one of their top commanders, he felt he was due the opportunity he had been promised by al-Baghdadi, to prove something even greater by leading an attack in Europe. However, he also had other reasons for wanting to make the journey, motives that were not lost on his superiors.

He raised the idea at each of their several meetings throughout 2016, including a secret meeting in late December held in the ruins of a burned-out slaughterhouse on the outskirts of Raqqa.

"I have a number of ideas on how I could lead another attack in Paris or a similar attack in London. And I think the time to strike again is now," bin Hakam said.

With a look of concern on his face, al-Baghdadi nodded his head, his massive gray and black peppered beard rising and falling with each nod, as he pondered his reply.

Finally, he said, "I'm well aware of your interest in London and your passion for avenging brother Nassim. There will be time for that, I promise you."

"Yes, I have sworn to avenge him, and I will. But that is not my only concern," bin Hakam replied. "The English pigs are the closest in the world to the great American Satan. We must strike them down at least as much as we do the French."

"You have a point," al-Baghdadi replied. "And I'm not against it in principle. But I cannot spare you, or anyone from here right now. Our spies tell us that Assad's forces are preparing for a new attack. And we are all still waiting to see if the new orange American president will make good on his promises to increase the scale of US attacks on us. We need every available man, especially brave leaders like you, to defend against the enemy in front of us right now. There will be time later to settle old scores and bring our fury to the English."

Bin Hakam tried one last angle. "My concern is that if we do not strike soon then this infidel may move back to USA or somewhere else where it is difficult to find him."

"Relax, my brother. Relax. Our German partner insists that he always knows where this man is. We will not lose him. His time will come—when it is Allah's wish," al-Baghdadi replied.

"I will be patient. But I'll have my revenge. He *will* die at my hand."

"Praise Allah. And so it shall be."

50

D*ecember 2016*
London, England

IT HAD BEEN over a week since Kelly left Mason at PJs, and neither had attempted to contact the other. Mason thought it best to let her cool down and hopefully realize that she had been unreasonable in jumping on him over something from the past. Kelly thought she needed time to think. Finally, against their agreed upon protocol at work, Mason entered her office one afternoon and closed the door.

"We need to talk."

A look of shock came over her face.

"Are you kidding? No way! Get out of my office," she said in an angry whisper.

"Come on, if we keep our voices down no one will hear," Mason replied.

"Not gonna happen. We agreed not to talk about us at work.

Now more than ever we have to respect that. Get out. I will talk to you, just not here. We can meet somewhere after work."

"Okay. It's a beautiful day. Let's take a walk in Hyde Park. How's six-thirty at the Albert Memorial, across from Royal Albert Hall?"

"Okay, okay." She shooed him to get out.

WHEN MASON ARRIVED, Kelly was already waiting in front of the memorial. When he saw her standing there he knew he loved her more than ever and that he would do anything to get her back. He walked up and kissed her on the lips.

"How are you doing?"

"Not great. I miss you, I miss us," she replied, as they turned and started walking into the park together.

Mason immediately launched into a passionate explanation.

"Listen, I get that you must be wondering how well you know me. But we always swore we'd be honest with each other, so I told you the truth. There has never been anyone else since we started dating—not for a minute. And you can't hold something against me that happened *before* we were dating. You especially can't hold something against me that happened at a time when I didn't know if I was going to survive to see another day. You can't know what that's like. Everything becomes incredibly short-term and primal."

"I know," Kelly replied. "I was going to apologize and try to talk with you about it, but everything has been going so fast that I thought it was a good idea to take a few days to get some perspective." She paused for a few seconds and then continued, "It's just a lot to take in knowing that there have been these other random women in your life since we first met two years ago at the French office. I haven't dated anyone seriously since then. In fact, I've believed you were the one since shortly after we met. I just knew you didn't know it yet. So it's hard now to be wondering if you feel the same way, or if I'll always need to worry when the phone rings that it's some other woman. I guess I'm just asking myself if I'm enough for you to never want anyone else."

"Are you kidding?! Mason interjected. "You are so far above and beyond anyone else I have ever known. And yes, I may have dated other women since we met two years ago, but since the very first day I met you in your office in Paris I have honestly never stopped thinking about you. I thought you were off limits because I was worried about dating someone at work. And frankly, I was worried down deep that you might be the last person I ever date. But if you knew how I feel now, you would know that I am willing to lose anything and everything in my life if it means being with you."

As he said these words, Kelly began to tear up. She reached over and touched his hand and then gently leaned into him and kissed him tenderly on the lips. Mason knew this was a huge effort for her because she was not a big fan of displaying affection in public, especially in an open place like Hyde Park. But with just one gentle kiss his entire world was made right. He knew he had not lost her. He had hope again that he could have a happy ending and finally not lose something great that happened to him. He hugged her with all his might, and she hugged him back. And they stood there embracing in the park for longer than either of them realized.

That night, while lying naked in bed together, both completely vulnerable, they shared everything either of them could think of that they had yet to tell the other. Mason even told her the story of being with Vicente when he accidentally killed Seamus Cole at the Black Rose in Boston, as well as what really happened at Sally's flat the night she died. Kelly had lots of questions, but she was also an amazing, sincere listener. She

knew Mason was not at fault in either case. And she could tell
that he was carrying a lot of pain and guilt from both incidents.

Mason also shared with her the enigma of his life. He made
friends and achieved goals easily, but often rushed decisions to
achieve something great that was not a good fit and ended up
finding himself alone—the outsider, yet again. He told her how
he had worried that he was going to add his current job to the
list after the frame-up the night of the Bataclan massacre.

"To me you have been the rock in our relationship this past
year as it has advanced," Mason said. "You never seem to waver
in your love. You can't imagine my horror at realizing that you
seemed ready to walk away last week. It was like my life's theme
playing out before me yet again, after I had gone to such great
lengths to avoid it."

Kelly put her hands on either side of his face and looked him
square in his eyes. "Listen to me. You are the most right, the
most perfect, the most obvious long-term decision of my life. I
love you. And I will never, ever leave you—ever. No matter
what."

He looked back into her eyes as she said it and he knew that
she meant it. He was overwhelmed with emotion from her love
and all that statement meant to him. They lay there in the
extraordinary warmth and silence of the moment, neither
saying another word, wrapped in each other's arms, until they
both fell asleep.

J *anuary 2017*
Paris, France

MASON AND KELLY resumed their relationship full force. A few weeks after having made up, they decided to go to Paris again for a three-day weekend. Strolling along the Seine, arm in arm, her head resting on his shoulder, they looked, and felt, as if they'd been in love forever.

On Saturday afternoon, Mason left her shopping in their favorite quartier, St. Germain des-pres.

"There is something I have to do for about an hour," he said. "I'll explain when I see you for lunch."

He walked over to Olivia's apartment. She was shocked to find him standing at her door, and she patiently listened as he explained the awkward situation. They had only spent a day and two nights together, and it had been a little over a year since she saw him, so she was long since over his disappearance, and friendlier than he had anticipated. She didn't believe him at first, but when he showed her his US passport which matched the name in news articles on the internet, she was convinced.

"Knowing the truth makes it a lot easier to understand why you vanished into thin air," she said. "To be honest, it's a little bit exciting. I'm glad I was able to help you, especially if the alternative was that you may have been shot by the soldiers that night." They both laughed. But it was a nervous laugh, given the scope of the tragedy that still weighed on all who understood how horrible the evil was that befell Paris that night.

The conversation grew awkward, and he politely told her he had to be somewhere, thanked her again for her kindness and for saving his life, and hugged her goodbye.

When he met Kelly for lunch at the Bonaparte, he explained the significance of where they were dining. He pointed to the TV behind the bar where he had heard the news of the attack that fateful night—and where he was wrongly accused of being part of it.

He also told her where he had just been.

She replied, "I get it. I suspected that might be what you were doing. The fact that you always make a sincere effort to do the right thing is one of the reasons I love you so much. Of course, that relationship, or whatever you want to call it, will always bug me a little bit. But it's part of who you are, and I know it probably saved your life, so I'll deal with it—or at least bury it and try to forget about it," she said in a very matter of fact way, neither smiling nor frowning.

"Thank you for that. It's all I feel like I have the right to ask," he said, picking up her hand and kissing her knuckles. "I just count myself lucky that you don't kick my ass all over the bar," which finally elicited the smile he was looking for.

After lunch, he said, "Hey, you wanna head over to the Louvre? I read that they have a special Roman antiquities exhibition going on right now. I'd love to check it out, just for a bit. And then we can have a drink at Café Marly and people-watch."

"Sounds great," Kelly said.

As they came out of the Bonaparte, Mason said, "Let's walk. It's only a few hundred yards and we can walk across the Pont Des Arts. It's my favorite spot in all of Paris."

"That's so funny. Mine too," Kelly replied. "I think the view back to Île de la Cité is one of the most beautiful vistas anywhere on earth."

They strolled on the Pont des Arts footbridge and stopped about halfway across the river to take in the view, arm in arm. As they looked upstream at the Pont Neuf and Île de la Cité, Mason turned to Kelly.

"Listen, uh, there is one other thing I need to tell you. It's pretty serious."

Looking concerned, Kelly turned to face him and hesitated. "Okay. What is it?"

"I don't know how to tell you this, so I'm just going to come right out with it," he said, deliberately pausing. "I don't know if it registered to you or not, but it has been over a year now since I showed up at your flat in London and you were kind enough to trust me and take me in. So, I guess that means that it has been over a year since I fell in love with you, although in reality I've loved you since the first time I met you. Anyway, this milestone has given me pause to think and reflect on you, and us, and life. And I've made a decision." Again, he stopped talking and left the uncertainty hanging there for dramatic effect.

"Okay. And?" Kelly was unable to breathe from the bizarre mixture of fear and anticipation.

"I want to spend the rest of my life with you. I don't want to ever be apart from you, not for a single day." He reached in his front right pocket and pulled out a small jewelry box. He opened it as he got down on one knee, exposing the flawless, round-cut diamond ring.

"Kelly O'Callaghan, will you marry me?"

Kelly gasped, totally caught off guard. Her hands clasped together, covering her mouth, as tears ran down her face. She was unable to speak. Tourists started to gather around, trying to get a glimpse of the ring, and taking pictures of the romantic couple. Finally, looking up at her helplessly, he raised his eyebrows playfully as if to say, "Please answer."

Realizing she had not spoken, Kelly nodded rapidly. "Yes. Yes. Of course I will marry you." Mason stood up and she leapt into his arms as everyone standing around began to clap.

52

March 2017
Al Qaim, Iraq

M

As UNIQUE AND bizarre a president as Trump was, he did follow through on the campaign promise to unleash the full power of the US armed forces on ISIS. By early 2017, the caliphate was in a life-or-death fight for survival. In the first few months of the new US administration, Islamic State fighters were brutally assaulted from the air and on the ground, day and night, by Kurdish fighters, Assad's fighters, US special forces, drones, and fighter jets. ISIS lost 98 percent of their territory within just a few months of Trump coming to power.

Against this backdrop, Abu Bakr al-Baghdadi and his chief lieutenant, Abdul bin Hakam, both of whom were miraculously still alive, decided that they urgently needed to come up with a plan to rebuild, as they had obviously lost this round and the physical caliphate with it. By their calculations they only had days left before they were completely overrun.

In order to rebuild they were going to need money, which was in desperately short supply. Al-Baghdadi had already put bin Hakam in charge of establishing trading partners and new channels of transportation for their human trafficking operations, shipping refugee women and teenage girls into the West —where they would end up hooked on drugs and forced into prostitution. The trade had been proving extremely lucrative and al-Baghdadi's recent messages to bin Hakam indicated he wanted him to increase his efforts in this area in order to generate the cash flow that would be needed for their rebuilding efforts.

In late March, the two men met in the middle of the night in an abandoned office building in the heart of Al Qaim, Iraq, a town that was just a shell of what it was prior to the rise of ISIS. About thirty minutes before the meeting, al-Baghdadi's ragtag band of advance security personnel arrived at the agreed upon location. They had to run off a group of homeless people living in the structure. And just before the men arrived, they chased off a lone teenage boy who was trying to steal the shoes from the week-old corpse of a man lying against the side of the building.

At the meeting, al-Baghdadi told bin Hakam, "We need you to expand the trafficking operation with great speed. In fact, we need to triple the income from this business within the next five or six months to have any chance to succeed in our goal of rebounding from this defeat at the hands of the great Satan."

"I understand. And I think that with Allah's help I can achieve this. However, in order to do so I will need to personally go to Europe to strike the business deals that will be required if we are to achieve such growth so quickly."

Al-Baghdadi thought long and hard about Abdul's suggestion. Finally, he nodded slowly and the two men began discussing logistics and timing. The only interruptions to their meeting came as each man took turns stopping to look out the window, up at the sky, to see if any US Predator drones were in the area. By the end of the meeting, they had arranged a plan to have bin Hakam travel to Brussels. Its location at the center of western Europe was strategic and they still had many contacts in the ghettos in the suburbs of the city.

Just before he left, al-Baghdadi turned to bin Hakam with a look of genuine pride on his face, and said, "I know you understand how critical this task is to our success. Go with Allah and do not fail in your mission."

Bin Hakam replied, "Thank you, great leader. I have not the words to express how honored I am to have been chosen for this task. I know that with your blessing, and Allah's will, I will succeed. And after I have succeeded, I will avenge my dear brother Nassim."

"Yes. I wanted to talk with you about that," al-Baghdadi replied. "As I mentioned before, our German friend says that the target of your revenge, this American, is still living in London but in a new location. I have blessed this additional mission because I know how important it is to you to avenge Nassim. I salute you for both your dedication to this, and your patience in waiting to achieve it. But you must swear to me that you will only kill this man *after* you have succeeded in your primary mission. You can do nothing to jeopardize the main mission before it has been achieved. In fact, we will not request this man's new location until we are agreed that the primary mission has first been achieved. I want your word that you will abide by this, and only avenge Nassim once I agree that the primary task has been completed.

"I swear," Abdul replied.

pril 2017
London, England

Shortly after they got engaged, Mason and Kelly had gotten out of the leases on their respective London flats and bought a completely renovated, two-story mews flat together on Phillimore Walk in Kensington. They had combined their money to make the down payment. It was a classic starter house for a well-to-do young family, in crazy-expensive London. Two bedrooms, one and a half baths, a tiny but modern kitchen, with a great little second-floor balcony just off the upstairs living room.

On the day they signed the agreement to buy the house they went with the real estate agent to see it for the third time. They had the good fortune to bump into the seller and his wife as they were collecting some final belongings. Kelly pulled the wife aside while Mason and the agent were talking to the husband.

"Are there any special features about the house or things we should know, positive or negative?" Kelly asked. "We've already committed in writing to buy it, and we're not backing out. I'd just love to know if there are any quirks we should know about?"

"Not really. We've loved our time here. I'm going to miss it," the woman replied. "The only minor annoyance you'll find is that the church bells at St. Mary Abbots Church at the end of the street can be loud on Sunday mornings. The clock ringing the time is nice, but the bells for Sunday morning service can take some getting used to. Over time it becomes part of the charm of the place. Other than that tiny issue, the place is as amazing as it looks."

"If that's the only drawback then I couldn't agree more."

"Also, the main sitting room is big enough that I used to use the far end of it as a workout area. You may have noticed that I left our full-length wall mirror there."

"I *did* see that. Thank you. It was a big selling point for us because I work out a lot."

"Yes, I can see you look quite fit. There's enough room there for you both to work out at the same time, if that's what you like to do."

Overhearing the conversation as he approached, Mason interjected, "Oh no. We don't work out together. I'm not in her league. Kelly's routine is extremely energetic and, how shall I say, quite special. I know better than to get too close when she's working out or I might get hurt."

Mason felt that for the first time in his adult life, everything seemed right. He was approaching the third anniversary of being kicked out of HBS. As he reflected, he couldn't help but recognize how far he had come: he was living his dream in Europe—successful in business and making good money, he'd found the love of his life, and they were planning a dream wedding in Galway in August.

. . .

A FEW MONTHS LATER, on a rainy Sunday morning in April, as
Mason was waking up, Kelly was sitting cross-legged on the bed
in their new flat, waiting for him to open his eyes. She was
holding a little white stick in her hand and she had an ear-to-ear
grin on her face.

"Why are you already awake? That's so rare for you. And
why so happy? That's even more rare for you this early in the
morning."

With her grin growing wider, and without saying a word, she
handed him the stick that was in her hand. It was a pregnancy
test and it said in big bold letters on the stick, "Pregnant." Mason
couldn't believe it. He jumped out of bed and hugged and kissed
her with all his might and they both cried ecstatic tears of joy.
They both very much wanted a family. And they were both
ready.

"Just when I thought I couldn't be any happier," he said in
between kisses. "I love you more than I will ever be able to relay
to you. You are going to make the most amazing mother."

"I love you right back, Mason Wright."

MASON BEGAN a tradition that he planned to continue
throughout her pregnancy—talking to her stomach, hoping the
baby would get to know his voice and come to know how much
he or she was loved.

"Your mommy needs to start doing less—starting today—
doesn't she? Yes, she does. She needs to relax and do absolutely
nothing," Mason said. "Don't even think about making breakfast. You just lay here and chill, and I'll run down to the coffee
shop on the corner and load up on your favorite stuff. I'll be
back with breakfast in ten minutes."

"I could get used to this." Kelly smiled and laid back on
the bed.

Just as he finished getting his shoes on and was heading out of the bedroom, Kelly said, "You know something strange? When I spoke to the wife of the owner a few months back, she mentioned that the church bells down at the abbey could be annoying. She said they rang the time each hour and were quite loud on Sunday mornings. But since we've been here, I've never heard the bells a single time. Have you?"

"Nope. And I confess I have not missed them either. Lucky us," he replied, without giving it a second thought.

Mason hustled down to the bakery and loaded up on croissants and quiche Lorraine. As he passed the electronics shop on High Street Ken, he noticed Sky News was broadcasting on the TV in the window. Although he couldn't hear the audio, he stopped just for a second to see the headlines that were coming on screen.

"UN spokesperson says human trafficking of refugees fleeing the war in Syria has increased threefold in the past year."

54

J une 2017
   London, England

"Honey, that dinner was spectacular. You really are an amazing cook," Mason said as he and Kelly were finishing supper at their kitchen table on a quiet Sunday evening. They both stood up to clear the plates and Mason grabbed her around the waist from behind and said, "You know what else you are? You are smokin' hot and I think I might just have to eat you for dessert." He began to tickle her as Kelly laughed uncontrollably.

The moment was interrupted by the sound of his mobile phone ringing. He could see from the caller ID that it was Hans.

"*Guten abend,* my old friend. How are you?"

"I am well. Thank you. Hey, I'm just calling to let you know that I have a board meeting this Thursday at that company in London my firm acquired last year. It was supposed to be in two weeks, but it just got moved up to this Thursday morning. I will only be in town for Wednesday night. I need to fly back the following afternoon after the meeting. If it is not an imposition, I would be very pleased to stay at Chateau Wright while I'm there and catch up with you and the beautiful Kelly."

"Of course. You know we'd be hurt if you didn't stay with us," Mason replied. "That's great. Text me your flight details and we'll have everything waiting. It'll be so great to see you, my friend. There is much we have to catch up on."

"*Sehr gut*. I should arrive at your place sometime around five p.m."

"Excellent. See you Wednesday. *Tschüss*."

THREE DAYS LATER, Mason and Kelly were relaxing on their second-story terrace waiting for Hans to arrive. Mason was reading the news on his phone and Kelly was casually thumbing through a recent issue of *Hello* magazine. Suddenly, something in an article caught Kelly's eye.

"Honey?" she said.

"Hmm," came the reply that was more of a grunt than a response.

Kelly leaned over to his chair. "Here, check this out."

As he picked up the open magazine and began looking at the pages he said, "What am I looking for?"

"The article on the right at the bottom. Check out the photograph."

"Yeah. It looks like an MI6 director named Seifert was given some award in the House of Commons last week. I think this guy is Spencer's boss. I've heard him mention his name before. That's cool. So what about it?"

"It's not the article but the photo of his family. Look at the girl just to his left. Who does she remind you of?"

"Wow. She looks a lot like Hans's friend Kristen."

"Now read the caption where it names his family members that were there with him."

"What the fuck? It says her name *is* Kristen. Are you sure that's her? She looks a lot like her but I'm not certain it's the same person. Could it just be a coincidence on the name?"

Kelly stood up and leaned over him, scrolling through the camera roll on her iPhone as she did. Finding what she was looking for, she put her phone on Mason's lap right next to the magazine picture. On her phone screen was the selfie she took of the four of them in Paris a year before. Mason zoomed in on Kristen as they stared at the photos side by side. He looked up at Kelly with a puzzled look on his face. She was already staring back with a look of worry on hers.

Just then the doorbell rang. Mason got up to answer the door. As he walked away he said, "Don't say anything about this to Hans. We need to talk about it first. It might not even be her. And if it is, I'm sure there's a logical explanation."

HANS AND MASON man-hugged at the door. It was always a joyous occasion when the two old friends were reunited.

"So great to see you, my friend. How was your trip?"

"Fine. Fine. Thank you. Traffic was bad coming in from Heathrow, but I know this is to be expected. And you? Are you and Kelly well?"

"We are, thanks. We're both doing great. Come in. She's upstairs."

As the old friends walked up the stairs to the living area, Hans smacked Mason on his behind—just like old times with Annabelle at SCI in Paris years before. They both laughed out loud.

As they got to the top of the stairs, Mason could see that

Kelly was rushing to finish a text. She quickly typed the last sentence, hit send, and then threw the phone onto the sofa.

"Hans! So very wonderful to see you. We've been looking forward to your visit since you called on Sunday." Kelly walked over and gave him a hug.

"Your mews house is so lovely. I have always preferred the charm of these to the larger townhomes here in London."

"Thank you, you're very sweet to say that. Come, we'll give you a tour," she said, reaching out her hand to take his. With the living space in the flat all on the second floor, the tour did not take long.

As they entered the final room Hans exclaimed, "I *love* this kitchen. All the modern appliances one would expect to find in an American kitchen. And everything appears brand new." Looking at the metal hood over the new modern gas stove he said, "I can even see myself in the exhaust hood. As the French would say, this is all très chic. Even an American-sized refrigerator. Wow."

As he said this Mason opened the fridge, saying, "And look what's inside our giant American-sized refrigerator. German beer! What else?" He pulled out two Bitburger pils and popped the tops off.

"Let's go sit on our little outdoor terrace off the back."

As Mason was picking up a third chair to carry outside for Kelly she said, "No, hon, I'm going to fix us all some dinner. You guys hang out on the terrace and catch up. I'll join you out there in a little bit."

As they walked out onto the terrace, Hans said, "Heeeyyy, this is nice! Very secluded back here away from the noise of the street. Now I'm jealous."

"Yeah, we really love it back here. We'll love it even more when the outdoor furniture arrives. We didn't get around to ordering it until a few weeks ago. It should arrive any day now."

Suddenly, a large black crow appeared on the roof immediately over Hans's head. The noise it made startled Hans, as he jumped several feet away from it.

"*Scheiße!* What the hell is that!?"

Mason laughed and said, "Yeah, that's the only drawback about the terrace. The damn crow thinks it's his. Kelly doesn't even like to come out here without me since that thing always scares her." They both laughed again as they sat in the chairs and clinked beer bottles.

After catching up on the latest news about mutual friends, Hans casually asked Mason, "Do you ever keep in touch with your crazy spy friends?"

Mason replied instantly and honestly, "They were hardly my friends, and no, I haven't spoken to anyone at MI6 in a year and a half, since all the crazy Bataclan shit happened. It seems they kept their promise and finally left us alone. Why? Have they been harassing your uncle again? I did tell them back then what we discussed, that you were sure your uncle was innocent and that a leak from a mole was more likely the source of their troubles. But I don't know what they did with that, if anything." Thinking back to the handwritten notes that he had seen in the baron's drawer, referencing info from someone named "Klug," Mason thought Hans could be right about a mole.

"I do not know. My uncle is convinced that he's still being watched. But if he is, they are wasting their time. He may have financial troubles, but he is not a criminal."

"Speaking of money, does he still go digging around the schloss from time to time?" Mason asked innocently.

"You know how it is. Old habits are hard to die—or however your expression goes."

Kelly stepped out onto the terrace and said, "Mason, we have a problem."

55

"What's wrong, hon?"

"I was going to make your grandma's mac and cheese recipe with German ham, but I just realized we don't have the right kind of cheese. You always use the extra sharp cheddar, and all we have is provolone."

"It's okay. We don't care which it is," Mason said, glancing at Hans.

"Why don't you run over to Waitrose and buy the right kind? It's only two blocks away," Kelly replied.

"I have a better idea. Why don't you relax and forget about making dinner and let's the three of us walk down to the pub and eat there." He turned to Hans and said, "It's our new local, just a few blocks from here. It's the quintessential London pub: right on a corner, with outdoor seating, hanging plants and ivy covering the walls. Inside, it's amazing. I think it's over a hundred years old, with wood paneling and leather upholstered seats. Plus, the food is like a real restaurant, not typical pub fare."

"Sure. This would be great," Hans said. "I'm happy to do whatever you both would like."

. . .

HEADING LAST OUT THE DOOR, Mason reached up on the coat rack and grabbed his trusty New England Patriots cap and popped it on his head. A few minutes later, as the three of them were strolling casually down Phillimore Walk towards the pub, Mason said, "Well, we have some pretty big news to share tonight." Smiling, he then waited a few seconds to let the anticipation build. "Hans, Kelly and I are so excited to tell you that... she's pregnant! We've known for a about six weeks but haven't told anyone yet, as she wanted to be further along before we broke the news. You're the very first person we've told."

Hans erupted in excitement, hugging Kelly and Mason and congratulating them both. He really was like a brother to Mason and his eyes teared up with joy for them at the wonderful news.

After their hugs and laughter died down, and Kelly saw how much the news had touched Hans, she said, "Hans, you are going to make an amazing husband and father some day when you find the right woman."

Hans shyly replied, "Stop. You two are as bad as my uncle. All he talks about is me carrying on the von Eiger name. He is obsessed by what he sees as my duty to continue the bloodline. I will marry. But just like Mason, I want to find the perfect woman first because I want it to last forever."

"Ah, you're so sweet, Hans. But I can assure you I'm far from perfect. Right, Mason?"

"I'm not taking that bait. I'm going to stick with Hans on this one," came the reply from Mason, as the trio arrived at the corner of Holland Street and Gordon Place and entered the Elephant and Castle Pub.

Hans seemed like a little boy on Christmas morning as he looked around the quaint little pub.

"You weren't kidding, this place is great. It feels like we have stepped into a bygone era. I love all the mirrors, the wood and brass everywhere, and the old bar along the entire wall. It is like something from a movie."

After they settled at the only open table, Mason said, "What are you drinking, *mien herr*?"

"I'll have whatever you're having."

"Then you'll be drinking Guinness."

Shortly afterwards, their very attractive waitress arrived with the menus and said, in a thick Polish accent, "Hi, Mason. Nice to see you back again. Can I get you all started with drinks?"

"Hey, Lena. Absolutely. We'll have two pints of Guinness, and what are you having, hon?"

"Just a sparkling water with lemon for me, please."

As they were finishing their pints, Lena came back around ready to take their orders. Mason and Hans were deep in discussion about the extraordinary rise of the young French president, Emmanuel Macron, who had just been sworn in a few weeks before. Kelly, sitting closest to where the waitress was standing, tried to get Mason's attention. But Mason was too deeply involved in making his point to be distracted. Eventually, she tugged on his sleeve and said, "Masey. Masey. We need to order."

After they placed their orders and Lena had gone, Hans could not resist having some fun at their expense. "So, I have to say that this is something new to me this evening."

"What's that?" Kelly replied, as she and Mason gave Hans a quizzical look.

Hans, suppressing a smile that was about to become a laugh, said, "Well, earlier I could not help but overhear Mason calling you 'hon.' And just now I heard you refer to him as, what was it, 'Masey'?" He then let out a hearty laugh, followed by, "No, seriously, I think this is wonderful. I am jealous. You two are so natural together. But surely you know that I will have to make fun of this 'Masey' name for many years."

They both immediately set upon him, trying to extract information in kind.

"Okay. Fair enough. So now you have to tell us a pet name for you."

"No. No. I have no pet name. And if I did, I would never confess this."

"Stop. That's not fair," Kelly said. "We've let our hair down enough for you to know ours. You have to tell us one for you. Come on. I'll never forgive you if you don't. Surely some girlfriend you have had over the years has given you a little diminutive name."

"No. Seriously. No one has ever given me one."

Kelly persisted, "No one? Not even when you were little?" She caught herself and realized that she had inadvertently raised the subject of his deceased family. She quickly said, "Sorry. I didn't mean…"

"No. No. It's okay. It was a long time ago." He sat silently for a few seconds, and then a peaceful look descended on his face—a look as if he were far away in another place and another time, enjoying a happy memory. The alcohol and the warmth of their friendship relaxed his normally cautious reserve. "When I was a small child my family used to call me 'clever' because I was the best in the family at playing hide and seek in the schloss."

Kelly, still fully engaged in the dialogue, and anxious to distance herself from the faux pas, asked, "How would they say it in German?"

Without changing the distant look in his eye he said, "Klug. They used to call me Klug. But no one has called me that in a very, very long time."

56

*O*ne week earlier

BARON VON EIGER sat on an ornate metal bench on a bridge over the Mosel River, about fifteen kilometers from Schloss Reichsburg, talking to his contact in Beirut about an upcoming shipment out of Syria. The baron knew him only as Ibrahim, but he knew it was unlikely this was his real name.

"I sorry. Many strange people ask questions about your ship. Too many. My contact tell me no one coming to boat tomorrow. Too much risk. We wait one month, maybe two before use you again."

"This is not acceptable. We had a deal. Arrangements have been made and costs have been incurred, costs that cannot be recuperated now. Who will compensate me for these lost expenses?"

"Sorry. Not our problem. No one coming to boat tomorrow."

As the man was preparing to hang up, the baron tried one last angle.

"Wait. I may have something else to trade that your contacts will find of value. Suppose I have the new address of the American in London who killed your colleague Nassim. What would this be worth to your boss?"

The man hesitated and then replied, "I no able to say. I think yes interested. What price you ask?"

"Make me an offer."

"I no able to say. Have to ask boss. Maybe ten thousand euro."

"You insult me. Is that all his friend Nassim's life was worth? I'll take fifty thousand—nothing less. Take it or leave it. I have already lost at least half this sum in expenses on the canceled shipment. I will need to know by ten a.m. tomorrow. You know how to reach me."

The baron hung up the phone and kicked the metal railing of the bridge so hard that he later thought he may have broken a toe.

After calming down, he dialed his partner from his regular smartphone via WhatsApp. "Hey, it's me. Listen, the news is not good from Beirut. Some asshole agents have been sniffing around our ship up in Latakia. So, the client is now too frightened to send their people. They just canceled the shipment."

"Damn it! That is seriously bad news. How hard are the Hamburg bankers pressuring you on the past-due note?"

"Very hard. Ten days ago they threatened to go before a judge and foreclose if I did not bring the interest payments current within a week. So, I am already past their deadline. We need to think of something today because the process may not be possible to stop once they start it. Listen, the Syrians asked again for the new address of our nosey American friend in

London. I did not give it to them, but I believe we are at a point that we must consider this as an option."

"Absolutely not. I did not agree to it the night of the massacre in France and you swore that you would never raise this subject again. It's not who we are. We don't kill people!"

"Stop being naïve. There is no such thing as getting your hands a little bit dirty. When you first suggested we go down this path I tried to tell you that there would be no going back, that you would not be able to pretend you were just doing something a little bit bad. This is the path we have chosen. A small step further down it makes no difference now."

"I disagree. I refuse to discuss it further."

"We will continue our discussion when you get home tonight," the baron said.

"Very well. Goodbye, Uncle."

LATER THAT EVENING, the baron waited patiently for Hans to finish his dinner at the kitchen table of Schloss Reichsburg before inviting him to continue seeking a resolution to their current crisis. Finally, he said, "Please, let's go into my office to finish our discussion."

As they arrived in the library, Hans said, "I'm sorry I lost my temper on the phone earlier. I understand what you are saying about our choosing this path, and that one more step down it seems like it's no big deal. But this is not just one more step for me. This man is my dear friend. I cannot be a party to taking his life. I don't care if we lose the schloss."

"Think about what you are saying. This man betrayed you and our whole family by spying on us for the English. Had you not found the device we would both have been in jail for the rest of our lives, and the schloss, our honor, our heritage would have been gone forever. It would have been worse than killing us. It would be erasing our entire history and the future of our family! You owe him no loyalty whatsoever. How do you know that he does not still work with the MI6 secret police to betray us? And besides, I'm not suggesting we kill the man. I'm only suggesting we sell the information of where he is. Who knows? It is quite possible that he finds some miraculous way to avoid being killed, yet again. This is no different than transporting weapons or a jihadi. *We* are not killing anyone."

Hans was half-leaning, half-sitting on the baron's desk, looking down between his legs at the floor, his face contorted with guilt, as he repeatedly opened and closed his hands into a fist. The baron stood over him, just close enough to be intimidating. His face was calm, but stern—not revealing a hint of doubt or weakness.

"I cannot separate the issue as easily as you can. When we first decided to do this, it seemed that any possible victims were nameless, faceless people that were part of some civil war where both sides were guilty. And they were so far away that they seemed anonymous. This is totally different. Mason and I completely trust each other. I don't see him as guilty as you do. I think he honestly struggled to do the right thing, and that it hurt him to betray us."

"So you are willing to continue being his friend, risking that he continues to betray us still. This is a fool's point of view. Your purity is long gone. You are kidding yourself if you think your conscience will be clear if you have no hand in doing this thing which we must do."

Hans paused and then replied, "I guess I just never—I just never thought it would come to this."

"It came to 'this' the very first time we shipped a single gun to a jihadi who we knew was going to use it to kill another human being. The *only* difference is you didn't know the person's name."

Hans pushed himself off the desk and walked over to the massive fourteen-foot-tall windows and looked out across the river at the beautiful moonlit countryside. It was a night much like the night that Mason had tiptoed through that very room to plant the listening device. After a minute or more of silence, Hans finally spoke, "I have to go to a board meeting at one of our portfolio companies in London in two weeks. I will try to see Mason while I'm there and assess whether he is still in contact with MI6. If I think he is, then I will agree to let the Syrians know his address, as long as they swear not to hurt his fiancée. If I believe he is no longer working with them then I will *not* consent to it—and we will just have to find some other way to raise the money or convince the bankers in Hamburg to give us more time."

The baron had maintained his patience as long as he could. With this response from Hans, he exploded in anger and slammed both open palms on top of the papers on his desk and slung them onto the floor.

"You do not understand! There is no more time! We are out of time! Why have we done everything we've done? Did we do it just to suddenly abandon all fortitude, second-guess ourselves, and throw centuries of our family heritage down the drain!?" he screamed, as he stormed out of the room and out of the castle, screeching the tires of his car as he sped away towards the main gate.

A SHORT TIME LATER, as the baron was still driving around to cool off, he received a WhatsApp call from Ibrahim.

"I speak to lead man in Europe. He say okay to fifty thousand euro. When we get address?"

"Our ship is docked in Latakia now," the baron replied. "Pier six. It leaves at two p.m. sharp tomorrow. Bring the cash by twelve noon. Ask for Captain Landolphi. He will give you the address and he will take the money. But there are two conditions: One, he is not, repeat, not to hurt the woman with the American. He must agree to only kill the American. And two, he must do it within the next seven days. After that there is risk of collateral damage from a colleague who may be with the American. If your man will agree to these two conditions, we have a deal. But he *must* agree to them or the deal is off."

"You wait on phone. I ask."

Ibrahim called Abdul bin Hakam, currently in Brussels, on a different phone while the baron held on the line. Speaking in Arabic he explained the terms as laid down by the baron.

"I will kill him within the week. This will not be a problem. But I did not realize there was a woman too. These Westerners are all so soft. Worried about their women. I will take care of this woman, for sure. I will kill everything this man loves."

Ibrahim and Bin Hakam both laughed. But Ibrahim stopped laughing long enough to say, "I feel I must ask you once more, are you sure you should make this decision without consulting al-Baghdadi? I understood he wanted to delay this action until later."

"Our great leader is in hiding. We have no way to reach him. He may not surface for many weeks. I am in charge of all things in Europe. And I say we strike while we have the chance. Besides, al-Baghdadi is pleased with us right now. I saved his nephew, Ziad, last month from arrest here in Belgium. He killed a local woman for fun. We have him hidden where he is safe. Our leader cares nothing about this American. I have made my decision. We act. Tell the German he has a deal."

Picking up the baron's call, Ibrahim spoke into the phone, "You have deal."

57

June 2017
London, England

MASON COULD NOT BELIEVE his ears. He tried to hide his horror at what Hans had just said, that his family called him Klug as a child. Taking care not to give himself away, he just nodded and smiled—a sick smile like he was about to vomit everything in his stomach. His brain was so busy racing that he just said nothing for fear of giving away his shock. *Clearly he doesn't know that the baron still refers to him by this name in his private notes, or that I saw those notes in his desk. Oh, Hans, what have you done? What could possibly have driven you to be part of this?*

While Mason was reeling from the shock, Kelly continued on without skipping a beat. "What's it like living back at the schloss after so many years away, first at university, then in Paris?"

"It's not too bad. I'm actually not there all the time. I rented a small flat in Koblenz near the office so I don't have to drive back and forth to Cochem every day. The road along the Mosel is indeed beautiful, but it's very winding, and it's easy to fall asleep from the boredom if I drive the speed limit. Therefore, I am tempted to go faster than I should. So the flat in Koblenz was a smart idea."

"And Mason tells me that you are seeing a young lady in Koblenz, in addition to Kristen. Is this correct?"

"Well, as I said, I do not see Kristen very often. It's more of a friendship these days. And yes, my friend in Koblenz is named Martina. She is very nice, and very pretty. You have to meet her. You will like her."

"Yes. We would *love* to meet her. We have to arrange that. And, of course, I guess Martina is another reason to have the flat in Koblenz." They all laughed.

"Yes. Yes, of course. Actually, the truth is, my uncle and I have not been getting along that well lately. It's nothing, really. Just the typical things that adults and younger people can disagree on, only a little more so in our case. That was my biggest motivation for getting the flat to start with." Looking to change the subject, Hans reached into the pocket of his sport coat as he continued, "In fact, thanks to a disagreement we had last Friday, I have stumbled across something quite amazing from my family history." He withdrew a small, exquisite, ancient-looking book.

"What's that?" Mason asked, squinting to read the cover.

"It is a very old, pocket-sized New Testament Bible. I found it hidden under a floorboard in my uncle's library yesterday. And if you look inside the cover, here, you'll see the handwritten name of none other than my famous ancestor Gerhard von Eiger," Hans said.

"You're shitting me! Let me see?" Hans gently passed the tiny Bible across the table. Mason carefully took it and thumbed through some pages and then passed it to Kelly to check out as well.

"It is in German but on the inside cover you can see the names of Gerhard's parents and grandparents, and of his kids. Back then, Bibles were important books in a family and they kept important dates and events in them."

"Where did you say you found it?" Mason asked.

"It is a crazy story. At one point in our discussion my uncle lost his temper as he was standing behind his desk, and his face turned bright red as if it would explode—which I found quite shocking because it is out of character for him. Suddenly, he put his hands on top of the desk and flung the papers across the room, then stomped out. After I recovered from the shock, I picked all the papers back up and tried to rearrange them on his desk. But a few of the papers landed under the large armoire in the corner. As I reached under it to grab the last of the papers, I noticed one of them was blowing slightly up in the air, as if air was blowing from under it somehow. So out of curiosity I slid the armoire away from the wall, and found a little hidden compartment in the floor under two very precisely cut floorboards that were clearly made for the purpose of concealing the compartment. There was nothing in there except this Bible, which I find quite bizarre."

"That schloss of yours is full of secrets. I love this. Secret compartments in the floor. So cool."

"I did not have time to tell my uncle about it because he had already left the schloss in anger, and I went back to Koblenz that night. In fact, I didn't even tell him that the date of my trip was moved up to today. I just didn't have the energy to argue anymore. So I didn't bother to call him."

"Hopefully, he will have cooled off by the time you get back tomorrow."

"Yes. I hope this too. And I know that he will absolutely love this little gem. He treats everything from our family history as sacred. I was reading it on the flight over here. I even Googled the edition. It is a very rare Calvinist Protestant Bible printed in the seventeenth century."

"What an incredible story. Why do you think Gerhard hid it in the floor? I'll bet you were thinking it had something to do with the myth of the treasure from the French gold shipment."

Hans started laughing as if he'd been caught.

"I must confess that this crossed my mind. But no. I have looked through it thoroughly. There is nothing about that in here. This is surely just a family myth anyway."

Kelly interjected, "Gold shipment? What's that all about?"

Hans replied, "It is just an old family myth that we laugh about sometimes. An ancestor of mine supposedly stole a great deal of gold from the French and everyone always wondered what happened to it. But there has never been a legitimate record documenting the existence of any gold in my family. I do not believe in such myths anyway."

AFTER THEY FINISHED THEIR MEALS, and shortly after Mason had ordered a third round of drinks from the lovely Lena, he noticed a man walking past the pub outside, carrying a strange case. Something about the man seemed off. Mason suddenly suggested to Kelly and Hans, "Let's go back and have a drink on our terrace. It's getting a bit too noisy in here for me."

After paying the bill, Mason said, "I've got to run to the loo before we go. I won't be but a minute. Wait for me here."

"Of course. We are accustomed to waiting for your bladder by now," replied Hans, as he and Kelly laughed.

Kelly noticed that Mason had accidentally left his Patriots cap on the table, so she picked it up.

"Mason and his Patriots cap. He doesn't go anywhere without it," Hans said.

"Yeah, I think he sees it as his lucky hat. Here, you wear it back to the house." Kelly playfully plopped it on Hans's head.

"No, I couldn't," Hans objected, taking it off and trying to give it back to Kelly.

She laughed and put it back on his head. "Don't be silly. He won't care. I insist."

Finding the whole thing amusing, Hans proudly adjusted the cap on his head as they both chuckled. He and Kelly stood by the side door inside the pub as they waited. But they were in Lena's way as she cleared their table, so they stepped outside to wait for Mason on the sidewalk.

Mason was drying his hands in the bathroom when his cell phone rang. He could see from the caller ID that it was Spencer.

"Mason, where are you right now, right this second?" Spencer asked in an urgent tone.

"I'm in the bathroom at the Elephant and Castle Pub on Gordon Place, a few hundred meters from our flat. We were just leaving to head back home."

"No! Stay right where you are! I'm in an unmarked police car coming to you on Kensington Gore. I know the place. We'll be there in four minutes. We'll pick you up. Do not walk home!"

"Okay. What's going on?"

Spencer proceeded to explain to Mason that he just found out that Abu bin Hakam had arrived in London two days before, and that Mason and Kelly's lives were now in danger, as he was seeking revenge for Mason having killed his friend Nassim eighteen months before.

After Spencer finished, Mason replied, "So that really is bad news, as bad as it gets. Listen, you say you have a picture of him, yes?"

"Sure, we have several."

"Can you text me one, like right now?"

"Roger that. Just give me a second to find it."

After three or four seconds, Mason added, "Spencer. I need it right now."

"Sorry, it's taking me a minute. Listen, I'm going to be there in three minutes. Besides, you don't need a picture to recognize this guy. He has a massive scar down the left side of his face. You can't miss him."

"Fuck!"

"Mason? Mason? Are you there?" The line went dead.

58

Abdul bin Hakam's sniper rifle rested on the top of the low wrought iron fence that surrounded the tiny front yard. He was nestled into the heavy bushes in front of one of the homes on Gordon Place, just one house down from where the street changes to a pedestrian path, forty meters from the Elephant and Castle. He had a perfect view of both the front and side doors of the corner pub. As Kelly and Hans, now wearing the cap Mason had worn walking into the pub, stepped out the side door, bin Hakam praised Allah. "A cleaner, simpler shot a sniper never had."

As he was adjusting his scope, an old lady opened a window on the second floor of the house.

"You there! What are you doing in our bushes?" She could make out the outline of a rifle. Frightened, she yelled, "I'm calling the police!"

He believed he had the man who killed Nassim in the crosshairs of his gun and nothing was going to jeopardize this chance to deliver his vengeance. He steadied his hands and looked through the scope. Just as he was preparing to pull the trigger, Kelly changed position as she was talking to Hans, suddenly walking behind him. It was then that bin Hakam had a twisted thought: *When I pull this trigger the bullet will pass through them both like butter. What better way to avenge Nassim than to slaughter this infidel and his whore with a single shot? My ISIS brothers will laugh for days when they hear what I have done.*

With a cocky grin, he aimed and gently squeezed the trigger.

MASON FLEW OUT of the bathroom and, not seeing Hans or Kelly inside, bolted towards the nearby side door to run outside. His hands were in the process of pushing the door open, when he saw a flash come from the bushes down by the pedestrian part of Gordon Place. A split second later, he heard the enormous *boom* of the gunshot. Blood exploded all over the wall and window to his left. Hans fell like a tree on top of Kelly, with a hole the size of a grapefruit blown out of the back of his head. Kelly's face and torso were so saturated in blood and brain matter that it was impossible to tell if she had also been shot.

From the sound and shock of the situation, Mason instinctively dropped to his knees and started to crawl the four-foot distance over to them. A man who had been eating at one of the outside tables was now lying flat on the patio, and said to Mason, "You'd better get back inside. There's a guy in those bushes shooting people."

Mason could tell immediately from the size of the hole in Hans's head that he was dead. Kelly lay under him with her eyes closed, appearing to be either unconscious or dead as well.

"Oh my God! Kelly! Talk to me," Mason yelled, shaking her.

Kelly calmly opened one eye and whispered, "I'm fine. I'm not hurt. Get back inside! Whoever is shooting is still out there. It's better that they think I'm dead than for me to move and give them a reason to fire again."

He did not retreat back into the pub. Instead, he spread out flat on the pavement next to her.

"Oh my God, are you sure you are not hurt?"

"Yes. I'm fine. I was just sitting down on the bench against the wall when the shot was fired. If I had stayed upright, I think the bullet would have hit us both. But I'm fine. Just get back inside."

Convinced now that she really was okay, Mason peeked out from behind Hans's body to see if he could spot the gunman. Just as he peered up over him for the second time, they heard a woman screaming at the top of her lungs from an open window. From what Mason could see in the distance, the sniper was hastily packing up his rifle. With the fear of being shot removed, Mason had a broader appreciation of what had just transpired, and he found himself filled with rage.

"Listen, Spencer called me when I was in the bathroom. He knows who this guy is. Abdul something or other, he's a sniper from Syria. Spencer is racing here in a marked police car right now. He'll be here any second. When he gets here show him which way I went."

"No! Wait! What are you thinking!? Stay here!" Kelly screamed as she sat up, pushing Hans's body off of her.

For Mason, doing nothing was a physical impossibility. He had already taken off running after the man.

The man abandoned the gun, bolted south on the path, and scaled the wall that surrounded St. Mary Abbots' gardens in one leap, disappearing on the other side. Mason followed, a few seconds behind him. As Mason lunged over the wall, he saw the man sprinting around the side of the church. Mason ran after him but lost sight of him as he reached High Street Kensington. Directly across the street was High Street Ken Tube station. Mason knew that a desperate man would have run into the station in an effort to disappear into the crowd. Running inside, he jumped the turnstile and bounded down the escalator three steps at a time. At the bottom, he had to choose left or right. He guessed left and ran onto the platform to search the outbound side.

Mason spotted the man about twenty feet away and tore through the crowd. The assassin saw him in the same instant, jumped down onto the tracks, and ran south toward the next tunnel entrance, several hundred yards in the distance.

"Call the police! That guy just killed a man!" Mason shouted to the crowd as he jumped down to continue his pursuit.

Mason sprinted after him at full speed, following the tracks as they gently curved out of sight of the platform. Just as he was closing in on him, the man abruptly came to a stop at the entrance to the left-hand tunnel. Seeing how narrow it was, he knew he would be running to his death if a train were to come through the tunnel while he was in it. He turned around, facing Mason, staring at him with an empty, soulless stare. Mason stopped about twenty feet away to catch his breath and figure out what to do. He had never been in the presence of someone like this—someone who exuded such an overwhelming aura of pure evil. The sniper reached behind his back and pulled out a large hunting knife.

It was only then that Mason realized he had chased after the man having no idea what he intended to do if he caught up with him. Mason was slender and well-built at six-foot-one. But he could see right away that his adversary had at least four inches and sixty pounds on him. The assassin was equally shocked to see Mason alive at all, as he thought he had just killed him back at the pub.

As the two men sized each other up, Mason's mind raced, trying to come up with a solution that didn't have tragic consequences.

59

H is first instinct was to run away. But Mason knew that he and his family would never be safe with this revenge-obsessed jihadi on the loose. And if the man were to escape, countless people would die through terrorist acts or have their lives destroyed through human trafficking. Mason knew he had to find a way to stop him—even if it meant risking his life to do so. He tried to quickly think of a plan, but there was no time. As soon as bin Hakam turned around and pulled the knife, he attacked Mason.

In an effort to defend himself, Mason reached to grab a large rotting stick on the ground between the tracks. As he bent down, bin Hakam dove at him. Mason leapt to the side to avoid the knife but was the recipient of a well-placed kick in the ribs as he rolled away on the ground. He got back to his feet, stick in hand, before bin Hakam could strike again. But the terrorist continued stabbing and slashing at him, keeping Mason on the defensive. Realizing that this approach was a losing strategy, Mason decided that going on the offensive was his best chance of survival. Perhaps he might get lucky and see an opening for a punch to the man's temple or throat. Rather than swinging the

stick to block the knife he began swinging it at his attacker's
head, connecting once against the man's elbow and a second
time against the side of his face. Mason could see the man was
more cautious in his attack now, fighting more defensively
himself.

Feeling emboldened by this turn of events, Mason escalated
his counterattack, swinging faster and more aggressively,
connecting more and more. Hoping to land a knockout blow, he
unleashed his next swing with all his might. The assassin
instinctively blocked it with his left arm. The blow from the stick
seriously injured his arm but it also broke the stick. And, purely
by accident, the shorter remaining part of the stick continued to
follow through the arc of his swing, hitting the man's right hand
and knocking the knife out of it onto the ground. In one blow,
Mason had miraculously managed to injure the guy's arm and
disarm him. But the stump of the stick that remained in his
hand was not worth much as a weapon now. They stared at each
other for a moment, each wondering which one of them was
going to try to retrieve the knife. Mason knew that if he bent
down to grab it the man would kick him in the face. Bin Hakam
had arrived at the same conclusion. Instead, Mason kicked the
knife back into the tunnel, so neither of them could easily get
to it.

At this point, bin Hakam had had enough. He knew he was
out of time and that others were going to come and prevent his
escape. Mason could tell by the look in his eyes that he wanted
to kill him with his bare hands. With that, bin Hakam charged
toward him. Mason faked left like he was going to try to run and
then quickly jerked back in place and punched bin Hakam in
his left eye with everything he had. The massive man took the
blow in stride, the pain temporarily forcing him to close both
eyes, but not before he tried to envelop Mason with his giant
arms. Mason knew he was done if this turned into a wrestling

match, so he forced his way free from the man's grip and jumped back several feet.

To Mason's horror bin Hakam was not incapacitated at all by his punch—he was still coming at him. So, he sprinted back towards the station, running in an erratic pattern to aid in his escape. After about twenty seconds of this madness, he looked back and saw that bin Hakam had stopped roughly ten yards behind him. He was hesitating. He looked at his watch. Mason suspected the jihadi was planning to sprint into whichever tunnel the next train either came out of or went into. It was probably a half mile or less to the next station. Mason saw him starting to walk back towards the tunnel entrance. He knew he had to think of some way to detain him.

"Hey, Scarface! I have a question for you. Are all you jihadis pussies? I mean, don't you have the guts to finish the job here?! You see, the only other one of you guys I ever met was your sissy friend, Nassim. That's right, NASSIM! What a pussy he was. You know he squealed like a bitch when I drove that big piece of glass through the back of his neck. Then he shook and twisted like a little girl as he bled to death."

The gamble of mocking his dead friend paid off. Bin Hakam went completely berserk, unleashing a primal scream as he ran towards Mason. Mason made his rage even worse by grinning and emitting a small laugh just as the angry man stormed towards him. But the smile quickly went away from Mason's face as he ran for his life back towards the station.

As he looked back to assess how close his pursuer was, he tripped on one of the rails, falling hard on the tracks. Just as he made it back to his feet, bin Hakam was on him.

The hand-to-hand fight that Mason had dreaded was now a reality. Bin Hakam punched Mason in the head. Mason saw it coming from the corner of his eye and was able to dodge some of the blow. But the men were now physically wrestling on the tracks. Bin Hakam outweighed Mason and was experienced at fighting. Mason was punching and maneuvering as best he could, but no easy kill shots were to be found. The outlook was bleak. Even with his wounded left arm, bin Hakam was landing more blows with more fury than Mason.

Laying on his side in the middle of the track, just as bin Hakam stood up to try to stomp on Mason's head, Mason was able to kick him with all his might in the left knee cap. He heard a grotesque crunch. This temporarily halted the attack long enough for Mason to get up and run in the other direction, which he soon realized was back towards the tunnel entrance.

At this point both men could hear the roar of an approaching train from within one of the tunnels, although neither of them knew from which tunnel it was coming. And since the tunnel tracks curve just before exiting into the open area where they were fighting, the driver would not be able to see anyone in his path until it was too late to brake.

Mason was tempted to gamble on which tunnel the train was about to exit—running in one to escape—but he'd be risking his life, as there were only inches of clearance on either side of the train. He opted to continue to try to fight and run. Just as he turned to see where bin Hakam was, he felt a crushing blow to the back of his head. His kneecap kick had not slowed the man for more than a second. He had been hot on his tail the entire time. Mason fell to the ground, disoriented by the blow, his body laying fully across the left-hand track, right at the tunnel entrance. Bin Hakam followed up with several more kicks for good measure, then halted his assault for just an instant to catch his breath. Mason, who appeared to be unconscious, was tempted to take advantage of this momentary lapse in the beating by rolling off the track. But he thought of Kelly laying in all of that blood, with Hans's corpse on top of her, and his rage boiled over anew. Instead, he swung his right foot up into bin Hakam's testicles with all his might. He connected with the full force of the kick, feeling the testicles collapse with a sickening popping sound. Bin Hakam shrieked an animal-like cry and doubled over in agony, as Mason screamed, "Looks like you won't be having any kids, scar-faced motherfucker!"

Just then the headlights from the approaching train came into view around the bend of the exact same track that Mason was laying on. As he tried to roll off the other side to get out of the way, bin Hakam, still bent over from the pain, grabbed his leg—holding him directly in the train's path. Mason kicked and jerked to try to break free from his grip, but it was no use. Testicles or no testicles, the jihadi monster was about to have his vengeance, and he would witness it up close and personal, as the train was about to obliterate Mason's body right before his eyes. Just as the roar of the train reached a deafening pitch, and the front of the train cleared the curve, bearing down on Mason, three gunshots rang out in rapid succession.

Mason, startled by the sound, looked through blurry vision and blood dripping down his face to see Spencer standing about thirty meters away, who had just fired three rounds from his nine-millimeter pistol at bin Hakam—all three of which had found their mark.

This miraculous turn of events inspired a burst of energy in Mason. In one violent movement, he jerked his leg free from the grip of the dying man and rolled off the track, at the very instant that bin Hakam fell into the train's path, where Mason had been lying one second before.

The train missed Mason's head by inches. But it did not miss bin Hakam. It shredded his body, scattering parts of him over the track, from the tunnel entrance all the way to the High Street Ken station platform. Once the train passed, the track looked as if it had been sprayed with blood and body parts from a hose.

Spencer had to wait for the train to finish passing before he could get to Mason on the other side. He ran up to him, yelling, "Are you okay?! Jesus, mate, I couldn't tell if you had made it out of the way in time or not. I knew the jihadi had not, thank God. But I was worried it got you too. You alright? Did it clip your head as you rolled off?"

Mason, still a bit groggy, and a lot bloody, mumbled through his swollen mouth and lips, saying, "I think I'm okay. The train didn't hit me, but I did get a right good ass-whippin'."

They both began to laugh. The extreme level of adrenaline pumping so fast through their veins at that instant meant they had to either laugh, or scream, or cry. Mason would later say that he thought they did all three.

SPENCER AND MASON sat there on the ground for the next few minutes as they tried to return their bodies to normal from this hyper-energized state. Mason asked if Kelly was okay and Spencer assured him she was. Shortly afterwards, other police officers started to arrive on the scene.

Eventually, Spencer said to him, "Mason, you've done the world an incredible service by taking this guy down. Had bin Hakam gotten away, who knows how many people here in London their attack might have killed, or how many thousands more would be enslaved in their human trafficking network."

"What are you talking about? I didn't take him down. You did. You saved my life. Don't thank me. Thank you."

"Okay, so I helped a little. But if you had not chased after him, we'd have lost him. We do indeed owe you a debt of gratitude."

Mason then thought for a second and added, "Just do me one favor. You can tell your bosses the truth about what happened here if you want. But please, *please* tell the cops and the press that you caught him by yourself. The last thing I need is to find that this asshole has some brother or cousin or other best friend who wants to have another go at me."

Spencer smiled as he leaned over to pat Mason on the back.

"That won't be a problem, mate. That won't be a problem. Now let's get you to hospital and get you patched up."

60

Kelly and Spencer patiently waited in Bupa Cromwell Hospital's emergency room reception for two hours as the doctors and nurses treated Mason. Even though Kelly had partially cleaned up, she was still covered in dried blood. While they waited, at least a half dozen clinicians asked her if she needed immediate assistance. Each time she politely declined, explaining that the blood was not hers. Finally, a doctor came out with an update.

"Mason has a concussion, two black eyes, a split and very swollen lip, a sprained left ankle, three cracked ribs, and more cuts and scrapes all over his body than we can count. But miraculously he has no major injuries. He's a very lucky man. You can come see him once we get him settled in his room. I'll send someone out when we're ready."

While they were waiting, Spencer filled Kelly in on everything MI6 had discovered about Hans. Finally, a nurse came out and escorted them to Mason's room. As she was leaving she said, "We have him lightly sedated because the doctor wants him to rest. You can have ten minutes but then the doctor has asked us to give him a further sedative to ensure he sleeps." Both Spencer and Kelly nodded in agreement.

"Hello, old man," Spencer said to Mason when they entered his room. "It looks as if they have you right well stitched up here. How are you feeling?"

Mason replied with just a grunt and a thumbs-up.

"Right. Well, as rude as it may seem, I actually can't stay. Lots to do to debrief others and write reports and such, but did want to stay long enough to hear for myself from the doctors that you were alright. It sounds as if they will let you go home tomorrow after a good rest and a final checkup in the morning." Putting his hand on Mason's shoulder, he looked at him solemnly and said, "Thank you again, mate. Our nation really does owe you a debt of gratitude for chasing that jihadi down—you crazy bugger."

He turned and nodded to Kelly and then headed for the door. Just as he was opening the door he said, "Oh, and one more thing. Just to be extra safe until we know the coast is clear, I'm going to post a guard at the door here tonight, and as I told Kelly, I'm going to have one of our agents in an unmarked car outside your mews flat tonight as well, just as a precaution. Kelly, Agent Crawley is in the lobby waiting to drive you home when you're ready. Cheers, guys."

As soon as the door closed Kelly threw her arms around Mason and gave him a big long kiss on his split, swollen lip.

"Arrrgh. That hurts." He groaned as she kissed him.

"I know that hurts, but I don't care. You deserve it. Although, I don't know whether to kiss you or smack you for being crazy enough to risk your life chasing that mad man. But I'll start with the kiss and we can talk about your insane streak tomorrow."

"Aoght id he shay arout Hans?"

"What? Sorry, I can't understand what you're saying, honey."

"What did he shay arout Hans?"

"Ah. Sorry. What did he say about Hans? He said that they

had discovered that he was indeed dating Kristen, Director Seifert's daughter, but that she had no idea who he was or what he was involved in. Apparently, Hans had visited their house here in London with her one time, two years ago when no one else was home. Kristen says she came into the living room and found him messing around behind the TV, where their Wi-Fi router was located. When she asked him what he was doing he told her the TV wasn't working and he was doing something to fix it. She never thought about it again. Spencer's men found a very small thumb drive plugged into the router which had allowed Hans to harvest information remotely from Seifert's computer whenever he was online."

Mason tried to ask another question but Kelly had trouble understanding him through his swollen lip and sedation. They were interrupted by the arrival of the nurse.

"So sorry, love. I'm going to have to shoo you off now. Doctor's orders that we give him the rest of his sedative and that he be allowed to sleep, if you want us to discharge him tomorrow."

Kelly nodded and turned back to Mason. "It's okay, sweetie. You can ask me your question tomorrow and I'll tell you everything Spencer told me."

Mason nodded and then pointed to Kelly, followed by the okay symbol with his hand, while simultaneously raising his eyebrows.

"Am I okay? Is that your question?" He nodded again. "I'm okay, honey. I'd be lying if I didn't admit I'm still freaked out by what happened to Hans, and to me, and to you. And I broke my iPhone when I fell. See?" She held up the device showing its lifeless, shattered screen, while shrugging her shoulders. "But I'm certain the baby's okay, and I'm not traumatized or catatonic, if that's what you mean. I may have a good cry when I get home tonight. But I'll pull it together and be ready to take care of you when you come home in the morning," she said with a smile that showed both tenderness and exhaustion.

She gave him a final, light kiss and held onto his hand for a few more seconds as she pulled away, looking back at him, until she gently pulled far enough away that their fingers no longer touched. Then she slowly turned and walked out the door to meet the agent waiting to drive her home.

SPENCER WAS WORKING LATE that evening. As tired as he was, he had an endless number of meetings and reports to file, especially since he had fired his weapon in a civilian area, and because a suspect had been killed. Around ten p.m., he was still in his office, speaking with a colleague when his office phone rang. He could see it was an internal call from a young research analyst name Greg, the same analyst who had alerted him earlier that evening to the fact that Abdul bin Hakam had entered the UK.

"Hi, Greg. I guess you've heard the news, that we got him. Can't thank you enough for—"

"I'm so sorry, sir, I have to interrupt you, it's urgent. Yes. I heard the news, and congratulations on taking him out. But something dawned on me this evening after everything happened. What if bin Hakam wasn't traveling alone? I know he walked off the boat alone, as the camera footage clearly showed. But all our intel told us that he was a very smart character. I thought, what if he had a colleague with him but was smart enough to not walk off the boat together? So I've been going over every photo that our surveillance cameras captured of every person that came off the *P&O* Ferry that day. The facial recognition system did not pick up anyone else disembarking from his vessel. But later that evening, on the last arrival of the Calais ferry, we got a match of one of his close associates. I've just IM'd his picture to you. The system positively ID'd him as Ziad Rahim. He is the nephew of none other than al-Baghdadi himself. Our intel says that bin Hakam personally trained him as an assassin. Anyway, he is now here in the UK. He walked off the same ferry as bin Hakam two days ago—just six hours after him."

As Greg was talking, Spencer's mind was racing. Before Greg could finish Spencer's eyes suddenly grew wide with terror.

"Oh my God!" he said under his breath as he grabbed his mobile phone and his gun and ran out the door.

61

Kelly mixed the perfumed bath salts, which she had been saving for a special occasion, into the piping hot water pouring into the tub in their luxurious, newly remodeled master bathroom. The day had been one of the most traumatic of her life. But rather than wallow in the memories of what she had endured, she decided instead to count her blessings. Mason was alive and going to be okay, the baby was fine in her womb, and the mystery of the leak from within MI6 had been solved, even if they lost someone they both considered a dear friend in the process. The world even had one less terrorist in it tonight. The fact that an agent was guarding her house outside gave her added comfort. And so she made the conscious choice to be grateful for what she had, and to try to put it all out of her mind as best she could, while she enjoyed the long, hot bath.

Afterwards, she put on her pajamas, wrapped herself in a big bathrobe, and slipped her bare feet into her furry bedroom slippers before heading into the kitchen to make a hot cup of tea. Her plan was to just lay in bed and veg out to a random Netflix movie until she fell asleep—and then sleep until whenever she woke up. With no landline phone at their mews house, and a broken iPhone, there would be nothing to disturb her slumber.

As the water in the pot on their new Viking stove was just coming to a boil, she noticed a strange smell. Standing with her back to the kitchen door, looking down at the stove, she could swear she smelled something resembling body odor. It reminded her of a crowded Greek market on a hot summer's day. She then noticed a slow movement behind her in the reflection of the silver exhaust hood over the stove. She did not turn around or give any indication she had seen it. Rather, she calmly removed her feet from her slippers so she was now standing in bare feet. Keeping a careful eye on the image in the reflection, she also removed her big bathrobe so she was only wearing her pajamas. Before tossing the robe onto the kitchen chair, she removed its long soft belt and wrapped it quickly around her left forearm. She turned around.

Ziad Rahim was standing in her kitchen just six feet away, with a long, unwashed beard and a bloodied, long-blade knife in his right hand. His six-foot, 180-pound frame towered over Kelly.

"I knew zee American had woman, but no one say she such a pretty woman. You a very pretty woman—bitch! We have fun before I keel you. And I gonna keel you nice and slow."

Kelly had assessed her situation in the first three seconds after seeing his reflection in the exhaust hood. She did not scream. She did not plead for mercy. She did not try to run. Her only reaction was to reach down with both hands to her thighs and slightly pull up the legs of her pajama bottoms so there was sufficient slack in them for better freedom of movement.

62

As Spencer pulled out of the underground car park at MI6 headquarters the first call he made was to MI6 central dispatch.

"Yes, this is Spencer Hughes-Smyth, MI6 security badge 67289. I need you to patch me through to the radio of Agent Crawley, on special security detail outside a flat at 38 Phillimore Walk in Kensington." He listened while the dispatcher tried to raise Crawley. As it became clear that Crawley was not answering the radio in his patrol car, Spencer smacked the steering wheel in his car and shouted, "Damnit!"

Accelerating his own vehicle to twice the legal speed limit, he turned on the siren and put the portable flashing blue light on his dashboard.

"I'm sorry, sir, I can't seem to raise him."

"Do you have his mobile number?"

"I can look it up, sir."

"Would you do that for me now, please. It's urgent," he said as he blew through the red light at the corner of Sloan Street and Brompton Road and turned left onto Knightsbridge.

The dispatcher dialed Crawley's mobile number and the phone rang out.

"I'm sorry, there is no answer, sir."

"Okay. Listen to me carefully. This is a terrorist threat level 'critical' event. I repeat, threat level 'critical.' I need you to send every available armed-police unit in the Kensington area to that address—38 Phillimore Walk—right now!"

Spencer was now back on Kensington Gore, the same road he had raced up earlier that day in a police car, weaving in and out of traffic. He arrived at the flat in three minutes. Other police units began arriving just a few seconds after him. Gun drawn, he looked in Crawley's car only to find him dead, his body slumped across the front seat. The dashboard and windscreen were covered in blood, and his throat was slit so deeply that his head was barely still attached to his body.

Spencer, with a look on his face resembling a snarling dog, ran to the front door of the house. Finding it slightly ajar, he pushed it open and quietly sprinted up the stairs three at a time to the main floor of the flat. Seeing nothing in the living area, he heard a noise coming from the kitchen and proceeded in that direction with two armed police officers immediately behind him.

Kelly was curled up on the floor in the kitchen doorway, softly crying to herself, blood coming from a piece of glass still in her back, to which she was oblivious in her state of total exhaustion. Looking past her into the kitchen he could see Rahim lying motionless on the floor. "Check on him, but be careful in case he's still alive," he said to the officer behind him. "If he so much as flinches put six in his head."

"O'Callaghan. It's Smyth," he said, kneeling next to Kelly and gently touching her shoulder. "Everything's going to be okay. Other than the glass in your back, are you hurt anywhere else?"

"I'm fine. I just needed a good cry. It's been a really long day."

Realizing she wasn't seriously hurt, Spencer let out a sigh of relief as he dropped backwards and sat on the floor next to her.

"This one's dead," one of the armed policemen in the kitchen said. "And it looks like someone took a sledgehammer to this kitchen."

The other, unable to contain his astonishment, said, "What the bloody hell happened to this bloke! Hey," he said, turning to Spencer, "You gotta come see this guy. The whole left side of his face is burnt to a crisp, and his right eyeball is out of its socket and dangling down on his bloody cheek. Two fingers on his right hand are bent backwards, almost broken off. And his neck is snapped clean in two. There's no way that lady did all this by herself, is there?"

Shaking his head and letting a small, knowing smile cross his lips, Spencer spoke into his handheld radio.

"This is Smyth. We have two agents down at 38 Phillimore Walk, Kensington. Repeat, two agents down. One deceased in his car out in front, the other in need of an ambulance. Get us an ambulance over here, right away."

63

The sound of the blaring siren made it difficult for Spencer and Kelly to talk in the back of the ambulance. She started to recount the details of the fight with Rahim but eventually just shook her head and pointed a finger at the roof of the vehicle.

"It's okay. Just rest for now. We can debrief later after they patch you up and you get a good night's sleep."

She just nodded in the affirmative.

The hospital staff was waiting to meet the ambulance when they arrived. Just as they were whisking her away, Spencer asked her, "Is there anything I can get for you, anything at all?"

"When they've finished sewing me up, I want to be in Mason's room."

"I'll see to it."

Ninety minutes later, Spencer was waiting in Mason's room when a nurse and an orderly wheeled Kelly in.

"How is she, Nurse?"

"She's going to be fine. She had a few cuts and bruises but nothing too dramatic. The doctor gave her ten stitches for the glass cut in her back, three stitches for a wound on her left forearm, and three more from a cut on her left shin. But other than this, I'd say she's in good shape, considering what she's been through. This is one amazing young lady."

The nurse and orderly left and Spencer walked over to her bedside.

"We can talk once you wake up. It's almost one a.m. Get some sleep. I'm going home to do the same. I have three agents outside your door and a female agent who will stay in the room with you guys all night. I'll pop in tomorrow after you guys are awake."

Kelly just nodded and softly mouthed the words, "Thank you." Lying on her right side, she reached her left hand over to Mason's bed, resting it on his left arm, and was fast asleep before Spencer made it out of the room.

RETURNING the next day around noon, Spencer brought his laptop with him so he could work while he waited for Kelly and Mason to wake up. Shortly after he started typing he looked over and noticed Kelly's eyes were open but she wasn't stirring yet.

"Good morning, or rather, good afternoon," he said quietly.

"Hey, there. Has sleepyhead here woken up yet?"

"Nope. You're the first."

After another minute or so of silence, she sat up in bed.

"How are you feeling?"

"I feel fine. A little sore, but fine, thanks." After a short pause, she continued, "Was yesterday even real? It's hard to believe all of that really happened, in a single day no less. It's even harder to believe that Hans is dead."

"I've definitely had that feeling before. But I can assure you, it all really happened. You know, like you, we never really suspected Hans was involved with his uncle's illegal activities— that is, until the night of the Bataclan attack, when Mason's mobile number ended up in the terrorist's apartment in Brussels. From then on, we believed he was in on it too."

"Why did that make you suspect Hans?"

"Because the von Eigers were the most plausible source for the jihadis having Mason's mobile number. But when Mason spoke to Hans afterwards to come clean about planting the listening device in his uncle's library, rather than admitting his uncle at least *may* have been involved in transporting jihadis, Hans swore to Mason that his uncle was innocent—even in the face of the evidence we had against him. This made us suspect that Hans was at least in some degree complicit. We knew he would slip up sooner or later. And he bloody well did, when you all met Seifert's daughter and finally made the connection through the *Hello* magazine article. "After you sent me that hurried text about it yesterday, we had Seifert call his daughter and she told him everything. She had no idea who Hans was. Apparently she only hid her friendship with him from her family because some older family members are still quite sensitive about Germans, given that they lost loved ones at Auschwitz."

"Either way, Hans's death really hurts, even if he was helping his uncle do bad things. And I'll never believe that he was in agreement with the idea of having Mason killed. No one is that good of an actor. If you saw Mason and Hans together you would have known that neither was acting. They really were best friends. Last night at dinner Hans told us that he and his uncle had been quarrelling a lot lately. I have to believe that one of the reasons was a disagreement over what to do about Mason."

"Perhaps. I guess we'll never know now." Spencer dropped his voice to a low whisper. "Hey, on a different subject, I've been warming up to the idea of allowing you to tell him that you've been an undercover agent for us for years."

Kelly's eyebrows rose approvingly, but before she could speak, Mason began to stir—speaking his first few sentences even before opening his eyes.

"Hey, guys. Wow. Whatever they gave me really knocked me out. What time is it?"

"It's around one-thirty in the afternoon, handsome," Kelly said, reaching over and gently rubbing his arm. "Did you have a good sleep?"

"I did, thanks. And I could have kept sleeping awhile longer if you two chatterboxes weren't blabbing away in here," he said jokingly, his eyes still closed.

Spencer's face showed slight alarm at this revelation.

"How long have you been able to hear us?" he asked.

"I heard the whole conversation. It's bizarre how your hearing comes back first after a sedative, even though your eyes are still too tired to open."

"Bugger," Spencer said.

"Why 'bugger'?"

Looking as guilty as a dog who just ate the bacon from the kitchen counter, Spencer launched into a classic English self-effacing speech.

"Because I assume you heard me, just a few seconds ago, discussing the fact that Kelly has been an MI6 agent for the last five years. I'm so terribly sorry. I fully appreciate that information of this magnitude is something that you both would have preferred she disclose to you in a private conversation and that it has all kinds of potential ramifications for your relationship, not that it should or needs to, mind you."

Kelly was shaking her head, smiling. Mason, also grinning, managed to finally open his eyes.

Looking at Spencer nervously rambling on as he stood at the foot of the bed, Mason said, "Yo, chief. Slow down. Just hit pause for a minute. I've known about her side gig with you guys for over a year."

"What? How could—"

"I know that she joined up after her boyfriend was killed by human traffickers in Greece five years ago. I know that you got her the job at SCI to try to get close to Hans to learn more about his uncle. And I know that she has studied karate since she was a teenager in Paris, that she's a third-degree blackbelt, and that she used to train your female field agents in self-defense right up until she joined SCI. How did I do, hon? Did I miss anything?"

"No. That was a nice summary," Kelly said slowly, looking towards Spencer as she guiltily clenched her teeth in a nervous grin.

Spencer's mouth was partially open in shock and he was glancing back and forth between the two of them in disbelief. Mason, without moving his head, continued looking at Spencer from his pillow, with a huge grin on his face.

Spencer's demeanor changed from guilty to indignant.

"Well that's a bloody massive breach of protocol. Why wasn't I informed about this?"

Kelly spoke up in her defense. "About a year and half ago when Mason and I became really serious, he confessed to me, among other things, everything he was doing for the agency. And he and I made a solemn pact that that there would never be any secrets between us. So, I told him everything. I knew it could get me in trouble with the top brass. But the agency had not been using me much lately, and more importantly, Mason is the love of my life. Then, as now, nothing is more important to me than him, than us. Besides, I knew that you would come around eventually, once you knew you could trust him as I do. I just accelerated the inevitable."

By the time she had finished, Spencer's frown had turned into a neutral nod. He finally spoke.

"Well, I...uh, I may have to ask that you cheeky buggers keep your premature disclosures just between the three of us. Given how completely you broke this case open for us, it is indeed a bit of a challenge to be mad at you right now."

"I'd like to change the subject for a second, if I may," Mason chimed in. "I've got a few questions that need answers. First, why is Kelly wearing a hospital gown and lying in a hospital bed next to mine? And second, I haven't talked to you guys about what the fuck happened yesterday at the pub! I saw my Patriots cap on the ground next to Hans and Kelly, covered in blood. Do you guys think my cap had something to do with why this Abdul asshole shot Hans? Because when I caught up with him on the Tube tracks he was clearly shocked to see me alive. So I assume he was trying to shoot me and made a mistake, yes?"

Spencer spoke first. "I think it was just a lucky twist of fate. As I understand it, Hans and Kelly were waiting for you to return from the loo, and you had accidentally left your cap on the table. So, Hans just happened to pop it on his head while waiting for you to come back. And it seems that casual decision cost him his life, and saved yours."

"Almost, but not quite," Kelly interjected. "I put it on his head. He kept taking it off but I insisted that he wear it."

"Why would you do that?" Spencer asked.

"Because you had briefed me on the contents of the case file from Mason's activities at the schloss. The file mentioned that the baron's personal notes said he'd received intel from 'Klug.' When Hans innocently divulged that Klug was his childhood nickname it solidified in my mind that he was working with the baron all along —especially given our earlier discovery that Kristen is Seifert's daughter. So, from that instant, I didn't trust him. I had no way to know there was a sniper outside, which he clearly didn't know either. But I knew that Mason wore that damn cap everywhere and I've always feared it was like a target on his head. I don't know, something deep inside, call it woman's intuition, told me at that moment to be scared. And I was. So, it just seemed like the right thing to do to put the target on Hans's head. It was just a lucky guess."

"Yeah, lucky for me. Good God, honey, you literally saved my life. Thank you."

"It's okay," she said as she gazed at him tenderly. "You have your whole life to pay me back. And I'll see that you do."

Mason reached over and grabbed her hand as he looked lovingly into her eyes. After a few seconds he said, "Okay. That's one of my questions. Now how about the other one? What the hell are you doing here, and what's with the bandages I see on your arm and leg?"

64

Mason listened intently as Spencer explained the discovery of the second jihadi, Ziad Rahim, and Kelly recounted her life-or-death fight with him in their kitchen.

When she had finished a modest summary of her ordeal, Spencer asked, "I still haven't been able to picture in my mind the scenario that required you to pull his eyeball out?"

"Yeah, it's my own fault that it came to that. I was in control from the instant I threw the boiling water in his face. But, at several junctures I offered him the opportunity to surrender. I didn't want to have to kill him, but he was determined to either kill me or die. I think in his mind there was no alternative. He preferred death to prison. Or maybe he just refused to believe that a woman was going to beat him in a one-on-one fight. Either way, after kicking, punching, and breaking more things on him than I could count, I gave him one last chance to give up. In hindsight I should have just put him out of his misery sooner. Delaying it almost cost me my life. He was on the floor, and I thought there was no way he had any fight left in him. And I got careless. He leapt from the ground and caught me by my throat, smashing my back into our new cupboard with the glass door. I knew I only had a few seconds before he choked me out, and that would have been the end for me. Only my right hand was in a position to do anything. His left eye was already burned closed from the boiling water, so I took the right eye out of the socket with a single, three-finger hit. Naturally, that caused him to completely freak out. He let go of me and started screaming and flailing like an animal, which gave me the opportunity to catch him from behind and break his neck. He didn't really leave me any choice."

Spencer couldn't resist adding, "I can't help but wonder what he was thinking in those last final seconds, as his life was slipping from his body and he knew it. For a man who had spent his life being so cruel to women, do you think he wondered if having his ass literally beaten to death by a woman was going to hurt his chances of getting into paradise?"

Ignoring Spencer's comment, Mason said, "God, honey, I'm so sorry you had to go through all of that, and I'm also sorry I wasn't there to help you—although it sure seems like you took care of matters just fine without me. Did he, uh, did he ever hit you or hurt you in your stomach area?"

"No. I'm sure the baby is fine. I never got hit or pushed into anything that touched my belly."

"Thank God for that. You are such a badass. I am so proud of you," Mason said, as he reached over and stroked her shoulder.

"It probably hasn't fully sunk in yet. But in my defense, this guy was pure evil. He made it so clear how much he was looking forward to torturing and killing me, that I have trouble feeling too bad about the fact that he died. There was no ambiguity about the situation; it was kill or be killed."

"Of course it was," Spencer chimed in. "This man was a sadistic murderer. Not only did you save yourself, but you and Mason have both saved countless citizens here in London from the terrorist attack these men were planning. You are both heroes and you must never forget that when you reflect on these terrible events."

Changing the subject, Spencer said, "Right. Let's move past this discussion if I may, because there is other news this morning, which I know you will both find of interest."

Mason and Kelly looked at each other and nodded and then turned back to Spencer.

"The media in the UK and on the continent carried the story of Hans's murder last night, including his name and photograph. It continues to be all over the news this morning, especially since bin Hakam was part of a terror cell. In addition, we gathered evidence from Seifert's router and the thumb drive Hans attached to it. The evidence shows the IP address the information was being sent to, after hopping through various other servers, and it matches the one at the baron's schloss in Cochem. So, this morning we sent an international warrant for the baron's arrest to our counterparts at the BND, the Federal Intelligence Services in Germany. When they arrived at the gate of his schloss, his security man called to let him know the BND were there with a warrant for his arrest. Apparently, he told his man to hold them up for a few minutes, which he dutifully did. It seems the baron used these few minutes to hang himself from the upstairs railing in the great hall of the castle."

"Wow!" Mason said, sitting up in bed.

"Oh my God," Kelly gasped as she put her hand over her mouth.

"The BND boys tried to revive him, sadly to no avail. I'm, uh, sorry, Mason. I know you knew him reasonably well, and I'm indeed sorry he chose that way out."

"Yeah, well, I won't say I'm sorry. But I will say the whole thing is incredibly tragic. Think about it. The baron failed completely at the only two things he wanted in life—to find

Gerhard's gold and to have Hans carry on the von Eiger legacy. I'm just relieved that this asshole, who tried three times to have me killed, is no longer a threat to me or to us. As far as Hans's betrayal, I still don't know how to process that. I guess you were right that first night you showed up at the Grenadier pub when you said how desperate people can become when trying not to lose what they have."

"Do you remember what else I said?"

"Yeah, that even with people who are generally good, if they get desperate enough, there is nothing they won't do."

65

_O_ _ne week later_

"I SPOKE to Spencer just now while you were in the shower, and he agrees with us that you should go to Hans's memorial service. In fact, the agency is not releasing any news about Hans or the baron being involved in trafficking with ISIS jihadis. They don't want to risk spooking other contacts in the network, who they have been cultivating for years."

It had been almost a week since Hans's death and both Kelly and Mason were recovering well at home from their injuries. Mason had been in touch with Hans's friend Flavio almost daily. Flavio was keeping Mason posted on when and where the memorial service for Hans would take place. Flavio confirmed what Spencer had also told them, that the schloss was headed into receivership and that the creditors had already filed their claims with the courts. None of the distant, next-of-kin cousins had the means to pay off the debts, so the banks were going to auction it off. Flavio said the most likely buyer looked to be a real estate development firm that had long wanted to turn it into a four-star hotel and spa, but the baron would never sell. Now it appeared that they would get it even cheaper than their prior offers.

A few days later, a date was fixed for Hans's service, to be held at the fifteenth-century St. Martin's Church in the heart of Cochem. Flavio had been handling the details with the parish minister, especially since he knew better than Mason how to reach all the folks that knew Hans. The service was going to be a reunion of all their old friends from the earlier party days when they both lived in Paris. In the back of his mind Mason was a bit worried that somehow some of their friends might blame him, since Hans had been killed while staying with him in London. The press had billed it as a random terror attack by a lone ISIS fanatic. Enough of those were happening around the world that it seemed plausible. Mason knew his concerns didn't make much sense; nothing made sense to him right now.

Kelly also thought of Hans as a brother. She wanted to go to the memorial, and to be there for Mason, but they both thought it would be best if she stayed behind, especially considering her pregnancy.

The day before he was scheduled to fly over for the service, a package was hand-delivered to Mason's front door with a return address from Bupa Cromwell Hospital.

"What do you think it is?" Kelly asked.

Mason opened the package and pulled out Hans's, or rather Gerhard's, family Bible, along with a handwritten note from the hospital that explained what had happened.

Mason knew that the ambulance had also taken Hans to Bupa Cromwell Hospital, the same one he and Kelly were at. He was declared DOA. The next day they had asked Mason to take possession of his belongings. In all the drama, Mason had completely forgotten about the Bible. Apparently, someone thought it was a hospital Bible and had put it in a drawer before Mason came to collect his things. When a nurse found it, and saw it was in German and had Gerhard von Eiger's name on the inside cover, she knew it must have belonged to Hans. She was kind enough to make a few phone calls to find Mason's address and personally dropped it off.

That night, he lay in bed looking through it. He spoke a few phrases of German but not nearly enough to read it. But still, it was fascinating to him to be holding in his hand this amazing, four-hundred-year-old Bible at the center of Hans's family history. What Hans had told him about it having been hidden in the floorboards of the library in the schloss didn't make any sense though. Why would Gerhard hide it? Mason didn't really believe in the old family myth about the buried treasure. But it was still curious that it had been in a hidden compartment for so long. Mason felt compelled to look through this amazing piece of history.

Kelly wanted to go to sleep and asked Mason to turn out the light. He complied and then turned on his iPhone flashlight to see as he flipped through the Bible, page by page, and got to the very end—but found nothing.

However, just as he was turning the very last page, the page that in most books is just blank white paper with nothing on it before the back cover, his iPhone flashlight illuminated something written faintly on the page. And then he realized that it was actually two pages stuck together so completely he believed that it was not by accident. Someone had glued the pages together to conceal the writing on the last page.

He carefully peeled the pages apart without tearing them. What he found on that hidden final page was both exhilarating and heartbreaking. A simplistic, hand-drawn map that resembled a picture from a children's tale. It was faded but still legible.

It showed the outline of the east wall of the schloss, the small church on the far side of the property, and neat rows of crosses just outside the church on the right, where he knew the old tombstone markers were in the ground. He and Hans had walked past the ruins of the little church a dozen times. He knew exactly where this was. The only thing out of the ordinary about this map was that one of the graves, denoted by a cross, had a circle drawn around it. There were seven graves in the row, and the fourth one, in the very center, was circled.

Mason believed that he may actually be holding the map to Gerhard's lost treasure in his hands. His exhilaration was tainted by heartbreak because if that turned out to be true, Hans had unknowingly been so close to the financial security that he, and particularly his uncle, had desperately sought for so long.

THE NEXT DAY, Mason flew to Frankfurt as planned, and rented a car at the airport. He drove to the memorial service at St. Martin's Church in Cochem. The day was overcast and a soft mist blanketed the Mosel River Valley. Despite the rain, Mason had never seen the valley look more serene.

At the church the old gang was all there. Some were married now, others engaged, some came alone. It had only been a couple of years since he had seen most of them, but everyone looked older, including Mason. The names of the families in attendance read like a who's who of European history: Saxe-Gotha-Altenburg, von Thurn und Taxis, Orange-Nassau, Fürstenberg, Schöburg, Orléans, Bourbons from France and Borbons from Spain, Borghese, Grimaldi; the list went on and on. Mason knew some of them from the old days, some he had never met. Véronique was there. In fact, she was incredibly supportive, giving Mason a huge, long hug when she first saw him, and insisting that Mason sit with her and her fiancé during the service. She invited Mason and Kelly to come visit them after Kelly delivered the baby.

The little church was packed to capacity, with people having to stand in the back to all fit in. He was pleased that no one appeared to blame him or be angry with him. Quite the contrary, everyone knew he and Hans were best friends, and they knew that it must have been truly horrible to have this happen right in front of him, with his own pregnant fiancée almost killed at the same time.

As they came out of the church after the service, the sky cleared and the sun gleamed through the clouds, which created a magnificent rainbow that stretched from the towering schloss to the neighboring valley on the other side of the river. Véronique walked up to Mason as he stared out at the sky in awe.

"That is the most beautiful rainbow I have ever seen in my life," Véronique said.

"I was just thinking the same thing," Mason replied.

After the service, about two dozen mourners walked over to Zum Kellerchen for drinks, just like the old days. Bourget, Le Lidec, Annabelle, and most of the SCI team were there as well. A core group settled in for a long night of drinking and reminiscing about Hans. Mason stayed for a couple of hours, but eventually told them he had to get up early the next day and excused himself. Bourget walked him out to his car.

"Don't worry about not staying. Everyone understands. We can tell that you're still not quite yourself. It's a lot to get over—for both you and for Kelly. Listen, take as much time as you need before trying to get back in the game. At least take the next week off at a minimum. Same goes for Kelly. Give her my best when you get back," said Bourget.

Mason thanked him, got in his rented SUV, and drove back to his hotel in Koblenz.

The next day he went to a local hardware store and bought a full-sized shovel, a large battery-powered flashlight, and several thick blankets. He spent the day casually driving along the Rhine and Mosel Rivers, taking in the sights and touring a few old schloss he had visited with Hans years before. He called home and talked to Kelly for a while. He had told her that he didn't feel he had the energy to do a one-day turnaround and that he was going to stay and relax for another day, reflecting on his thoughts and seeing some old familiar sights, before coming home. She understood. She knew he had been through a lot and she was worried about his health from the stress and the loss of his friend. He did not mention to her what he was considering doing that evening, primarily because he still hadn't decided whether or not he was going to go through with it.

By dusk, he found himself pulling into the dirt service road on the back of Hans's property that led up to the ruins of the tiny old church. As he drove his rented SUV past the overgrown bushes that obscured the entrance to the road, he second-guessed his plan yet again.

Am I really going to dig up a graveyard in the middle of the night? There's no guarantee that this is even a map to the treasure. And what if I find it—is it stealing if I take it?

He sat in his SUV for twenty minutes wrestling with these issues.

Fuck it! I've come this far. I'm going to at least find out if there is anything there. If there is, I'll deal with the moral dilemma then.

He pulled out the flashlight and the shovel and before he knew it, he was standing in front of the centuries-old grave that had been circled on the map.

The stone tombstones for all the graves were laid flat on the ground, not upright. Most of them were partially or fully overgrown with earth or grass. Mason scraped the shovel across the dirt on the fourth one over, the one that had been circled on the map in the bible. The others had names on them; this one was marked only with the year that changed everything for the von Eigers—1792.

He dug nonstop for about thirty minutes. If he had bothered to think about it, he would have realized he was tired. But driven by the excitement and the risk of his task, he continued to dig at a relentless pace. He had no idea what the punishment was in Germany for desecrating a grave.

Forty minutes in, he had opened a hole that was about four feet deep and three feet by four feet wide, when suddenly he hit something hard. He scraped away the dirt and revealed the outline of a chest about the size of a large coffee table.

Most likely some poor bastard's coffin. Don't get excited. This proves nothing.

He propped his flashlight on a mound of wet soil above his head. As he cleared away more dirt, he could see it was some kind of old-fashioned chest or strongbox. He continued to clear around it and down the sides. He tried to lift the box, but it didn't move a millimeter; it felt like it was welded to the earth. A hinged metal strap hung loose because there was no lock.

He lifted the metal strap and pried open the heavy lid. The rotted hinges on the back gave way and the top came off in his hands. He heaved the cover aside and the contents of the box shimmered in the beam of his flashlight.

66

Mason sat in the hole he'd just dug and stared in a combination of amazement and disbelief. He had found Gerhard von Eiger's treasure. The strongbox was full of brilliant gold coins that looked like they were minted the day before. Mason knew very little about gold, except that it was incredibly heavy, and that it never tarnishes. It stays that beautiful golden color forever. Now he faced the ethical dilemma. He was sitting in a muddy ditch, in a graveyard, in a foreign country, on government property, staring at a fortune in gold. And the longer he sat there the more likely it was he would get busted and be in serious legal trouble for what he was crazy enough to have just done. But he was already too far in, and too excited about the riches in front of him to be able to think straight.

He decided he would ask Kelly what to do. As silly as it sounded, he knew she always did the right thing. In the meantime, he had to move the gold somewhere safe. Whatever he was going to do with it, he wasn't going to leave it in the ground. And he didn't feel any pressing obligation to notify the German authorities, or the French authorities either, for that matter.

The case was too heavy for five men to lift, let alone one man by himself. Mason went to the SUV and brought out one of the blankets. He spread it out at the top right-hand side of the ditch and started tossing handfuls of coins up onto it. Every five minutes or so he would bundle the blanket up, drag it over to the SUV, and dump its contents onto the backseat floor. He evenly distributed the coins between each of the two backseat floor wells with each trip.

Mason had not done manual labor in years and he was starting to feel the effects of his crazy endeavor—his back ached, his wrists felt like someone had hit them with a hammer, and his thighs burned as he crawled in and out of the pit and dragged the heavy blankets across the graveyard.

Over the next hour and a half, he made fourteen trips to the car to get all the coins out of the strongbox. By his rough estimate he had about eight or nine hundred pounds of gold. He could see the SUV was riding low from the weight. He spent another forty minutes filling in the hole at the grave, tidying up the area, and covering his footprints. He neatly covered up all of the contents of the backseat floor with the blankets, and slowly drove back to Koblenz. On the way, he stopped to dispose of the shovel. Checking that no one was in sight, he dropped the shovel off a bridge into the Mosel and watched it disappear into the black water. He thought to himself that it was likely the same bridge from which Hans had thrown the listening device he had planted in the baron's library.

Back in the hotel garage, he locked the SUV, checking it multiple times. *If someone steals this rental car tonight, then it's God's will, and it's truly their lucky night.* As he walked away, he let out a loud, carefree laugh. He was utterly exhausted from the physical labor and stress of his escapade. As he lay in bed, he struggled to fall asleep. His mind was racing from the evening's excitement. *The fucking fairy tale about the gold was true! I can't*

believe I have an SUV filled with gold downstairs in the garage. Two
hours later he eventually drifted off to sleep.

THE NEXT DAY he woke up, ate a huge breakfast, and showered
and shaved and dressed in his nice coat and tie that he had worn
to Hans's memorial service. He grabbed his MacBook and began
to research the top private banks in Switzerland. He didn't want
to call any rich HBS friends to ask them, as he didn't want any
association between anyone who knew him and the bank he
chose. Afterwards, he got in his loaded-down SUV. The gold was
still under the blankets on the backseat floor. He stopped at the
nearest gas station to fill up and set out for the six-hour drive to
Zurich, Switzerland.

He arrived at Bank Julius Baer about an hour before closing
time. He asked to meet a private banker right away, on a matter
of some urgency. He was introduced to Herr Stefan Gruber, a
middle-aged, rotund, balding man with thick round glasses. He
explained to Herr Gruber that he wanted to rent a number of
their largest safety deposit boxes. The banker arranged it in a
matter of minutes. He also loaned Mason a special rolling
strongbox to shuttle his cargo from the rental car to his new
depository. Herr Gruber agreed to keep the bank open past
normal hours in order to allow Mason to complete his
transaction.

On his first trip back from the car, Mason asked if they could
weigh the contents of the rolling strongbox. It was close to 150
pounds, per case load. He had been conservative with his estimate the night before. Mason made eight trips back and forth to
the SUV in order to move all the gold into three large safe
deposit boxes. This meant his total haul was somewhere near
1,200 pounds of gold. At the current rate of approximately $1,500
per ounce, he was looking at somewhere between $28 and $29

million in total value of the gold alone, without accounting for its possible historic value.

When his transaction was finished, Mason said goodbye to Herr Gruber and assured him that he would see him again very soon. He was anxious to get home to Kelly to get her advice on what to do with the gold. Maybe she would tell him to give it back, although to whom would be unclear. Maybe she would tell him to give it to a charity. What he did know was that she had the best moral compass of anyone he had ever met. He also knew he would be praying for guidance from above.

He returned the rental car at the Zurich airport and caught the last flight to London. On the flight he couldn't help but think of his Granddaddy Wright's words about how God rewards those who do the right thing in life, in ways you never imagined. But Mason felt like he already had the only reward he ever wanted with his beautiful fiancée, the child growing in her womb, and a great life, albeit one that would be lived without his friend Hans now.

The last thought that drifted into his mind as he started to doze off in his seat was, *Man, everything about my life seems surreal right now. My childhood back in sleepy little Richmond, Virginia, feels a long ways away, like a lifetime ago.*

67

When Mason arrived home, Kelly was waiting up for him. She met him at the top of the stairs with a long, slow hug. The hug, and the love that flowed between them, felt like pure energy, replenishing their depleted bodies. They stayed there savoring it for a minute before either of them said a word.

Even though it was past midnight, Mason opened a bottle of Bitburger Pils. He offered a second, unopened one to Kelly, hoping to have a toast.

"You know I'm not drinking but I'll have a couple of sips of yours," Kelly said. "Let's talk out on the terrace. I have a surprise for you."

When they got outside Mason said, "Wow, the furniture came. It looks amazing! And planters with flowers too. You're such a natural at this stuff." He looked around, appreciating how she had arranged the terrace.

"Hey, how is it that you've been out here without me to protect you from the crazy crow?"

"Ah, that's the best surprise of all. No more crow."

"What? How's that?" Mason asked.

"Someone scared him away." Kelly walked to the edge of the terrace and waved her arm like a game show presenter towards the nearest tree branch about twenty feet away.

Mason walked over, put his arm around her, and squinted into the darkness. He spotted the reflection of dark eyes atop a hawk-like beak. Mason's pupils adjusted and he could make out the rest of the feathered body.

"Good Lord. That's the largest wood owl I've ever seen!" Mason whispered. "Where the hell did he come from?"

"I don't know, probably from over in Hyde Park, but he seems to have made that tree his new home. And I've decided he's my new best friend, because that crow is long gone."

Mason laughed and kissed her. They sat down on the new outdoor sofa, and he took a long, slow sip from his beer. He and Kelly sat in silence for some time. She curled up next to him on the sofa, her head resting against his shoulder while she ran her hand through his hair. Finally she asked, "So, how was it?"

"I guess it went as well as could be expected. The service was incredibly moving. The church was filled to capacity with a crowd of aristocratic families from all over Europe, and the minister was nothing short of poetic. It was really a special service. It was also nice to see the old gang, only I sure wish the circumstances had been different. Bourget was there, as was most of the company. He insisted that we take at least another week off to just decompress from it all. Also, as bizarre as I know this sounds, in the middle of the service I got this powerful feeling that Hans is at peace in heaven with his brother and parents."

"That's a nice thought. I'm sure you're right. Even if he was flawed. We both know he was also a really good person."

"I agree. I can't imagine the hell he must have been living in

—for someone who had that much goodness in them to have to live with the knowledge of how far into the darkness he had strayed. It just blows my mind that he was willing to work with his uncle and be involved with those evil bastards, just for the cash. I guess it's like he and I used to talk about. It's one level of lust to want to be accepted in a club. But the desire to not get thrown out of the club once you're in it—or in his case born into it—is one hundred times greater. I guess people will do anything to avoid that humiliation. Lord knows what I might have been willing to do if I'd had an option to stay at HBS and avoid the public humiliation of being thrown out. Shit, I don't even want to think about it. All I know is that as long as I have you I don't need to be in any other club, not even Harvard."

Kelly squeezed his hand and kissed him. "Funny you should mention HBS. A letter came from them while you were gone. I couldn't resist the temptation to open it. It was just a one-pager. I didn't know you were trying to get reaccepted right now?"

"Oh yeah, as crazy as things have been, I forgot to tell you that I sent them a letter a few weeks ago, before all this shit happened. Professor Bellini called out of the blue and reminded me that we were coming up on the three-year anniversary of my looping out. He said that Le Lidec had kept him up to date on our success at growing the company and that he thought I should update the committee at Harvard. So, I just wrote two quick pages outlining what we've done over the last three years. I didn't really give it a lot of thought. Anyway, what did the letter say?"

"It said you've been accepted to go back this September! Congratulations. You must be excited about that."

"Wow, okay, well, we've got some decisions to make," Mason replied, with a look that was more thoughtful than excited. "To be honest, I'm not really sure how I feel about it. I kind of just wanted to know if they would ever let me back in. I'm not even certain that I should go. I meant what I said a minute ago. From now on you and our children define me. Not achieving some degree or being in anyone else's fancy-pants club. I now belong to the coolest club on earth: the Kelly and Mason Club."

Looking into his eyes, her head tilted slightly, Kelly leaned in and gave him another long kiss and said, "Exactly. And you have a lifetime membership."

"So, the crazy bastards made good on their promise," Mason said, switching back to the letter. "Good for them. Maybe I should just look at the last three years as having been a long sabbatical."

"Yeah. And a wild one at that. Don't misunderstand. I'm happy for you. And I will support you 100 percent if you want to do it. But there's one pretty big problem," Kelly said.

"What's that?"

"How can we possibly pay for it? I mean, we put everything we had into buying this house. The real estate commission alone, if we sold it now, would take all of our equity, so selling the house won't help. And if we don't sell it, how will we pay the mortgage if you're not working because you're in school in Boston? We already agreed that I'm taking some time off to take care of the baby. So I'm not sure how we will afford the tuition for the year with neither of us working."

Mason's demeanor shifted and a faint hint of a grin appeared.

"Why do I get the feeling that you're not telling me something, or maybe that you're about to tell me something?" Kelly said, after several seconds of funny looks between them.

Before he could answer, the bell in St. Mary Abbots' tower chimed a single dong, indicating that it was one a.m. Momentarily distracted, they both looked toward the end of the street where the sound had come from, and then back at each other with raised eyebrows, as if to say, *Hey, the church bells work!*

Kelly nuzzled into Mason's arms and said, "You were saying?"

No longer able to contain his secret, a mischievous smile slowly spread across his face. "Yeah, I think I might have the money thing figured out. Honey, we, uh...we need to talk."

ACKNOWLEDGMENTS

Writing this book over the past three years has been an extraordinary adventure. It's hard to comprehend how far it has come since my, truly primitive, first draft. One thing for certain is that I could not possibly have succeeded in this endeavor without the help of friends and loved ones who took time from their busy lives to read my humble manuscript and give me thoughtful, direct feedback. In no particular order, I will always owe a debt of gratitude to: Kim Miles, Paul Duke, Jeff Andrews, Dr. WD Taylor, my brothers Otho and Preston, my dear mom, Alice, my lovely wife, Kerry, Laura Kroky, Rusty Sullivan, Pat Murray, Bruce Tyler, Henri de Perignon, Mark Kessler, Charles Robinson, David Moore, Joni Evans, Doug Ranalli, Axel Majert, Sara Thwaite, my editor, Candace Coakley, and finally, extraordinary authors, Daniel Palmer, John Hughes, John Gray, and Pamela Kelley, whose sage advice regarding this crazy industry has been of incalculable value.

ABOUT THE AUTHOR

Ben was raised in Virginia and received his BA from the University of Richmond. After graduating from Harvard Business School, he spent the next 6 years living in France and England - opening the European offices of a telecom startup in the UK, France, Germany, and Italy. While living in Europe he learned to speak French and Spanish fluently and became a passionate practitioner of the European café culture. Over the past 25 years he has been the founder or CEO of 4 tech startups, in industries ranging from eLearning to online music. He is currently the Founder and CEO of a B2B learning solutions company where he oversees scriptwriting and production of corporate communication, training, and marketing videos. Besides writing, he spends much of his free time traveling, reading, watching old movies, and enjoying time with family and friends - often at a sidewalk café. Ben lives in a quiet village just outside of Boston with his wonderful wife and children.

Made in United States
North Haven, CT
30 June 2022